Arthur L. Ford

Shunned

UnTapped Talent

Shunned
By Arthur L. Ford

Copyright © 2008 by Arthur L. Ford
All rights reserved.

While this novel's premise is loosely based on a real-life shunning more than thirty years ago, the story and characters in this work are purely fiction. Any resemblance to persons living or dead is purely coincidental.

Library of Congress Control Number: 2008935784

ISBN 978-0-9820834-0-6

Published by
UnTapped Talent LLC
Hershey, PA 17033-0396
www.UnT2.com

Set in 11-point Adobe Caslon™
Cover design and illustration by Linda Dows-Byers
Printed in the United States of America

For Mary Ellen

Shunned

~≪~ Overture ~≫~

It was a heap of splintered gray wood and torn black canvas. The only recognizable object in the debris by the side of the road was a woman in a dark purple dress, face down, lying to one side of the heap, her hair splattered with blood already soaking through a white bonnet. Off in the field of early, foot-high corn, a horse shrieked, its cry rolling wildly over the neat rows and across the long stream of cars moving slowly along the two-lane road.

Andy and Beth Simpson had left New York City three hours earlier, escaping through a Friday morning, planning to spend this early spring weekend in the "Amish country" of Lancaster County. They were inching along the Old Philadelphia Pike—the link to Lancaster before the newer, wider Route 30 tore Lancaster County in two.

"My God," Beth said, "I can't look at that. What is it?"

"I think it's one of those Amish buggies," Andy said. "Something must have hit it. Looks like it's made of tinder."

"That poor woman."

"She has to be dead," Andy said.

As they moved slowly past the accident, Andy rolled down his window and heard two rescue workers talking.

"The man's over in the field," one said.

"Must've been thrown fifty feet," the other said.

Someone covered the woman with a coat.

Meanwhile, the horse in the field continued to bolt wildly, staggering on a crumpled leg, its screams streaking the air, shrieks of pain and fear piercing the rescuers, the bystanders, the motorists, Andy and Beth. The men did not even attempt to catch it.

Beth began to shake.

"Let's get out of here," Andy said as he rolled up the window. "Maybe we can get off this road."

He looked ahead at the intersection and saw several signs. One said "Paradise four miles." He thought about turning but decided against it. The irony was too much. He had to go on.

They drove silently for a few minutes.

Beth said, "I'm sorry. I don't know what got into me. It's not like I never saw an accident before. But that poor woman, and that man somewhere in the field. They never had a chance. The buggy was nothing. It's just a pile of sticks. Why do they do that? Why do they ride along a road like this? They're asking for trouble."

"It's their road," Andy said.

Andy and Beth were in their late thirties. He was average in all ways, light-brown hair trimmed neatly, brown eyes, just under six feet tall. She was light haired, slim, her sunglasses in her hair. They had been married for ten years or so. Beth was from the New York area. Andy had grown up in this part of Pennsylvania, fifty miles north of Lancaster on the Susquehanna River, and had visited the area many times with his parents, so he knew something of the Amish who lived here. He had seen the Amish and their buggies before, but he had never seen this. He had never seen this vulnerability or this total devastation, just for being Amish.

"Do you want to go back to New York," Andy said, shifting in his seat, trying to settle in again.

"I don't know. Do you?"

"We could." Andy half hoped she would say yes.

"No," Beth said, shading her hand with her eyes. "Let's stay.

This is the first time we've had together in months. Let's see how it goes. Let's give it a try."

"Okay. Maybe we can work things out."

"Yeah," Beth said, and then added, turning to look back in the direction of the accident, "We're not off to such a good start though."

"No," Andy said.

"Besides, I really do want to see all these things you've talked about. I know this part of the country means something to you. Maybe I can see what that is, or why it means so much. Maybe I can know you then. Oh, I don't know. I'm not making sense. Maybe this was a mistake. Maybe we shouldn't have come. Maybe we should have just had a quiet weekend in Manhattan."

"No such thing," Andy said. "We're here."

The traffic began to move more quickly. Soon, however, they slowed again, this time for a small town.

"Intercourse! That's the name of a town?" Beth's mood lightened.

"Yeah," Andy said. "It comes from its location as a commercial center at one time. Traffic crossing at the intersection. That sort of thing."

"Right," Beth said. "You mean people actually live here and keep a straight face?"

"Oh, they don't have any trouble keeping a straight face except when they see the New York tourists gaping and shelling out big bucks for the wooden mailboxes."

"But Intercourse. What a wonderful name. It's sort of like giving the finger to the world or something," Beth said. She was obviously feeling better. Andy also relaxed.

"No, it's just a name down here," he said, "just like any other name. Strasburg, New Holland, Blue Ball."

"Blue Ball! My God, what are these people doing?"

"How about Bird-in-Hand?" Andy said. "Or Virginville?"

"You're kidding."

"No," Andy said smiling. "Other people make fun of the names, but not the people who live here. I had a roommate in college from Delaware. He drove through here on his way home. One time I got a touristy postcard from him with a picture of a buggy and a sign for Intercourse on it next to the buggy. He wrote on the back: 'I'll bet this is the first time anyone ever stopped in the middle of Intercourse to send you a post card.'"

They both laughed.

Andy continued, "And right next to Intercourse is, what else? Paradise!"

They suddenly grew silent, remembering the sign back at the accident, remembering the irony of Paradise, remembering the woman with the bloody bonnet and the horse screaming in the field.

"Let's stop here, in Intercourse," Andy said. "You'll like the town. We can stand on the street corner and watch the buggies, other buggies, go by. The horses really are beautiful."

They pulled to the side of the road, in front of a hardware store, and walked to the corner.

"Look," Andy said, "Here comes a buggy."

They watched as the buggy drove by them. They saw a man and a woman, probably in their thirties, sitting at the front of the gray buggy. The man wore black pants and a purple shirt. He had a beard and a straw hat with a wide black band. The woman wore a dress similar to the one the other woman wore, the woman by the side of the road, purple and black. She also wore a white bonnet with thin white strings hanging from either side. Beth and Andy watched as the buggy passed them. Peering out the open rear window were two small children, a girl with pigtails and a bonnet, and a boy with the same type of shirt and hat his father wore. They smiled.

Beth winced like someone had hit her.

"What?" Andy asked.

"I wonder," she said.

"What?"

"I can't help wondering if there were any children in the other buggy. Oh God, I hope not."

She began to shake again.

Come on," Andy said. "There should be a restaurant down the road. We can get something to eat. We haven't eaten since breakfast."

They walked slowly back to their car.

"Isn't it early to eat?" Beth asked. She stopped walking and began looking at some quilts hanging in front of a house.

"Not around here," Andy said. "People get up early and work hard all day. They're ready for dinner at 4:30."

"But we're tourists," Beth said, fingering the needlework on one of the quilts.

"Let's go native," Andy said.

Finally, Andy got Beth to the car, and they drove a short distance to a place called The Seven Sweets and Seven Sours, where they ordered an all-you-can-eat dinner of "Pennsylvania Dutch Specialties." Andy ate everything, from the boiled pot pie to the chow-chow to the shoofly pie.

"So you're going to tell me the pie is called that because they used to shoe flies around here when they ran out of horses to shoe," Beth said.

"Good," Andy said. "But no, that's not it. I can tell you, however, on very good authority just how this name came about. One of the primary ingredients of shoofly pie is a heavy, dark, sweet molasses, so sweet in fact that the flies used to hover over every pie. The baker had to shoo the flies away."

"Oh, so it's spelled with two o's." Beth was obviously amused.

Andy helped himself to more chicken and mashed potatoes.

"Where are you putting all of this?" Beth asked.

"It's good," Andy said. "I never get food like this at Nick's Deli."

"Thank God," Beth said. "I would starve."

The dinner had taken Andy's mind off the accident. He

assumed it had done the same for Beth, although she was silent again. They returned to their car.

"Let's find a place to stay," Andy said, turning the key to the car. "I'm beat."

"Beat? I don't see how you can move after all that food."

They eased out into the traffic.

"There's a place over on Route 30, a big motel in the shape of a steamboat."

"Spare me."

"No, really. Robert Fulton used to live around here somewhere."

"Let's find a motel on this road. It should be quiet at least."

They stopped at the first motel they came to, a small one, The Leola. The man at the desk, fifties, graying, overweight, told them yes, he had a room. Lucky it's still early in the season, he said. Another month and they would need reservations. Andy felt guilty enough to apologize for their thoughtlessness. The owner walked with them to the end unit and opened the door.

"Here's the keys. Nobody's gonna disturb you down here. Quiet. Check-out's eleven."

Andy thanked him and carried the suitcase into the room, placing it on a small folding stand beside the bed.

"We should have looked at the room before taking it," Beth said, testing the dresser for dust with her finger. "It smells like a motel."

"It is a motel," Andy said. "I like authenticity." He snapped open the suitcase.

Beth said nothing. She began to take her things out of the suitcase. Andy noticed he didn't recognize most of the toiletries, and then he turned and switched on the television set.

"Hey, it has cable," he said.

"Good," Beth said. "Does that mean we are privileged to watch a baseball game?"

"No chance. They don't get the Mets down here. Maybe the Phillies though."

Beth sat on the edge of the bed, her back to Andy. She didn't move.

"I'm just kidding," Andy said. "We can watch a movie."

He went over to Beth and sat down, putting his arm around her.

"Or maybe we can find something better to do. We have the rest of the evening to ourselves."

"I'll be back," Beth said.

She took some things and went into the bathroom, closing the door behind her.

"Jesus," Andy thought. "I don't know."

Andy undressed and lay on the bed, his head propped on his arms, looking at the ceiling. Soon Beth returned. She had put on the t-shirt she usually wore to bed. Andy liked to see her this way. She was slim with nice legs. Her hair was down. Beth walked over to the dresser and sat down at the mirror. She started to brush her hair. Andy came up close behind her.

"You really are beautiful," he said.

"You know I'm not, but thanks for saying it," she said. She put her brush down.

"No, I mean it. I always have."

She leaned back against him and then looked at him above her in the mirror. She smiled slightly.

"I think I would like to make love," he said.

"I noticed," she said, still with her back to him. "But are you sure you want to make love?"

"What do you mean?"

Beth paused and then said, "I mean, are you sure you don't just want to have sex?"

Andy slowly pulled the t-shirt over her head and threw it in a corner of the room. He had missed the distinction, the tone of her voice.

"Whatever," he said.

"Whatever?" Beth looked at him again in the mirror. "You really don't have a clue, do you?"

He put his hands on her breasts.

"About what?"

"About love," she said.

"I told you I love you." He was getting impatient.

"You don't know what love is, do you, Andy?"

Andy didn't know how to respond.

"If you don't know what love is, how can you know if you love me? Or anyone?"

Beth turned around on the bench and faced Andy, looking up at him. Her face softened. He leaned down and kissed her. She held him to her.

"I don't know, Andy. I want you. I want you now, but I'm not sure about tomorrow."

"Now is enough," Andy said and led her back to the bed by the hand. They lay down together and held each other tightly. Andy's hand explored Beth as he had not done since their early nights. Beth responded, pushing herself against his hand.

Finally, Andy said, "Okay?"

"Okay."

Sex that night was good. Andy felt Beth respond to each need he had, easily, without holding back. She moved hungrily, filling him with a satisfaction he had not remembered.

And then it was over, too soon. Andy and Beth lay on their backs, looking at the ceiling.

"God," Andy said.

"Is that a prayer?" Beth asked.

"Of thanks," Andy said. "That was . . . very satisfying."

"Yes," Beth said, pulling the sheet over herself.

After a few moments of silence, Andy said, "I think we can make it, Beth. I mean, that should prove something."

"What does it prove, Andy?"

"Well, I mean. We're really good together."

"Oh."

More silence. And then Andy turned to Beth, and in the light shining through the window from a lamp outside he saw she was quietly crying.

"Why are you crying?" he asked.

She did not respond, did not move.

"Beth, can't we talk? Can't you say something?" Andy was clearly baffled.

"I don't know," she said. "The sex was good. I needed that. It's been a while. But, Andy, sex isn't life. There's more, and I'm not sure we have that anymore. I don't know if we ever had it."

"Is it the accident?"

"No. That was upsetting. I can't get it out of my mind, but there's more."

"Like what? What do you mean more?"

"I don't know. Maybe we should wait and talk about it in the morning. We're both tired."

Andy lay awake in the darkness for hours. He knew Beth was also awake.

Finally, he fell into a deep sleep, and when he awoke Saturday morning, he found Beth dressed and sitting at the dresser table, combing her hair, putting it up.

"Hi," he said.

"Hi."

Andy pushed his pillow up behind him and leaned back against it. He wasn't sure what to say.

"Early riser today?"

"Yes." Beth volunteered no further information.

"Going somewhere?"

"I thought I would go for a walk. It's a nice morning."

"The only place to walk is down this country road. Probably lots of traffic."

"That's okay," she said. "I'll be back in half an hour or so."

She came over to the bed and kissed him on the cheek.

"Bye," she said.

"Bye."

Andy lay in bed for a few more minutes, trying to think of what was wrong. It was never really right, he thought. He got up, shaved, showered, and put on a pair of jeans he had not worn since he had moved to New York several years ago. They were tight. For the first time in months he and Beth had gotten the same weekend off from their jobs, he with a newspaper, she with an ad agency. The goddamned fast lane, he thought. He turned on the television and watched a news show until it was over. Beth had still not come back. It had been forty-five minutes.

Finally, Andy went down to the motel office to see if he could get a *Times* and found Beth sitting on a bench outside the office.

"I was just about to come in," she said. "It's really beautiful out here. I like the farm land."

"It's cold," Andy said, rubbing his arm.

"It's not so bad," Beth said. She was hunched over. "It could be worse."

"Yes."

Andy and Beth spent the rest of the day driving around the Amish countryside to the west of Lancaster. They saw other buggies, but neither said anything about them as they passed. They drove silently most of the time, Beth playing with the radio, finally giving up.

At one point midway through the afternoon, they stopped at an Amish farmhouse, either original or restored; neither could tell. The house contained rooms full of simple, wooden furniture. A woman dressed much like the woman by the side of the road told of the simple lives and principles of the Amish. Beth was fascinated. Andy had heard it before. After the tour they walked down a path to the edge of the field and sat on a bench, looking out over the rich and rolling farm land.

"So this is where you come from?" Beth said.

"Well, not exactly," Andy said. "My hometown, Sunbury, is north of here, actually pretty far from Amish country, now that I think about it. No Amish up there. But I used to like to come down

10

here as a kid. They have some sort of theme park over on Route 30, and my dad took me for a buggy ride each time we came down."

"You rode in a buggy?"

"Sure. There was an Amish man just down the road who would take us out on some of the back roads for a couple of dollars. Do you want to go for a ride?"

"No," Beth said. She pulled her arms in around her.

"We don't have to."

"So are all these people here Amish?" Beth seemed to want to keep the conversation going.

"Not all of them. Some are Mennonite, and even the Mennonites come in different types. Some of the Mennonites are almost Amish; others are more like us. Well, maybe that's not the way to put it. I mean they're all like us in a way, in certain fundamental ways."

"Like what ways?" Beth asked.

"I don't know. Emotionally, maybe." Andy wasn't prepared for subtle distinctions.

Beth pressed on. "I doubt it. This is a different world. This isn't New York, or even Lancaster. These are simple people who are happy without electricity or automobiles. They probably don't even know that the Phillies exist. I envy them." Beth looked out over the fields and smiled, to herself, not to Andy.

Andy could not decide if he should agree or disagree with Beth. He could not even decide if she was serious.

"You're probably right," he said finally. "But I don't think we should romanticize them. I'm sure they hurt too sometimes."

"I suppose so," Beth said in a tone that suggested they drop the subject.

After leaving the Amish farm, they drove into Lancaster. Beth had read about the farmers' market in the center of the city and wanted to see it. They parked near the center square, the old one with the Civil War statue, and wandered around until they found the market. It reminded Andy of a huge brick barn with a concrete floor, poor lighting, and row upon row of stalls. Behind many of the stalls were the Amish, old men with white beards, young girls with hair pulled back in a bun, their faces smooth as ivory, older women standing around chatting with each other or pleasantly waiting on a customer. The tourists were there, clearly so, but the sense of community transcended all of that.

"Look at that woman over there," Beth said.

She motioned toward a stall which had some sort of smoked bologna hanging behind it. The woman was young, mid-twenties perhaps. She smiled pleasantly at each customer, but seemed shy. Her black hair was pulled back severely, the effect softened by her large, dark eyes and white teeth.

"She's beautiful," Beth said. "Do you think that's her husband there beside her?"

"I think so," Andy said. "Probably. But I'm no expert, you know."

The man wore a purple shirt and black pants held up with wide suspenders. He also wore the usual wide-brimmed straw hat with the broad black band, and he had the beginnings of a beard. He stood to the side of the stall, talking with the young woman.

"They seem happy," Beth said. "They must be married."

"Yes," Andy said, and wondered what one had to do with the other. He said nothing to Beth.

They decided to have dinner at one of the upscale restaurants in the center of town, forgoing another Pennsylvania Dutch meal. The restaurant, Lockard's, served mainly French dishes. The wine was excellent. They could have been in New York.

They returned to their motel exhausted and slipped into bed.

"So," Andy said, "have you had enough of the Amish? Should we leave first thing in the morning or would you like to look around some more?"

Beth had turned over.

"No," she said, "I think we can go back. I have some work I have to do before Monday. Good night."

"Beth," Andy said, "Do you want to talk?"

"No, I don't think so."

"Good night," Andy said and turned off the light. "It was pretty good today, wasn't it?"

"Uh."

"I mean after we got past that terrible accident yesterday, things got better. This really is a good place, don't you think?"

Beth did not answer.

"Maybe things really will get better," Andy said to himself.

He turned over and settled his head into the pillow. Just before falling asleep he thought he heard Beth crying softly.

When Andy awoke Sunday morning, Beth was gone. She left a note: "I went for a walk. You were sleeping so peacefully I didn't want to wake you. Be back soon and we can go. B."

Andy was confused because he knew Beth hated getting up in the morning, but he was also relieved and he didn't know why. He shaved and showered quickly, got dressed, and went out to the office. Beth was not on the bench.

"She'll be back soon, I guess."

The voice belonged to the motel owner, a man nearing retirement. He held a cup of coffee in his hand as he stood in the doorway of the office.

"Name's Ben," he said, "Want some coffee?"

"Oh, thanks," Andy said, taking the mug. "She likes to walk early in the morning. Me, I prefer to sleep in if I can."

"I know what you mean," Ben said, blowing on his coffee. "But being in the motel business I get up early and go to bed late."

"Tough way to make a living."

"Not so bad. Could be worse. Course anything could be worse."

"Except death," Andy said. He meant it as a joke, but it didn't come out that way.

"Don't know," Ben said. "One of my customers said one time the only thing worse than dying is living. Blew his brains out in the room next to yours. I guess I can tell you that since you're leaving today. How'd you sleep?"

"Fine," Andy said, but he shivered in the cold wind.

Ben sat down in one of the two wooden chairs on the porch, putting his cup on a small white, plastic table.

"Take a load off," he said.

Andy sat beside him, cupping his mug in both hands.

Ben leaned back in his chair and said, "Did you get to see the Amish?"

"Yes," Andy said. "We had a good tour yesterday, visited a farm, spent some time at the farmers' market in Lancaster, but mostly we just drove around and saw the farms and the buggies and the men working in the fields."

"Yeah, their busy time's starting, started a month or so ago in fact. They'll work hard till the harvest in October, out in the fields while there's light."

"It's a hard life," Andy said, "but it looks like a good life. They must be good neighbors, good people."

"They're good neighbors all right, the Amish, the Mennonites, all the people here that farm the land. They mostly keep to themselves, only mix with the world—that's what they call everyone else—to sell their things. Probably no better or worse than most of us."

"They look a lot better to me," Andy said. "They seem to have a lot more respect for each other." Andy paused and then put his mug down on the table. "Probably resist temptation a lot better than most of us," he added.

Ben sipped his coffee. "Maybe," he said. "Don't know much about that. Except, of course, for the stories we hear."

"What do you mean, stories?"

"Just stories. Probably nothing to them. But you do hear things, living here and all."

"What sorts of things?" Andy was embarrassed to appear so eager, but he wanted to know.

"Things just like most of us. They're not perfect either. None of us is. At least I'm not."

Andy nodded.

Ben continued when Andy said nothing.

"Every once in a while you hear about one of the girls disappearing for a while. Having a baby and then giving it up for adoption or more likely keeping it as a brother or sister. Don't know if that's true, but that's what you hear. Or one of the men chasing after someone's wife. The older men usually talk him out of that, but it happens. You never hear about divorce though. They work it out. Course some of the young people do leave and go live in the world. But I think it's just because they don't like the restrictions. More and more of them see the fun that's out there and that they can't have. They want it so they go get it. But that's different. There's lots going on with those that stay. No, I don't think you could say they're perfect. No more than the rest of us. Just human I guess."

"Yeah," Andy said and thought of his own marriage.

"It's hard on them," Ben said. "Every so often you hear about a suicide. Especially the women. Just can't take it, I guess."

"It must be a terrible strain on the women," Andy said.

He had not thought about it before, but now he realized how painful it must be for the women, how much pressure there must be for them to conform, how restrictive their lives must be. And how little he could understand it.

"Look," Ben said, "there's one of the women now. Sometimes they're out this early walking to a neighbor's farm or to a roadside market."

The figure grew closer and Andy watched, thinking what kind of life this woman must have, how difficult it must be. Then as the figure got closer he saw it was Beth.

He continued to watch her walking slowly toward him, and when she got to him, they went back to the room.

"Did you have a nice walk?" he asked.

"Yes," she said, smoothing her hair with her hand.

"I had an interesting talk with the owner," Andy said. "He told me stories about the dark side of Amish life."

"I don't believe there is a dark side," Beth said. "He was just entertaining you."

"Maybe so," Andy said. "You're probably right."

They packed their things and put everything in the car. When Andy was ready to turn the key, Beth reached over for his hand.

"Wait," she said. "I want to talk now. I can't talk when we're moving in traffic. We should concentrate on this."

"On what?"

"On us."

"Us? What about us?"

"There is no us," Beth said. "We've tried but I don't think so."

Andy was confused. "What don't you think?"

"I don't know. We can't even understand each other when we're talking about not understanding each other. It's crazy."

Beth looked straight ahead, through the windshield to the road, already beginning to fill with morning traffic.

"Lots of tourists already," Andy said.

Beth just looked ahead. "Lots," she said, finally.

"Beth?" Andy turned to look at her.

"What?"

"What should we do?"

"I don't know." Beth looked down.

"Keep trying?"

"Maybe."

"Harder?"

"Maybe. But I'm not sure."

"Beth, what if I said I love you?"

She did not respond.

"Wouldn't that be enough?"

Beth turned to Andy. "Andy?"

Andy didn't respond. Instead he sat there for a moment and then started the car. They drove back to New York in silence.

16

One

A year later Andy Simpson was back in central Pennsylvania, alone, sitting in his Carlisle office, surrounded by the leftovers of his weekly edition of the Carlisle *Courier*, and by the leftovers of his life. His divorce was final, quick and clean, almost before he could realize what had happened to him. Beth was right. They had lived side by side for twelve years, but that was it. Why should anyone be at fault? These things happen. Often, too. Only, one part of his life was still empty.

Thirty-eight years old, he had been working in Carlisle for just a month, putting together a weekly newspaper that was mostly ads and local news. Last month he had been city editor of *The Long Island Daily*. It was his idea to leave, he told himself. He was happy to be back in central Pennsylvania, but he wasn't sure why he was here. Was it simply to get away? To start over? To get back to where he began? It probably wasn't any of those things. It was just restlessness, rootlessness. Beth had been something of an anchor for him, something that could hold him in place. He knew he needed her. He just wasn't sure he loved her. Wasn't need enough? He thought it was, but he also knew it wasn't enough for Beth.

He turned back to the article he was writing, an article he had promised the publisher in Harrisburg he would have to him in fifteen minutes. Even weeklies have deadlines, and Andy needed to get the article on last night's school board meeting to Harrisburg by e-mail. The Harrisburg *Capital* published his paper. They had bought it from the previous owner, a Carlisle native who had owned and edited it for forty years. That's when they brought in Andy and told him to give Carlisle the local news each week. They would cover the big news. That satisfied Andy, particularly now when he no longer cared about the big news. Or much of anything. He turned back to his article, determined to focus on it until it was done. Pretty routine stuff.

Andy became aware of a man standing beside him, but decided to ignore him until he finished the final two or three paragraphs. The man shuffled his feet. Andy grew impatient.

"Are you the newspaper editor?" the man asked.

Without looking up, Andy said, "Yes, but I'm busy right now."

"I was wondering . . . ."

Andy looked up, still impatient amid growing frustration. The man's face was dark brown and furrowed from the sun, but his eyes were a deep blue-gray. For some reason, the man's eyes reminded Andy of the sheen on the dark soil turned up by his grandfather's plow, that dark, shiny surface that looked more dark blue than brown. The man had white hair, a firm, square face, a solid build. But it was his eyes that fixed Andy. He looked deeply into those eyes.

The man began again, "I was wondering if you could help me."

Andy looked away and said, "Yes, well, like I said, I'm busy right now."

He then looked back, gazed into his eyes, and then said, "What kind of help?"

"Advice," the man said. "I need advice on how to get my story out so people will know."

"What story? Know about what?" Andy forgot about the school board, leaving the two paragraphs hanging.

"About my wife." The man looked down at his heavy, worn boots. Andy too looked at the boots and then back at the man.

"What about your wife?"

"She shuns me," he said.

Andy looked back at his screen. My God, he thought, another story about an abandoned husband. Just what the public wants. He wondered how he could get out of this.

"Look," Andy said, "I'm sorry your wife left you, but — "

"She did not leave me," he interrupted. "She still lives in the house. She shuns me."

"Shuns? What do you mean 'shuns'?"

"She avoids me."

"I'm sorry," Andy said. "Lots of men have trouble with their wives. You can't always keep them interested."

Andy knew about trouble, about not keeping them interested. Maybe that was the problem. He couldn't keep Beth interested. Hell, he thought, he couldn't even keep himself interested. He still can't. He looked at the man again. He looked strong, determined, but Andy was losing patience.

"I'm sorry," he said, " but I have a story to finish. I don't think I can help you."

Andy turned to his screen, about to end the article with a summary of the dispute over a certain book the board wants to keep out of the hands of children.

The man didn't leave. "I think you can," he said, pausing until he had Andy's attention, and then added, "I need publicity. Once people understand what they are doing to me, they might stop."

They? Now it's a conspiracy, Andy thought. He looked back at the man and noticed again his wide-brimmed straw hat and black shirt and pants. His suspenders hiked his pants halfway to his chest.

"Amish," Andy thought. He knew he was near Amish country, but he thought the Amish were over in Lancaster County, back where he and Beth had spent their last weekend together. That's Amish country. Why would an Amish man walk into a newspaper office in Carlisle?

"Are you Amish?" Andy asked.

"No, Reformed Mennonite," he said, his face hardening. "They will not let my wife have anything to do with me."

"Is 'they' the Reformed Mennonites?"

"Yes. The bishop. It was his decision."

"And your wife can't talk to you?"

"No. She is forbidden to have any relationship. My children too."

Andy looked away, pushing some papers to the edge of his desk. The man stood still.

"Look," Andy said, "could you come back later and we'll talk about it?"

"When?"

"I don't know."

"This afternoon?"

This afternoon, Andy thought. He had meant later as in never, but the man missed the message. He could think of no way out of this predicament. He wasn't even sure he wanted out.

Finally he said, "All right, this afternoon."

"When this afternoon?"

"Uh, two. How about two? Will that be okay?"

"Yes," the man said, and left. Andy didn't even get his name.

He finished the article and sent it off to Harrisburg, a bit late but close enough, he thought. It was time for lunch.

Andy looked around his office and then called into the adjoining room, "Sue, how about something to eat? We can go down to Harry's. I have something I want to talk to you about."

"Sure, give me twenty minutes."

Sue was the ad exec at the newspaper. She got the money to pay the bills. She had grown up in Carlisle and had worked at the *Courier* for the past twenty years. That's what made her good. She kept the place going with the money she brought in. In the short time he had been there, Andy had noticed Sue liked to replace news with another quarter-page ad.

She called to him, "Do you really need that story on the school board?"

"Yes," he said.

"Something has to go."

"Take out the story on Reider's new travel agency. We can run it next week."

"OK. I'm going to replace it with an ad for Reider's new travel agency."

"Perfect," he said, "I like the irony."

"Right," she said, "I like the money."

Andy had liked Sue from the start. She is slightly older than he, mid-forties he guessed, and competent, no airs. She liked to talk and didn't seem to mind that he did not. She never took it personally. Although she was only a few years older than Andy, he thought of her almost as a mother. And he liked the way she knew the county, something he found mystifying after his years in New York City.

When Sue was finished with the ad, she walked into Andy's office. "Ready?" she said.

The *Courier* office was located on Pomfret Street, across from the Pomfret Book Store. Andy often stopped there on his way home to look over the thousands of used books stuffed into every cranny of the shop. He and Sue didn't stop this time. Instead, they walked a half block down Pomfret Street through the warm, spring day to Hanover Street and then turned right. One block up they crossed the intersection of Hanover and High streets and the park that marks that intersection. Shortly after arriving in town, Andy was pleased when he found a small marker commemorating the achievements of Jim Thorpe, who had been a student at the Carlisle Indian School, the same school where Marianne Moore had taught. Andy also liked the fact that the square was bounded just two blocks out by four streets called North, South, East, and West. It's impossible to get lost here, he thought. Moving north on Hanover Street, he and Sue walked past a series of small-town shops, places Sue never even looked at anymore but that Andy still found somehow comforting. The Carlisle Tavern and the Molly Pitcher Hotel side by side, the Olde Thyme Farm Shop and the Thomas Sewing Center. Across the street, the Market Cross Tavern next to the Global Empire Restaurant and then the Cumberland Valley Bible Book Center.

"Harry's okay?" he asked, as though there was another choice, like the Burger King at the end of High Street.

"Yeah, sure," she said.

Harry's, a small-town family restaurant, fit the ambiance of Hanover Street perfectly. Sue said that Harry had died some years before but that they still call it Harry's anyway. No point confusing people, she said. His widow, Mary, ran the place now, did the cooking and hired local girls, the ones that got married right out of high school and now needed a job. He looked around the restaurant. The paneling was beginning to bow and pull away from the wall, but the checkerboard tablecloths were comforting, and Mary insisted on using matching cloth napkins. Andy and Sue sat in one of the half-dozen booths that line one wall; another eight tables, napkins waiting expectantly, occupied the center of the room. As usual Harry's was empty, except for one man sitting at the counter, drinking coffee and chatting with Mary.

"How does she do it?" Andy asked Sue.

"The mortgage is paid. The overhead is low. She doesn't need much volume. Enough people around here come in for dinner around 4, 4:30, especially the older people. You should see it at 5:30 in the morning when she opens. Not much like New York, is it?"

"No, not much," Andy said. He felt good sitting there. "I like it this way. I can't imagine a deli in the City getting by without hordes of people pushing and shoving for a pastrami sandwich or something. Here we get a hot meatloaf sandwich and fries for a couple of dollars and no one even yells at us."

Andy had been trying to avoid condescension ever since

arriving in Carlisle. He knew how easy it is to make comments about the locals after having lived in New York for fifteen years. He didn't want to do that. He didn't need to do that . . . so he told himself. He especially had no reason to feel superior to Sue. He at least knew that much. And everyone here in town seemed to be something like Sue: kind, understanding, solid, reliable, a bit suspicious of outsiders. Everyone here seemed married. Everyone in New York seemed divorced. When they separated, Beth said she wanted to stay in New York and work at her ad agency. She was good and she made money. He told himself he wanted to get out of the pressure. They never had much in common, so divorce seemed like a good idea. He didn't know why; he never really questioned it. He did know, however, that the *Courier* was not the *Daily*, but it was fine.

"You're awfully quiet," Sue said. "What are you thinking about?"

"Nothing in particular," Andy said. He ran his finger around the top of his water glass. Sue watched this for a moment and then said, "Let me guess. Are you thinking about your wife?"

"My ex-wife."

"Your ex-wife."

"No, I wasn't," he said. He began to stir his coffee, hoping not to talk about that. Especially not with Sue. She was a good listener and he knew once he started he would never stop. I don't mind spilling everything for $200 an hour, he thought, but doing it for free just didn't seem right somehow.

He looked at his coffee and continued stirring.

"What do you know about the Reformed Mennonites?" he asked.

Sue seemed surprised by the suddenness of the question.

"Not much," she said. "I know there's a church just south of here. Kreider's, I think. But I don't know anyone who goes there. They keep pretty much to themselves. Most people think they're Amish because they dress sort of like them, but they're not. They're

Mennonites, just more conservative than most Mennonites, and less friendly. At least they seem that way to me. Have you been to the big roadside market down on Route 15?"

He had not.

"A Reformed Mennonite family owns that. All the relatives take turns working there. Souders. Best fruits and vegetables around. That's all I know. Like I said, they keep pretty much to themselves."

"That's good. That helps."

"Why do you ask? That's a strange thing for a city boy to wonder about."

"Oh," he said, "it's just that a man came in my office this morning."

She said she had seen him.

"I think he wants to get a story in the paper. He said the bishop in his church—Reformed Mennonite—is keeping his wife and children from having anything to do with him."

"Yeah," she said. "Shunning. That's what they call it. I've heard about it, but like I said I don't know anybody, so I don't even know if they still do it."

Andy assured her they still do.

"I suppose you're right," Sue said, "but I'm surprised he wants to talk about it, and even put something in the paper."

"Can they really keep them apart like that, even if both want to be together?"

"I don't know," she said. "Most churches I know try to keep couples together."

"Most churches I know don't care one way or another," Andy said with a cynicism that ended that part of the conversation.

As they finished their lunch, Andy used his bread to soak up the remaining gravy, just the way he always did as a kid. He found it satisfying, comforting. When they left Harry's, Sue went back to the office. Andy decided to take a walk around the town.

He liked Carlisle, Andy told himself. He especially liked the slow pace and the nineteenth-century architecture. Carlisle had been important during the Civil War, the wounded of Gettysburg spilling over into the homes and buildings of the town. Because of that many of the old buildings were preserved, and Andy always enjoyed walking past them. He even liked the trendy little boutique-like flower shops and dress shops carved out of the fronts of the buildings: Winnie's, Trish's, the usual names.

By two o'clock Andy was back at his office. The man was there, outside the door, waiting.

"Come in," Andy said.

The office was small, with a single window, the office of a journalist: piles of newspapers, his and others; a bookcase filled with reference books and favorite novels; awards on the walls; three chairs, unmatched; a desk covered with papers; the computer, cursor blinking.

"Please sit down," Andy said. He had decided to start over with the Mennonite, on a more cordial note.

"I'll stand, thank you," he said.

So much for cordiality, Andy thought.

"I'm Andy Simpson." He held out his hand.

"I know."

"I don't know your name,"

"Jacob Weaver." Jacob took Andy's hand, hard, and shook it.

"That's a start," Andy said, wondering already if it was going to be worth it.

"You said your wife is shunning you."

"Yes."

"Look," Andy said, "I have to be truthful with you. Half the marriages today end in divorce. A man losing his wife is one of the great non-stories in today's news."

"I will not lose my wife. We will not divorce," Jacob said. "I love my wife. She loves me. We just cannot be together as man and wife."

"You said you live in the same house, with your wife and children."

"Yes." Jacob's response was formal, clipped, almost military. The antiphony began.

"Do you eat there?"

"Yes. We eat together."

"At the same table?"

"Yes."

"But you don't talk to each other?"

"No, they shun me."

Andy had many questions, but he wasn't sure which were appropriate. He decided to plunge.

"Do you sleep there?"

"Yes, but we do not touch."

"Oh." Andy didn't know where to go from there. "And this is because of the bishop?"

"Yes. The bishop—Bishop Souders—forbids contact."

"Why?" Andy asked, sincerely perplexed. It seemed to him like a logical question.

Jacob ignored the question and instead asked if Andy could come with him.

Andy had wrapped up the paper for the week and had the afternoon free. He certainly had nothing better to do.

"Why not?" he said, surprising himself, and followed Jacob out of the office into the street.

"We'll take my car," Jacob said.

Andy looked at the car. It was a ten-year-old Buick, painted completely black, even the chrome. He got in. It smelled of hay and dirt, just like his grandfather's car used to smell. He decided that he liked the car and the smell, and settled back for the ride.

Andy asked where they were going.

"You will see. It is not far," Jacob said as he turned the key and forced the gear into first.

Pretty primitive, Andy thought. Not even automatic.

They followed a winding back road through the countryside. In the short time he had been here, Andy had discovered he loved these roads. He watched the farms, each seeming more comfortable than the last. Finally, they turned south onto the busy Route 15, a road that crawled past fast food restaurants, used car dealerships, paint stores, farm equipment centers, opening up to the occasional farm field. Beyond that Andy could see the hills that rolled, he knew, to the Susquehanna River. These were the remains of a mountain range, once higher than the Rockies. Tired, Andy thought. Even mountains wear out.

He also knew that beyond those hills, sitting in the middle of the Susquehanna, was Three Mile Island, TMI, the nuclear power plant that almost melted down back in '79. He had been away at college at the time, but he followed it on the news. His family up in Sunbury thought about evacuating and would have, if a nice man had not come on television to calm everyone down. What the nice man did not say is that fumes laced with radioactive material spewed out over the countryside and poisoned the air and probably the ground soil, to say nothing of the people. He remembers how they talked about the half-life of the material. Half-life. He liked the phrase and wondered if the air around here was still poisoned somehow. He thought maybe it was. Jacob said nothing for the five miles it took them to get to where he was taking Andy.

Then Jacob slowed and pulled over to the left side of the road, swinging the car around at an angle so they could see across the road.

Andy asked why they were stopping there.

"I want you to see the market," Jacob said, "over there."

The market was one of the many roadside fruit and vegetable stands that dot the landscape, farmers selling off extra produce. This market, however, was larger, a family business. A sign, "Souders," hung over the stand. Three cars had pulled alongside the stand. A half-dozen or so people milled around, picking up vegetables, talking with the help.

"That is her," Jacob said.

"Who?"

"My wife, Sarah. She is the one on the left."

Two women were waiting on customers. They both wore long, dark purple dresses and white bonnets. The one on the left, Sarah, smiling shyly, was waiting on a well-dressed couple. She gave them change, put their produce in a paper bag, and gave it to them. When they left, she stepped back, waiting for the next customer, her hands at her sides.

"That's your wife?" Andy said, not knowing what to add. She was pretty, looking younger than her forty or so years, slim. The other woman was older and heavier.

"That is Esther," Jacob said.

A man walked over to Sarah and asked her a question. She smiled.

"But why are we here?" Andy asked.

"I come here to watch her work," Jacob said, adding after a moment, "I come here to watch her smile."

Jacob began to talk. Andy watched Jacob's wife moving among the people.

"The other woman, Esther, is Sarah's sister," he said.

Andy nodded and asked Jacob if the bishop owned the market stand.

Jacob said he does own the stand and the farm behind it, and then he added, "I . . . we live a mile down the road."

Andy was more confused than ever. He understood everything Jacob told him, but he didn't know what it all had to do with him. He said to Jacob, "I still don't know what I can do for you. What help do you want from me?"

Jacob responded almost as though he had been waiting for an invitation. "I want you to tell the truth about all this, so I can get my wife back. It is unnatural. She belongs to me. The Bible says that. The bishop is blaspheming against the Bible. He is violating the teachings of Paul. Paul said the man is the head of the house, and he must be obeyed. You tell the people that, and my family will be restored."

Andy thought perhaps he should be back-pedaling on this one.

"Maybe so," he said, "but I don't think anybody really belongs to anyone else, no matter what Paul said. I don't think I would get far with a story like that."

"The people would listen."

"What people?" Andy was thinking of his readership.

"The people of the church. The believers. They would see that the bishop is wrong, and I would have my wife back."

Those people? Andy wondered how many of those people bought the products his paper advertised, or even bought his paper. He saw that Jacob simply wanted to use him as a propaganda tool, and he wasn't interested in that. At the same time, as he thought more about the situation, his newspaper sense began to take over, and he realized there might be a story here. The individual conscience against the authority of the church. The story of the little guy. Maybe. He decided to let Jacob talk and see where it might go. Even if it went nowhere, Jacob was interesting, and it was pleasant enough sitting by the side of the road watching local people go about their business. A steady stream of customers pulled over, felt the melons, held up the celery, and bought the produce. Sarah never looked across the road. Andy couldn't tell if she even recognized Jacob's car.

Jacob told his story. "Everyone thinks the bishop speaks for the church, but I can tell you he is not blameless. His parents were feuding and he did nothing. He lies. About me. And about other people too. And he has done things I cannot talk about. He has gone against the teachings of the church. I told the congregation about it. I stood up in the church and I told them all about him, about how he was not following the teachings of Menno Simon. I had facts, but he said I should obey him. I told him I obey God and that he was not God. He met with the elders and they excommunicated me. Now my wife must shun me. Sarah loves me. I know that. She cannot say it and she cannot do anything, but I know. I can tell it in her eyes. Besides, one night she came to me.

She was unclothed. And in that one act she repudiated the bishop. She says it never happened, but it did, and it showed the lies the bishop has been spreading. It shows what he says are all lies, and it shows that the shunning is empty."

Andy allowed the words to wash over him as he watched the activities of the vegetable stand. Jacob sat with his face down, talking. Sarah and Esther continued to wait on customers but were soon joined by a middle-aged man, tall, with a graying beard. He too was dressed in black with a wide-brimmed straw hat. He seemed to be supervising the women, nodding to a few customers, waiting in the background.

Jacob raised his head.

"That is him!" he said, his eyes even fiercer. "That is the bishop. He usually does not come down to the stand. See how he tells everyone what to do."

He looked like a typical proprietor to Andy.

"He cannot do that. Sarah must know the truth."

Suddenly Jacob opened his door and jumped onto the berm of the road. Before Andy could say anything, Jacob was striding across the highway, heading for the vegetable stand. Andy sat there, not sure what he should be doing, watching as Jacob moved quickly behind the counter, up to the bishop.

Andy saw but could not hear Jacob shouting at the bishop, standing close to him, their faces almost touching, bordering on pantomime. The two women tried to ignore Jacob; the customers were clearly embarrassed. The bishop walked around Jacob, trying to avoid contact, but Jacob stood there, then turned to the bishop and shouted something. The bishop shouted something back, Jacob punching the air with his arms. Finally, the bishop turned and walked back up the hill toward his house as Jacob kept shouting after him until he was out of sight. Jacob then turned to the two women and said something to them. Esther glared at him, but Sarah turned her back and lowered her head. Finally, they too walked up the hill, leaving the customers bewildered, several pretending nothing was happening. Others simply left. Jacob stood for a while, looking lost, confused, and then he sat down on a tomato crate. During all this activity, Andy never even wound down his window. He just sat there, watching a show with the sound turned down. After several minutes, Andy decided to go to Jacob and try to get him back in his car. He checked the traffic and crossed the highway.

"Do you think we should go now?" he asked Jacob. Jacob stared ahead.

Andy tried again. "Let's get back in the car."

Jacob turned to Andy. "I know she loves me, but the church will not let us be together. What kind of a church would destroy a family? She obeys the bishop and not me. The Bible says she should obey me."

"Maybe she should obey herself," Andy said, but Jacob just looked through him for a few seconds. They walked slowly back across the highway to the car, and once inside sat for a few moments in silence. Andy wasn't sure whether to say something or just let Jacob start the car.

Finally, Jacob said, "Now, do you see what my life is? It is a life in hell. That is what it is. That is what I wanted you to see. That is why I need you to tell my story."

Andy thought more about the story in all this. He could make Jacob admirable, even if he did not like the righteousness that came through so strongly. Andy knew he was always uncomfortable in the presence of religious certainty, perhaps because of his own uncertainty, but he thought he could be objective. Maybe it would make a good story, maybe even make the newswire, but he also knew he would have trouble making Jacob into a David, and he certainly did not want to make a Don Quixote out of him. But beyond all that, beyond the newspaper possibilities, he was sure there was more to it, more to Jacob, more to his predicament. He was not sure, however, he wanted to get the rest of the story.

"Let me think about it," he told Jacob as they headed back up Route 15. "Give me your phone number and I'll get back to you."

"I do not have a phone number," Jacob said.

"Oh, right," Andy said. "How can I contact you?"

"You cannot. I will be back."

Back in his office, Andy sat among the wares of his trade, all that which made his job possible. He stared at the blinking cursor and thought of Jacob and his wife. How could the church do this? How could someone so obviously certain be a victim? How can certainty and victimization be so unattractive? Andy had many questions, many related to his own uncertainties. He did know, however, one certainty in all this. Jacob would be back.

Two

About a week later, Thursday, the day after the *Courier* came out, Jacob was back. Andy was in his office on the phone, busy lining up stringers for all the school board and township commissioners meetings he needed to cover next week. The book banning debate was continuing over in Conewago, and the Cumberland County commissioners were planning to raise taxes, probably six or seven mills. Always something. He would cover those two stories, but he knew he would need more help. Maybe, he thought, he could get a couple journalism majors from the local college to help out. He couldn't pay much, but clips are clips.

Andy felt someone watching him and looked up.

"Hello, Mr. Simpson."

"Jacob. How are you? Have a seat." Andy had almost forgotten about Jacob during the last few days, but not completely.

"I did not see the story," Jacob said.

"Your story?"

"Yes."

"No, I decided not to do a story. There's just not enough there, at least not yet. I mean it just doesn't have a hook yet, an angle. It's sort of dog bites man. You know, husband loses wife." Andy turned back to his screen, but Jacob persisted.

"I have not lost her. I told you, the church forbids contact.

My suffering can be your story. I suffer because the church tries to control me. But it cannot. I do not give in to the church. To give in would be to admit they are right. And I know they are wrong. I have the word of God on my side. They have the word of the bishop. I am right, and they beat me down because of it. I told you, my life is a life in Hell. Your readers will be interested in that, and I will have my story told."

He's right, Andy thought. He should be in PR somewhere. Suffering always makes a good story, especially when it's the little guy suffering. Suffering David. Maybe that's the angle after all.

Andy swiveled around and asked Jacob to sit. He refused, so Andy went over to the shelf with the coffee pot and poured himself a cup, motioning for Jacob to have one. Jacob shook his head.

"You might be right," Andy said, "but I still need more information, more detail, and I should have the other side of the story too. Even if I don't use it, I should know what it is. I need background. Could I talk with the bishop?"

"No."

Andy walked over to Jacob. "Are you forbidding my talking with the bishop?"

"No," Jacob said, "he will not talk with you. You are an outsider, and he is afraid of the light."

"The light?"

Jacob's eyes flashed. "The light of truth. The truth of what he has done to me, what they have all done to me. He will not talk with you."

Andy went back to his desk and sat, but Jacob remained standing. Andy thought for a moment, staring at his screen, and then he said, "Maybe I could do some research. There must be something written about the Reformed Mennonite Church. Books, articles, something."

"There is a history, but it is old," Jacob said, "and there is another book."

"Another book?"

"Yes, about the church today and what it does to people, to me."

Andy was surprised. "There's a book that describes your situation?"

"Yes."

"Who wrote it"

"I did."

Andy swiveled again to Jacob and said, "You wrote a book? Then why do you need me? What's an article when you have a book with your story in it?"

"No one reads my book. I wrote it and no one would print it, so I paid my own money for copies of it. No stores want it. No one reads it. But you can read it. It is all there."

Andy was sure it was all there, and just a bit slanted. He was also sure he could not read the book while working on the article. Any vestige of objectivity would be gone completely.

"Maybe I can read it later," he said to Jacob. "Right now I think I should try to gather the information on my own. Could we talk more about it? You say you live on a farm just off Route 15 near the vegetable market. Can I come see you there? Maybe I could talk with Sarah too."

"You cannot talk with Sarah," he said.

"For the same reason I can't talk to the bishop?"

"Yes."

"Well, at least I could talk with you there."

"Yes."

Andy got directions from Jacob for later that afternoon, third farm back the road, and Jacob left.

"Way to go, Andy." Sue was standing in the doorway to Andy's office. She had obviously been listening to everything Andy and Jacob had been saying.

"It's pretty hard not to hear in these two small rooms," she said by way of explanation.

Andy didn't respond. Instead he kept watching Jacob as he walked to his car.

Sue walked into Andy's office and leaned against the wall beside the door. She too watched Jacob until he drove away.

"I don't think you'll get any information from any of the Mennonites," she said. "Like I said, they pretty much keep to themselves."

"Jacob did not keep to himself," Andy said, turning back to Sue.

"No, Jacob needs you. He's not your average Mennonite."

"No, I suppose not," Andy said. He looked out the window again and then back at Sue.

"So do you believe him?" Sue asked.

"I don't know what to believe. He seems sincere enough."

Sue turned away, as though to leave, and said, "He seems cracked enough to me."

"I don't know. I think his point about being shunned is true. I just don't know how much he deserves it, and I don't know what he really did to deserve it."

"He's too certain for me," Sue said, "too rigid. I wouldn't want to get in his way."

Andy agreed.

"But you're going to go see him anyway, aren't you?"

"Probably," Andy said. "I'm curious now. At least I'll look into it some more."

Andy got up and sat on the edge of his desk. He turned to Sue.

"Do you want to go along?"

Sue did not hesitate. "No."

That afternoon Andy drove down Route 15, past the hills that lead to TMI, turned in to the narrow road past the vegetable market, and then took the third lane, dirt and rutted. It was a long lane, a row of pine trees lining the left side, and he had to go slowly because of the ruts. The fields on both sides had been recently plowed; if it had been seeded, nothing so far was showing. He could smell the freshly turned earth. It smelled good to him, reminding him of his childhood and the summers he had spent on his grandfather's farm. He loved the smell of fresh earth. As he rounded the final curve to the farmhouse, he saw a woman in a purple dress, walking on the left, eyes down. He remembered Sarah from the week before at the vegetable stand. She never looked up at him, just kept walking slowly. She must be going down to the market to work, Andy thought as he slowly passed her.

Andy pulled his car into the yard, parked it under a tree, and got out. He looked up the slight slope of land to the farmhouse near the top and beyond it to a large wooden barn with white slats. The square brick house had two storeys with small attic windows of some sort at the peak and a large wooden porch across the front. Laundry, all black and purple, hung from a line attached to the side of the house and then to a large pole in the yard. Andy had seen hundreds of farmhouses just like it spread all over central Pennsylvania, including even his grandfather's house. He looked forward to getting inside again and began to walk toward it.

"I am over here," he heard someone shout. He turned to the voice and saw Jacob standing in front of what looked like an old house trailer, the permanent sort with a cement block base, the kind that tornadoes always destroy. He walked toward the trailer but stopped short of Jacob.

"I am living here now," Jacob explained. "I just could not take it anymore, being in the house but like I never existed. It was just terrible, so I moved here. Sarah's grandfather used to live here before he died. A good man. He never wanted to be a burden, but he could not take care of himself, so we bought this for him. Now I am here."

"I'm sorry," Andy said. "I saw your wife just now, walking down the road."

"Yes, she is going to work at the market. She always walks. It is only a mile."

Both men stood standing, Andy looking around, not knowing what to say, where to begin. Finally, he just plunged in.

"What did she say when you told her you were moving out?"
"Nothing."
"Did you tell her?"
"No, I just moved out."

Andy walked the last few steps to stand with Jacob as they both looked out over the land to the hills beyond. Jacob told Andy about the farm. It had been in his family for 150 years. Never changed much. Always grew potatoes. Jacob said he had just finished putting in the last of them. He asked Andy if he would like to walk around the farm a bit.

"Sure," Andy said, and then as they started to walk, Andy told Jacob about his grandfather's farm.

"I used to love hanging out in the barn," Andy said, "especially in the fall when the hay was in. Some of the other kids would come over and we could play in the bales, make forts, that sort of thing. They were good times."

"Yes," Jacob said, "I remember good times." He quickly changed the subject back to his farm.

"I want to walk over and see how the potatoes are doing," he said and asked Andy to come along.

Andy agreed. "I could use the walk," he said.

The potato leaves were barely out of the ground. Andy knew they were fine. They walked slowly along the rows between the raised potato mounds, Jacob stopping occasionally to kick the dirt or kneel to look more closely.

"My grandfather never grew potatoes," Andy said, "mostly wheat and some soybeans. Is it difficult to grow potatoes?" Andy was straining for small talk.

"No," Jacob said, "it is not difficult. The secret is in the eyes. You have to have at least one eye in each piece of potato you plant. The eyes are important."

"Yes, I know," Andy said, thinking of Jacob's eyes.

"Nothing grows without the eyes, Mr. Simpson."

Jacob stopped walking and stared again across the potato field to other fields in the distance and to the hills, now light blue in the haze. Andy did not want to interrupt his thoughts, so he leaned up against the rail fence and waited. Jacob seemed like such a combination of gentleness and fierceness to him. He spoke softly but could shout heatedly. He spoke of love for his wife, but expressed clear hatred for the bishop. He lived his life by the Bible, but could use it to beat someone into the ground. Now, foregrounded against the blue haze of the hills in the distance, he looked vulnerable and very sad.

Andy thought of his own sadness, but his, he realized, came not out of certainty but out of doubt, out of confusion. He and Beth separated, then divorced, because he could not say he loved her, even to himself. It wasn't so much that he did not love her; it was just that he did not know what love was. He could not recognize it, and therefore could not function within the context of love. Jacob, on the other hand, knew what love was, even, perhaps, when it wasn't there. Andy knew he missed Beth, missed the someone who was Beth, and he knew he had no alternative but to come back here, back close to where he had been a child, hoping somehow to discover something, something that would help him make some sense of his life. He thought maybe he wanted to start over somehow, but he wasn't sure. He didn't know how to do that.

Finally, Jacob interrupted their reveries.

"It is pretty here, is it not, Mr. Simpson?"

Andy was startled. "What? Oh, yes," he said. "It's peaceful too. I can't imagine anything unpleasant happening around here. This is why the poets like the phrase, idyllic, I suppose."

"I suppose so, Mr. Simpson, but unpleasant things do happen here."

"Look, Jacob," Andy said, trying to change the subject, "do you have to call me Mr. Simpson? Just call me Andy."

"If it is all the same, I will call you Mr. Simpson."

"Then should I call you Mr. Weaver?"

"No need to. Suit yourself."

Jacob began to walk back to his trailer. Andy followed. When he drew even with Jacob, Andy asked directly, "Why did you do it, Jacob?" he asked.

"Move out to the trailer?"

"No. Why did you oppose the bishop? I can't figure out if you really had a theological dispute or if you were just being difficult."

Andy expected a strong reaction, a defensive attack of some sort. Instead Jacob just kicked gently at the dirt and turned his eyes to Andy, shattering his directness.

"Mr. Simpson," Jacob said softly, "I am always difficult when defending the true church. That is what God wants me to do."

Andy asked if the Reformed Mennonite Church is the true church.

"It is, but it has gone wrong," Jacob said.

"How did it go wrong?" Andy determined to push this as far as he could.

"The bishop has taken it in the wrong direction. It has gotten away from the truth."

Andy asked which truth.

"The truth that Paul preaches."

"That the man is the head of the house?"

"Yes, that and other things."

"But that's the main thing?"

Jacob stopped walking and turned to Andy.

"That is the basis, the foundation," he said. "Any person who destroys a family is not following the teachings of Christ. We have two children, and they are not allowed to be with me. I have a wife, and she is not allowed to be my wife."

"Maybe that's her choice," Andy said, pushing Jacob, still expecting an explosion.

"No, that is not her choice. I know that. She obeys the bishop."

"Why?"

"Because she has been taught to obey the church and its

representatives. She was taught that when she came into the church."

"Who brought her into the church?"

"I did. We were to be married."

Andy realized then that Sarah had not grown up in the church, but had joined as an adult. He asked Jacob what she had done before joining the church.

"She was in school."

"What did she do there, besides go to class? I mean what was her life like? What was she like? Was she popular? Did she go out on dates?"

"People liked her," Jacob said calmly, almost with pride. "She was a good student. And she was a cheerleader."

"A cheerleader? My God, look at her now. She wears long purple dresses and a bonnet."

"She has learned modesty," Jacob said, also with pride.

Andy was puzzled. Jacob was responsible for bringing her into his church and now he accuses her of collaborating in a plot to destroy their marriage, even though he says she loves him. She apparently believes she must obey the church, even when it means making their marriage hollow. She must be willing to sacrifice her love for Jacob to a higher calling. There is something admirable in that, Andy thought. But, on the other hand, Jacob says she is obeying the bishop and not the church. It sounded hopeless to Andy, so he decided to try another approach and asked Jacob when Esther, Sarah's sister, had joined the church. Jacob said she had joined the church after he had married Sarah.

"Tell me about the bishop," Andy said. He was curious about the power this man apparently held over the congregation.

Jacob's eyes flashed. "He is an evil man," he said.

"I know," Andy said, "but what's he done that's so evil? Isn't he also doing what he thinks is God's will? Isn't he making the people in the church shun you because he thinks that's what the church says he must do? Isn't that the teaching of the church?"

Jacob remained adamant. "Yes, but he is wrong to accuse me of heresy to the church, and he is wrong for imposing the ban and making others avoid me."

Andy asked Jacob about the purpose of shunning, what it is supposed to accomplish.

"To keep the faithful from the unfaithful," Jacob said, "and to bring the unfaithful back to the church."

Andy asked if the people in the congregation want him back.

"Yes, but only if I admit I sinned in opposing the bishop?"

"Do they try to get you back?" Andy asked. "Does anyone talk to you?"

Jacob paused for a moment, again looking at the soil before saying simply, "No." He then continued, "But once the bishop tried. This will tell you what kind of person he is. Once he tried to get me to admit my wrongs and to come back to the church. Do you remember when I told you that once my wife came to me in our bed, unclothed?"

"Yes." Andy had thought of that often, unable to fit it in with everything else he had discovered.

"She came to me that way because the bishop told her to do it."

"The bishop told a wife to go naked to her husband's bed? I suppose most bishops wouldn't actually say that, but it doesn't sound exactly unorthodox either."

"She sold her body to the church. She wanted me to come back and she thought her body would make me do it. She offered me her body if I would sell my soul, and it was the bishop who made her do that." Jacob became more excited. "She acted like a harlot, doing and saying things she never did before. I cannot tell you."

"No need to," Andy said. Jacob's eyes sparked, and his jaw became firmer, more set. He was not the gentle man of a few moments earlier. He was angry.

"It did not work," he said, "I did not resist, and in that act, in her coming to me that way, the ban was lifted. The bishop destroyed the ban when he himself told her to violate it, and now, for the church, it is no more."

Andy asked how he knew it was the bishop's idea. Jacob responded immediately. "Sarah would not have done that alone."

Jacob reached down and picked up a handful of the moist, dark earth. He slowly shaped it with his hands into a ball. "This is what the bishop can do to the people of his church, but he could never do this to me." He flung the ball of soil into the ground where it splattered.

On the way back to the trailer, Jacob talked more of his frustration and of his loneliness, but mostly of the farming and the coming summer.

At the top of the hill, Jacob asked, "Are you married, Mr. Simpson?"

"No," Andy said, "Divorced."

"Oh, then you know."

"No," Andy said, "I don't know."

They walked the rest of the way back to the trailer in silence. Andy thought more of Sarah. He had only seen her briefly, but he knew she had a side of this story to tell as well, just as Beth had her side to tell. He wondered what Beth's side would sound like.

When they reached the trailer, Andy thanked Jacob for his cooperation.

"Do you have enough now for a story?" Jacob asked.

"Perhaps," Andy said, "I'll have to think it over."

Back in his office later that afternoon, Andy thought more about Jacob and Sarah and the bishop. There's a lot more here, he thought, but I'm not sure I want to get into it. He realized he would be living in this community, perhaps for some time to come, and he might have to deal with these people.

After a moment, he shrugged his shoulders, sat down at his desk, and clicked on the terminal. The cursor blinked at him and he began to type, his journalistic instinct taking over. I'll see what

I write, he said to himself. After all, I don't have to print it. He started with the first sentence, the lead, the way he usually did. He knew a good lead would write the story for him.

A Cumberland County potato farmer has recently been shunned by his church, Kreider's Reformed Mennonite Church....

That isn't it. No hook. No angle. Besides, it's in the passive voice. This isn't a straight news story. As he told Jacob, this is a non-news story. Even shunning isn't all that unusual here. Sue knew about it.

"My life is a life in Hell," said a Cumberland County....

Better, but starting with a quote is too easy. Everybody does it. It's a cliché.

What's it like to live in the same house with a wife and children and yet never communicate?

Sounds like half the families in the country these days. Sounds like my loft without the kids.

Jacob Weaver has a mission. He wants to reunite his broken family, but his church says no.

Okay. That's better. It's a start. It says something and it makes you want to read more. It also identifies the direction of the article. Suffering, that's where it's going. Andy kept typing.

Kreider's Reformed Mennonite Church has shunned a Cumberland County potato farmer. As a result of the official church act, Weaver's wife and children are prohibited from having any contact with him.

Weaver has recently moved out of the house and into a trailer on the property. "It was just too painful to be there. It was like a life in Hell," he said. "I was with my wife and children, but they acted like I did not exist."

In a recent interview Weaver talked about his ordeal.

"The church has decided I no longer deserve to be a member. The shunning means that no members of the church can talk with me or have any kind of intercourse with me."

His crime, Weaver said, was his opposition to church authority, particularly that of the bishop, John Souders. Under church doctrine any person opposing the official position of the church can be excommunicated. The procedure is also known as shunning or banning.

"They want to destroy me," Weaver said, adding, "They know they cannot destroy my mind, so they want to destroy my life. I will not let them do that."

What keeps the 48 year-old-Weaver going? "I know I must obey God and the teachings of Jesus," he said, "and the church is going against those teachings, against the truth. They want to force me into agreeing with them, but I will not do that because it is not the truth."

The dispute arose originally over a disagreement between Weaver and Bishop Souders. According to Weaver, Souders administered a church sacrament to members who were undeserving. When Weaver called him on this, Souders instituted the excommunication procedures.

As a result of the shunning, Weaver's family must not talk with him or have any other form of communication. Until he moved out, the family ate together at the same table and spent evenings together.

"It was like I was dead," Weaver said. "It is terrible when those you love act like you are not even there."

Weaver vows to get his family together again. He cites Biblical authority.

"The Bible says what God has put together let no man put asunder. Paul said that the husband is the head of the house, not the bishop or any other man," Weaver explained.

For now Weaver expects to continue his fight for his family.

"No I will not give up," he said, adding confidently, "The word of God is on my side. I will keep trying until I get my family back."

Meanwhile, Weaver lives alone in his trailer and works the family potato farm.

Andy published the story in the next edition.

Three

"Why are you doing this?"

Andy looked up from his computer. It was Sarah. He was wondering how he might get to talk with her, but now that she stood before him, he didn't know what to say. She stood there in purple and black, a white bonnet on the back of her head. He was surprised at his initial reaction. She's pretty, he thought. Her face was smooth, and her dark hair, pulled back severely, gleamed. His second reaction was to her austere, clearly religious demeanor. The combination produced in Andy severe embarrassment, and he had to look away. Like letching after a nun, he thought. She stood there, waiting for Andy to respond; he did not.

"Mr. Simpson, please answer my question." Her voice trembled slightly.

"Oh, I'm sorry," Andy said, adding, "I didn't mean to be rude. Please sit down. May I take your . . . anything? Shawl?"

"No, thank you. I am quite comfortable," she said and sat on a chair at the end of Andy's desk. She was obviously uncomfortable but composed. It must have taken enormous courage for her to come here, Andy thought. Or maybe desperation. As Andy tried to remember what she had asked, he noticed Sue sitting in the other office, watching them. She smiled and gave a thumbs up sign.

"I would like to know why you are telling the public about our private affairs." She lowered her eyes. "I would like you to stop doing it."

"I just did the one story," Andy said.

Puzzlement crept into Sarah's expression. She adjusted her shawl. "Will there be more?" she asked.

Andy thought for a moment, looked to the side, and then back to Sarah. "I don't know," he said. "Maybe."

"Please do not." Sarah raised her eyes to his. They were pale green. Andy felt compelled to look at her, at her eyes. "We do not like the world to intrude into our lives," she said. "Our religion is very important to us. It may seem strange to outsiders, but we live by it. Our church is our life. When you tell others about us, you show great disrespect to us and to our religion."

Andy tried to reassert himself. "You know your husband came to me with the story."

"I know. He is no longer a member of our church. He is lost to us. We expect him to do what he does, but we do not want you to help him."

The bishop must have sent her, Andy thought. He was intrigued. She spoke so calmly about this man who is her husband, almost as if he were already dead. Perhaps he is.

"I'm just doing my job," Andy said. "It's a good story."

"It is not a story. It is our lives."

"All good stories are someone's lives," Andy replied, too quickly, too flippantly. He regretted it immediately. That was the cynical journalist speaking. He thought she deserved better.

Sarah kept her hands in her lap, looking at them. "Is there nothing we can do?" she asked quietly.

Andy took a moment before responding. She looks too vulnerable, he thought, and then his professionalism kicked in. "I'm sorry," he said, "but I am a journalist. If I stopped every story that made someone uncomfortable, I would be out of a job."

Sarah did not hesitate. "There are other jobs."

Andy stood and walked to the window, where he fingered the cord to the plastic Venetian blinds. "Not for me," he said, finally. "This is what I do, what I want to do."

Again, with no hesitation, Sarah said, "To hurt people?"

Andy felt himself on the defensive through the subsequent rapid exchange.

"No. To tell the truth, at least as best as I can understand it," he said.

"Do you know the truth?"

"Sometimes, I think I do. Most times I'm not so sure, but I try."

"Do you know the truth about our church?"

Andy felt the checkmate coming.

He countered: "Do you know the truth?"

"Yes," she said.

"What is it?"

"Our church."

"How do you know that?" Andy asked.

"Through the teachings of our church and the teachings of Jesus."

Andy thought about arguing the logic of her position, of challenging the premise her argument rested upon, but he realized that would be irrelevant to her. Her church and her truth are the same.

"Then you're absolutely sure?" he asked.

"Yes."

Sarah did not waver.

There it was again. Andy had never encountered such certainty before. Where he came from, at least recently, uncertainty, doubt, skepticism, even cynicism were all the rage. He doubted everything, certainly the church, but also his relationships, especially his marriage, now failed, and even the possibility of fixed values. He was not sure what was good, what was right, where he was going, what he wanted. The one thing, however, he was sure about was his ability as a journalist and his conviction that this is what he should be doing. He also wasn't sure that was enough for him. And now this woman sat before him, quietly convinced of everything, but she was also part of a decision that was bringing great pain to another human being. Jacob was suffering because of her. He sat quietly for a few moments, thinking to himself, wondering what he should ask her. He knew he wouldn't stop the story. Should he tell her that?

Andy returned to his desk and sat down. He picked up a pencil and began to twirl it in his fingers. Then he looked up at Sarah.

"Look, Mrs. Weaver, Sarah. What should I call you?"

"My name is Sarah."

Andy relaxed a bit. "My name is Andy," he said.

"I know." She was now clearly in control.

"Sarah," Andy said, "you must understand that what you ask me to do is impossible."

"Mr. Simpson, nothing is impossible."

Certainty again, Andy thought, and then he said, "I know, trust in the Lord."

Sarah apparently did not hear the sarcasm. Andy was glad. She stood and faced Andy, still sitting behind his desk.

"You are an outsider," she said.

Andy interrupted, "I was born just forty miles from here."

"You are an outsider to us," Sarah continued. "We do not expect you to understand and to accept the teachings of our church. We are unknown to you and you are lost to us. But we do ask you to respect us and not to bring shame to us."

Sarah stood there, eyes down, while Andy tried to think of something to say. He wanted more of the story, but he couldn't get through her gentle wall. He wanted to talk with her, but there seemed nowhere to start.

"Please, Sarah, sit down. Let's talk some more and see if we can agree on something, anything."

She paused and then sat down, her eyes again looking at the hands folded in her lap. Andy looked at her, closely. Her eyebrows were too dark, too full, but her skin was almost porcelain, smooth, unwrinkled, seeming to glow from within. It had been a long time since Andy had seen a woman without makeup. Even his wife had never been completely free of it. Sarah looked up at him. He averted his eyes, embarrassed to be caught staring at her. She's a nun, Andy reminded himself.

"Do you know that you are deeply hurting another human being?" he asked.

She did not respond, did not look up.

Andy thought he might have an advantage here, and so he continued, "I've talked with your husband, and I know he's grieving. Do you bear no responsibility for that? Does that have nothing to do with you, with your church?"

She looked up at him and softly replied, "He has chosen his way."

Andy persisted, trying to hold the advantage, knowing already it was lost before this quiet persistence. "But he is a human being," he said. "He is hurting deeply, and you choose to ignore him. How can you do that and still call yourself a religious person? I don't understand that."

"If he suffers, that is because he has chosen to disobey the church. That is his choice."

"But isn't there some way you can forgive him? Even Christ forgave the sinners." Andy was not too sure of that, but he seemed to remember something about it from his Sunday School days back in Sunbury.

"I am not Christ. I too am a sinner. I can only obey the teachings of my church. My husband . . ."

Andy interrupted her again, "Then he is still your husband?"

"Of course."

Sarah seemed confused by the question, looking at Andy with wide eyes.

"And you still think of him as your husband?" he asked.

She did not hesitate. "Yes."

"But you ignore him?"

Andy thought he might have her in an inconsistency here. This, after all, is not far from the final stages of his own failed marriage.

"He ignores us," Sarah said quietly, "by choosing to be outside the church. We must have contact only with believers."

Andy wanted to ask more. He wanted to know what life was like from her perspective. How did she avoid contact? Did they never talk? What did she tell her children? Did she really sleep in the same bed with him and still avoid contact? Did she come to him unclothed that night, as Jacob had insisted? But he asked none of these things, and Sarah sat there, quietly defiant but clearly uncomfortable. Andy had no idea where to go from there, but he didn't want the conversation to end.

Suddenly, Sue was at the door. Andy looked up.

"Can I get you anything?" she said to Sarah. "Coffee, tea, soda?"

"No, thank you," Sarah said. "I must go. Thank you, Mr. Simpson, for listening to me. I hope you respect my request."

She stood up, nodded to Andy, then to Sue, and left.

Andy watched her go through the outside door, sat for a moment, and then swiveled to Sue.

"Dammit, Sue. You never offer to bring coffee any other time. Why did you interrupt us?" Andy was fascinated by this person from another world.

"I was watching her and listening, Andy," Sue said. "She made her point, and she was in pain, but you seemed oblivious to that. I did it for her, and I would do it again."

With that Sue turned and walked back to her desk.

Several weeks later Andy had to go to New York City to see about some new software for the newspaper. He had been putting it off, until Beth called him to ask about their loft in the city. She had been living in it since the divorce, but now she planned to move out and wanted to discuss the sale and financial arrangements. He told her he would be right up, using the software inspection as an excuse.

He thought about taking the train to New York but decided to drive instead. He knew the City well enough to find a place to park, and besides, he thought it might take his mind off of Jacob and Sarah.

Before leaving town he stopped at Harry's for a cup of coffee and leafed through a copy of the Philadelphia *Inquirer*. He saw it on page 17: "Mennonite Shunned by Church."

"My God," Andy said as he read over the two-paragraph article. "He doesn't need me. The *Inquirer*. He's really reaching big-time. I wonder how he got it in there."

Andy knew the *Inquirer* would not have published it based on his story, at least without contacting him. Jacob must have gone there and somehow convinced them to do a story.

All during the three-hour drive, Andy kept thinking of Jacob and Sarah, unable to understand, unable to forget. He sympathized with Jacob because he stood up to an authoritarian organization. He told the truth as he saw it, and he had guts. He did what Andy could never bring himself to do, act on his convictions with total certainty. He didn't agree with Jacob's attitude toward his wife, but that after all is part of his culture. It seemed clear to Andy that the Reformed Mennonite Church remains a patriarchy. The man rules. The woman obeys. He didn't like it, but that was the way it was.

He also liked Sarah. Even though they had met just that once and even though he disagreed with just about everything she said and believed, he admired her calmness. Whereas Jacob's certainty resulted in rage, Sarah's certainty resulted in a peace at the center of the storm. Nothing could shake her. She was quiet, humble, simple; and yet she was also firm. She confused him because he had never before been defeated by someone weaker than he. Beth always won because she was simply stronger, smarter. That was not confusing at all. But Sarah had asserted control of the situation without really trying. She was simply sure of everything, and she was calm. That combination intimidated Andy, although he didn't know why. He thought about it all the way to New York.

At the parking garage he phoned Beth at work.

"Hi . . . yeah, I'm here, in New York. . . . No, that's okay. I have to see someone at Foster's first. About the new software. . . . No, it shouldn't take long. . . . Lunch? Yeah, okay. I can do that. . . . I know where it is. . . . Then I have to head back. . . . One? . . . Right."

He hung up. That wasn't so bad. She sounded fine, like she wouldn't mind meeting with him, at least for lunch. He immediately began to feel nervous, a slight fluttering in his stomach.

Andy took care of business and wandered around Manhattan for an hour, waiting for one o'clock. He then went over to the small restaurant on Second Avenue where he had agreed to meet Beth. He had known about it but had never been there before. It was the usual tiny brick-front restaurant trying to make it despite exorbitant rent, relying on local business people and the occasional tourist. Andy went in, checked for a reservation. They had one, in Beth's name, her maiden name. She had not said she would make a reservation; it was just a hunch. He sat at the last table by the window, a table with two chairs. When the waitress came over, he said he was waiting for someone but that he would have a Heineken. He sat and watched the people walk past the window and got increasingly nervous, the fluttering in his stomach increasing despite the Heineken. He didn't know what recently divorced people talk about, except the terms of the divorce settlement. He had felt good about letting Beth have the loft until she wanted to move somewhere else. It was a generous gesture, he thought with considerable self-satisfaction. He also knew, however, that this meant they would have to get together some day and discuss the financial arrangements of the loft, and he wondered if that was the reason he had been so generous. Fifteen minutes later Beth walked through the door, looked around, saw Andy, and came over.

"Hi," she said, and sat down, placing her handbag beside her chair, resting it against her leg, the usual City precaution against thieves.

"Hi," he said, not knowing what else to say.

Andy thought Beth looked good. She always looked professional on the job and did now with her gray suit and flowered scarf. Her hair looked different, more swept back, lighter. Life without me agrees with her, Andy thought.

"Thanks for coming," she said.

"No problem," he said. "I had to come to the City anyway." And then Andy remembered he had already told her that. Something about protesting too much, he thought.

"Yeah, I remember you said that. I guess I could have come to see you, but I thought you might like an excuse to get back to the City. Do you miss it?"

"No."

"Really?"

Andy shifted in his seat and glanced at the couple sitting at the next table.

"I guess I've always been a small-town boy," he said.

"Maybe. That's good," Beth said. "It's a lot healthier there than here."

Neither spoke for a painfully long time. Beth picked up her knife, inspected it, appeared to brush something from it, looked again, and replaced it.

"But I do prefer it here," Beth said, finally.

More silence. Andy played with his glass and drained the remaining beer.

"Well, this isn't going very well, is it?" Beth said.

"I'm sorry," Andy said and determined to try again. "You're looking good, like life agrees with you."

"I guess it does, generally. Good days and bad days, you know."

"Yeah, I know."

"How have you been doing?" she asked. She sounded genuinely concerned. Andy relaxed for the first time since he had left Carlisle.

"Okay," Andy said. "Busy. It's amazing how much time a small-town weekly takes. I don't seem to have time for anything else."

"You're not seeing anyone?"

Andy was taken off guard by the question. He didn't think they would get into this.

"Who, me?" he said and then added, after a pause, "Are you?"

"Not really. Once in a while. Nothing serious. I don't want to rush things. I'm sorry I brought it up. It's really none of my business."

"Yeah," Andy said, "mine either. How's your job going?"

"Good. I mean fine. It's going really well. We've picked up a few new accounts. I got two myself."

"Good."

Beth seemed to be relaxing now, warming to the conversation. "I really do love this work. It's such a rush, even when it goes badly. I don't think I could live without it."

"I'm glad," Andy said. "You were made for it."

"How about you?" Beth asked, again with apparent concern.

"Oh, I don't know. I like what I'm doing all right."

"No, that's not what I mean." she said. "You never answered my question. You're really not seeing anyone?"

Andy was confused again. He thought they had decided to drop the subject.

"No," he said, "I'm not really seeing anyone, even once." Andy didn't know why he added that last phrase. Sympathy? He wasn't sure, but he wished he hadn't said it.

"Really?" Beth seemed puzzled.

"No," he said. "I haven't been doing much of anything lately."

Their lunch came. Vegetable quiche for Beth. Tuna salad sandwich for Andy. No meatloaf on the menu, Andy thought. They ate mostly in silence.

"You okay?" Beth asked, again catching Andy off guard.

"Yeah, sure." he said. "What do you mean?"

"I don't know. You seem . . . preoccupied. Like something's

wrong. Anything you want to talk about? Are you handling the divorce okay? I know it's tough. I get really down sometimes. Like I've failed big-time. But I get through it."

"No," Andy said, "it's not that." He thought he knew what she meant, but he wasn't sure himself what was wrong. "It's just work," he said, not knowing what else to say.

"But you said that was going well."

"It is," he said.

"So?"

Andy wished Beth would get off this line of questioning. "It's nothing," he said, hoping that would end it.

Beth persisted. "Come on. Tell me. It's okay."

Finally, Andy decided to go with it. Perhaps, he thought, he might figure out what's going on by talking about it.

"It's this story I did," he said. "I'm still doing it. I just can't figure out what's going on."

"What do you mean?"

"Do you remember last year when we saw the Amish in Lancaster County?"

"Yes," Beth said and shuddered slightly. She still had not gotten over the Amish woman by the side of the road.

"Do you remember I said there were Mennonites there, different kinds?"

"Yes. You said some were even like us. I remember."

"Well, the most extreme Mennonites, the most conservative are the Reformed Mennonites, at least that's what Sue says."

"Sue?"

"My ad executive."

"Oh."

"So, anyway, I can't get these people off my mind."

"Reformed Mennonites? You can't get Reformed Mennonites off your mind?"

"Yeah," Andy said and then added, not sure if he should, "At least two of them. Jacob and Sarah."

"Jacob and Sarah," Beth said slowly. "What's so special about them?"

"I've never met anyone like them," Andy said. "They're really different, especially Jacob. He disobeyed the church, and now his church has excommunicated him, which means his wife, Sarah, and their kids can't have contact with him. He's shunned. She's even forbidden to sleep with him. Well, she can sleep with him; she just can't do anything else."

"You mean they're in bed night after night and don't even have sex?"

"Yes."

"How do you know that?" From the expression on her face, it was clear that Beth was having trouble comprehending such a situation, but Andy did have her attention.

"Jacob told me. It's forbidden by the church."

"And you believed him?" Beth asked. By now she was simply staring at Andy.

Andy continued, unaware of Beth's reaction, absorbed in his thoughts. "Yes," he said, "he's shunned by the church, even by his own family."

"Shunned?"

"Yeah. Shunned. Banned. Cut off."

"And you did a story on them?"

"Yeah. I just published it." Andy hesitated, unsure of how far to take this. Then he plunged in. "Maybe I'll do another story. I don't know if I'm done. There's lots there."

"Like what?" Beth also pushed it.

"Like who's right. Like what's right. I don't know. It just seems like everyone's right, and everyone's wrong."

"That clearly can't be, Andy. I know you have a difficult time deciding things, but somebody has to be wrong. This guy should not have disobeyed his church."

"But he thought the church was wrong. He stood up for what he believed."

"Then he should take the consequences and not bitch about it. What about her?"

"Sarah?"

Andy was taken off guard once again. He did not want to get into this. He sensed that Beth was beginning to return to her usual argumentative self.

"Yes." Beth said, "Sarah. If she wants to be with her husband, she should stay with him."

"But then she must disobey her convictions," Andy replied, "her belief in her church."

"Well, it's simple then. You can't have it both ways. What's the problem?"

It's not simple. Andy knew that. He looked around, and he saw people, mostly couples, and he knew they all had problems too, and none of those problems were simple. He didn't know why Beth was doing this, or even why she was interested, but he explained anyway, just the way he had always done.

"The problem," Andy said, "is that we have two people here, both doing what they believe is right, and both suffering for it."

"Maybe so," Beth said, "but that's not exactly uncommon, is it? Look at us."

They looked at each other.

"I'm sorry," Beth said quickly, dropping her eyes, "I shouldn't have said that. Forget I said it." She lifted her cup to her lips and then put it down before adding, "Which one do you side with?"

"Side with?"

The questioning resumed.

"Yeah, which one do you sympathize with? Empathize with?"

"I'm a reporter. I don't empathize. I'm objective. I'm just a reporter."

"Sure. Really. You know what I mean."

"Well," Andy said, returning to the explanation he thought he had left, "I think I agree with Jacob. He's the rebel. He knows what he wants, and he fights for it."

"Like you."

"That's not fair." Andy was suddenly angry. Beth was reasserting her superiority of wit, and Andy knew he could not match her.

"Sorry." Beth refolded her napkin and placed it on the table. "Go on."

Andy went on. "He's the one who's taking on the establishment. Thoreau. Martin Luther. You know what I mean. That's really appealing, at least to most readers. I think that's what made it a good story."

"So what's the problem?" Beth asked. "He's right; she's wrong."

"I haven't finished."

Beth apparently sensed Andy's emotional involvement and waited for him to continue.

"Sarah is good," he said quietly. "She's kind. She's unassuming. There's no ego at all there. I don't know if she's right or wrong. I only know I really admire her. Maybe she's right, at least partially right."

Andy leaned back in his chair, exhaled, and hoped the topic was closed.

"What does she look like?"

"Look like?" Andy leaned his chair back down and looked directly at Beth.

"Just tell me. What does she look like? Describe her."

Andy tossed his napkin on the table and shook his head. He thought of leaving but did not. Instead he tried to visualize Sarah, what she looked like, what he remembered about her.

"I don't know." he said. "She's about forty or so, thin. She pulls her hair straight back and always wears a white bonnet. She smiles. And her skin is remarkably smooth, like a China doll."

"Is she pretty?"

"What do you mean pretty?"

"You know what pretty is. Is she attractive?"

Andy was not sure just how to respond. He looked around and then blurted out, louder than he intended, "My God, Beth, she's a Mennonite. She wears long purple dresses and a bonnet. She doesn't wear any makeup."

Several customers glanced over at them, but Beth ignored them.

"Is she pretty?"

Andy replied, hesitantly, softly, "I suppose so."

"You suppose so. Andy, you really are genuinely naive."

"Right." Andy gave up.

"No, I mean that as a compliment," Beth said. "Really. It's one of the things that I found attractive about you. Still do."

Andy didn't see it as a compliment but just more of Beth's big-city condescension, and besides, he thought he might be quickly losing that naiveté.

Beth smiled and then changed the subject to the disposition of the loft. Andy agreed with her decision to sell it and split the profits. He really didn't care what she did. He also realized they could have done this easily by phone, so he had just wasted a day. As they said goodbye and went in opposite directions on Second Avenue, Andy's mind was back in Carlisle before Beth could turn the corner.

"So," Sue said, "welcome back. How'd it go?"

Andy entered the office, just as Sue was about to leave.

"Not so good," he said, putting a newspaper on the desk, the one he had picked up in New York. "More of the same," he added.

"More of the same software?"

Andy suddenly realized he had not told Sue of his plan to meet with Beth.

"No," he said, "I mean good. I ordered the software. You can layout your ads right on the screen. What you see is what you get. Right? Isn't that what you wanted?"

Sue was at the door, ready to leave.

"So you had lunch with Beth," she said.

"Huh? Well, yes. But . . . how did you know? Did I tell you?"

"Andy, you're pretty transparent."

Andy smiled, mostly to himself.

"Is that the same as being naive?" he asked.

"No, of course not. Why do you ask?"

"No reason," he said.

Sue was clearly in a hurry to leave, but she paused for a moment.

"You're the one with the words," she said. "I just mean you don't hide things very well, even if you rarely talk about them. You probably should open up more. Get things off your chest. I'm a good listener, just in case you need one."

Andy knew Sue meant well, but the last thing he needed right now was to talk about Beth. In fact, he had not even been thinking about Beth. He had been thinking about Sarah, all the way home from New York.

⊰ **Four** ⊱

For the next two days Andy concentrated on getting his newspaper out. He knew he was overqualified to run a small-town weekly, and he was often bored by the stories he did, but he still found satisfaction in the right phrase, even if it was in a rewrite of a garden party. He never put in a local press release—and there were dozens every week, some little more than notes in pencil—without editing and usually rewriting it. Even if no one else cared, he did. Everything had to be right. Pride, he would say. Anal-retentive, Beth would say. Whatever. It made him a good journalist. But probably a lousy husband, he admitted.

When the last piece for the week finally went to Harrisburg, Andy settled back in his chair and fiddled with the old metal ruler he still kept from the pre-computer days, the kind that allowed the editor to measure out the column inches manually. He thought about Jacob and Sarah. The differences between them are huge, he thought, and yet they're still married. Why? Is it their religion? The church has divided them, and the church keeps them together? That's some power. And then you have to put in one other ingredient: they love each other. What a mess. Andy could not imagine their misery. To love someone, to be that close, and then no further. It's much better to be separate, and not to love.

Then he thought of himself and Beth. It was easy. There was

nothing to keep them together, so they parted. Sensible. No church, no kids, no reason not to. Very modern. He thought about love for a while, and wondered what that had to do with anything. They parted on fairly friendly terms, no real bitterness. Disappointment, yes. A sense of failure, yes. Regret, he supposed so. But did he still love her? Had he ever loved her? He didn't know. He enjoyed being with her. He missed her when she was not there. He missed her now. Is that enough for love? She is pretty, he thought. He liked the way she looked. She was interesting in the sense that he never knew what she might say or do next. He cared for her. He cared what might happen to her. He still did care. Does that mean he still loves her? He didn't know.

He was sure, however, that Jacob loves Sarah. That came though clearly and powerfully. Despite the rejection and humiliation, he persists in his love. He wants Sarah at any cost, except, of course, at the expense of his own principles. He admires that in Jacob. But then he remembered the part of Jacob he did not admire. Jacob wants to be the master of his house again. He quotes scripture—Paul—to prove that he as a man must be in charge, that his wife must obey him, because that's what the Bible says wives must do. Sarah was clearly not doing that. How much of the macho stance motivates his desire for reconciliation? How much is this a threat to his manhood? Andy knew that he himself had passed through that point of chauvinistic insistence, less strident than Jacob certainly, but it was there at one point early on. Beth had helped him see that neither the man nor the woman should dominate. By that he thought Beth meant neither should place unreasonable demands—perhaps any demands—on the other. If he had ever said anything like he was head of the house to Beth, she would have laughed. He could not imagine two marriages more dissimilar than theirs. He could not imagine two people more dissimilar than he and Jacob.

Women simply mystified Andy, although Sarah seemed straightforward enough. She obeyed the church. All else was secondary. Even her love for her husband. But what was she feeling? Did her certain faith bring her emotional peace or did it simply ratchet up the agony? What was she feeling beneath her faith, as a woman? How could she continue as she is? And Beth. Who the hell is Beth anyway, Andy thought. What does she want? A career? She had it. Andy never interfered with her career. He thought he supported her. All those evenings watching the Mets and Knicks on TV while she was entertaining a prospective client. He never complained, and she never seemed to want another man. Andy never suspected that. Even now she says she's not seeing anyone in particular. So what went wrong? Why did she suggest they separate? Why did he agree?

At any rate, Andy thought, I'm done for the day and no meetings to cover tonight. He decided to take in a ball game. Pittsburgh had a minor league team in Harrisburg, and he had wanted to see them ever since moving to Carlisle. He liked baseball, had played all through college. He was nothing special.

"Sue," he called to the next room.

Sue came to the door. "Hi, want something?"

"I'm sorry. I didn't call for you to come. I just wanted to ask you something." Andy was particularly careful to avoid the boss-obedient secretary syndrome, especially since Sue was not his secretary. Technically, she was the ad executive. He never asked her to bring him a cup of coffee, which she sometimes did anyway. He was always a bit embarrassed but secretly pleased.

"I just wanted to know if Gary's busy tonight. I'm going to see the Senators and thought he might like to go along."

"He would love to go along, but he won't because he's going with me to see his mother. She hasn't seen the kids in a while, and I finally got him to go."

"Okay, that's fine. Just tell him I asked."

"Do you mind if I don't tell him?" Sue smiled. "It would ruin the evening for him."

"Sure," Andy said, and then he thought, maybe that's love.

The Senators play on an island in the Susquehanna, the ballpark taking up most of the land. It looks like a grown-up version of the park Andy used to play in as a kid, except for the modest bleachers down both baselines and a row of rectangular advertisements hemming in the outfield. He loved the crispness of the grass, the white precision of the foul lines, the perfect fit of the dimensions, the finality of the rules. The game is being played now as it was 100 years ago.

He remembered last summer seeing Amish kids outside a one-room schoolhouse playing softball, boys and girls together. The girls hit the ball and then ran with their long skirts tugging at their ankles. The boys, no matter how fast they ran, never lost their straw hats, the flat ones with the wide brims and black bands. They laughed and giggled throughout the game. One thing at least never changes, Andy thought, although he couldn't imagine Jacob and Sarah sitting here beside him having a beer and chewing on a hot dog.

Andy chose a bleacher seat—$3.50—behind the home team dugout along the first base line. You would have to be a top exec at a Fortune 500 company to watch the Mets from here, he thought. He watched several of the players tossing a ball in front of the dugout. They looked young to him. My God, he thought, some of these kids are still in their teens, and I pay good money to watch them play a game. Maybe I should try to get some comps. I won't tell them we never cover the Senators. Like most kids in Little League, Andy once thought he would play professional ball. He had been big for his age—5'10" in eighth grade—but in tenth grade he was still 5'10". One of life's early disappointments, he thought. One of many more to come. He should have been prepared.

This isn't a bad level of ball, he thought as he watched the third baseman make a one-handed stop of a screamer down the line and flick it almost nonchalantly to first. Shortstop to second, to third, and the third baseman flipped it underhand back to the pitcher, trotting back to his position, admired by all, secure in that admiration. The kid was probably twenty-two, just out of college, but he had that self-assurance, that cockiness that the good athlete has. He made an incredibly difficult act look easy, look like anyone could do it.

Just once in my life, Andy thought, I would like to do something with that ease and that competency. It didn't matter what; he just wanted to be that good at something, anything. Even writing did not come easy to him, although it was the only thing that he was even remotely good at.

At the end of the scoreless first inning, a heavy-set man pushed past Andy and wedged his body into the next seat. He wore a Senators shirt and hat, and had a sausage sandwich in one hand and a beer in the other. When the Senators took the field again, he yelled something about getting the Generals and bit into the sausage.

"Should be a good game," he said to Andy.

"I hope so," Andy said. He was always tentative with small talk.

"Just got off work. Came straight to the game."

"Oh," Andy murmured, hoping the man would concentrate on the game. Instead he took a large bite out of his sausage sandwich and chewed while he spoke.

"You follow the Senators?" he said.

"I guess not," Andy said. "This is my first game this season." He took a long swallow of beer.

"That so? Don't worry about it. I'll fill you in. This is my team. I never miss a game. Got season tickets. My seats are up there, under the roof, but I don't like it there, so I come down here, where the real people are. These are the fans." He took another bite as he drained his beer.

"These are good seats," Andy said. "You ever go see the Phils?"

"Naw," he said, "I don't like the Bigs. Too much money. Too much ego. I like it here because this is where the kids are. They have dreams, so they play hard. They're all good too, or they wouldn't have made it this far. Hell, they wouldn't have signed at all." The man called for another beer and while he was paying, he continued, "See that kid at third?" He motioned with his beer. "He just came in from the University of Texas. All-American there. Looks like he's sixteen, but he can hit and he's slick in the field. He'll be triple-A by the end of the season. In two years he'll be starting for Pittsburgh, and I can say I saw him when he started. That's why I come here. This team is my life."

Passion again, Andy thought, but he didn't respond to the man.

The man found a more willing listener on the other side, filling him in on the details of each Senator's career. Meanwhile, the game turned routine for Andy, his mind returning to Beth. At first he remembered their life had seemed fine. Beth was interesting. She was fun. And he was impressed by the fact that she felt he was worth her instruction. Even in sex, particularly in sex. He remembered the first time, in a friend's bedroom, the party going on outside the door, the door not even locked. "It's okay," she said, "Breathe deep." It was no good that first time, but it got better; he got better as they fell into a routine. "Hey," she would say, "you're a fast learner." "Hey," he would say, "where did you learn that?" She would smile at him, "You're the scholar. Don't you read books? The *Kama Sutra*. It even has pictures." Then she told him about the copy she used to have with pop-ups. They dissolved in laughter.

There was something comfortable in their early relationship. He liked the idea of having someone there, someone dependably there, and so he said let's get married. She said, sure, why not, and so they got married at a church they never attended. Their relationship got even more dependable, and Andy thought he was happy.

But he was never entirely comfortable with her expertise, with her openness, just as he was never entirely comfortable with the offhand way she could use the word "fuck" and its variants, although rarely with him. At dinner with friends, she could say of someone, "He's so fucking straight I can't stand it." Or once he overheard a conversation with a client when she admitted a deal was "all fucked up." That sort of thing. He knew the term was used so much that it was now worn out, had lost any impact it might have once had. "Screwed up" had the same origin and underwent the same process. He didn't feel uncomfortable with that either.

He knew that Beth was patient with him, and she never judged him, just as he never judged her. At parties she liked to roll a joint, or better yet have one rolled for her. They never had the stuff at home. He would take a few puffs—to avoid being a jerk—and pass it on. She smiled at him and had another, inhaling deeply, relaxing back into the sofa. It was fine with him. He knew later the sex would be great. Another page from the *Kama Sutra*.

The crowd cheered, and Andy came back to the ballgame. The Senators fan beside him jabbed his elbow into Andy's side and said, "Did you see that catch in right field? Saved three runs, easy." The Senators trotted off the field and into the dugout. Andy ordered another beer.

"Some game," he said with feigned enthusiasm.

"Yeah," the man said. "You're seeing a good one for the first one."

The next inning turned routine, and Andy settled back, again letting his mind wander, back to his life in New York.

Andy wondered if Beth still entertained so much. It was part of her job, but she also liked to have people back to their place, a few people with similar interests, at least similar to hers. Andy often drifted off to the bedroom to watch a game and would be sitting there when Beth came to bed.

"You're some host," she would say, not really angry.

"I thought you were having a good time and didn't really need me."

"Yeah, well, it looked pretty stupid with me out there trying to rev up the conversation and you nowhere to be seen. At least you could sit there and try to look interested. You really are something," she said.

And so their conversation went. The wine let Beth say what she thought, and she usually ended up using words like "wimp" and "lump" and "boring." Andy knew it was the wine talking, but he also knew at some level she meant it. Usually he just watched the game or, later, pretended to be asleep.

They had occasional arguments, but most of their marriage passed in silence, a dependable silence for Andy, but a silence. Even before marriage, when they were sharing the loft they eventually bought, they seemed to see each other rarely. Each was pursuing a career. He started early in the morning to get the afternoon paper out. She worked late to finish up projects or entertain clients. Sunday he got up early, went out to have a cup of coffee, and brought back a *Times*. They spent the morning in bed reading it. He started with the sports section. She started with the business section. He always had to straighten out the section she had just read. Toward the end of the morning he would put his hand on her, to see if she was interested. After they were married, she seemed less and less interested, but Andy didn't mind; at least it was comfortable.

And so they drifted. Toward the end Andy saw it coming, but he didn't know what to do about it. He thought of counseling, but he knew what the counselor would say: "You two have to communicate. Here are some games to help." He had never been to counseling, but he had read about it, in novels mostly, and he was sure that's what she would say. It would have to be a "she." Beth would insist on that. So would he.

Finally, halfway through one Sunday morning, Beth turned to him and said, "Look, we have to talk about this."

"What?" Andy said, still looking at the sports section.

"Us," she said simply.

Andy put the paper in his lap and looked at Beth. He was confused.

"What do you mean? What about us?"

"There is no us," Beth said, turning to Andy, propping her

elbow on the pillow. "That's the problem. There's you, and there's me. There's no us."

Andy could think of no response. Finally, he said, "So what do you want to do about it?"

Beth looked away and said, finally, "I think maybe we should separate. Just for a trial, just to see what happens."

"Is there someone else?" Andy knew there was not.

"No."

Andy responded with uncharacteristic resolution. "Okay. I'll move out," he said.

And so he did, just like that. By the middle of the week, he had found a three-room apartment out on the island close to where he worked, and three months later the divorce was final. They agreed on everything.

"It's a pleasure working with you two," her lawyer said, her office filled with oak furniture and large volumes of matching books.

"Yeah, you wouldn't believe what some of these people drag themselves through," Andy's lawyer said.

"I had one that went on for months," her lawyer said, "because they both wanted the dog. Months. The only way we settled was when the dog died."

"The dog was the only sensible one, right?" his lawyer said.

The lawyers laughed.

Beth and Andy said thanks and left. It was all very civilized.

Everyone in the ballpark began to stir, and Andy realized the game was over. He looked up and saw the large Senators fan standing next to him, waiting for him to move. Andy asked him who won. He looked at Andy strangely and then with disgust. "The Senators," he said and pushed past him to the aisle. Andy didn't leave. Instead he sat there until most of the crowd had gone and they started to put out the lights.

"I hope she's going to be all right," he said to himself. "I hope she finds someone."

As he left the ballpark and walked in the dark back to his car, he paused to look across the river at the bright skyline of Harrisburg. It's not much like Manhattan's skyline, he thought, and then decided he liked it better. Somehow it seemed more to human scale. He always felt overwhelmed in New York, even outside looking in. Here he felt part of the landscape. He sat on a bench for a few minutes and watched the lights from the city dancing on the water. A paddle-wheel steamboat, or at least a replica of one, the Pride of the Susquehanna, drifted down the river, heading for dock further down the island. Andy watched the people milling about on deck, chatting, laughing, some singing, glasses clinking. He almost wished he were with them, but instead he got up, stretched, and walked back to his car, driving all the way to the music of the local classical music station.

Back in the small house he was renting on the outskirts of Carlisle, Andy poured himself a beer, a Budweiser. He never drank beer from the bottle. Beth did sometimes. But he did not think of Beth. He thought of Sarah, the mysterious, forbidden, nun-like Sarah. And he continued to wonder about her. What has her life been like? What is life like with her? Beth was easy to live with. She made no demands really. She just got bored and wanted out. When he was with Sarah, however, even briefly and under somewhat adversarial circumstances, he sensed something like the presence of love in her, of deep commitment to something at least. And he knew its emptiness in himself. She cared about her faith. She cared about her church. He was sure she cared about her children, and he suspected that she cared about Jacob too. What went so terribly wrong that could cause so much suffering? By comparison, his experience with marriage had been painless. Their world was foreign to him, as alien as if they had been from Mars, or he.

He opened another bottle, refilled the glass, and drank slowly in his kitchen until he went to bed.

∝ **Five** ∞

"How was the game?" Sue asked Andy as he walked though the door, a bit later than usual.

Andy was startled. "The game? Oh, last night? Fine. Good game. The Senators have a good team this year. Good night for a ballgame."

He kept talking all the way to his office, then looked quickly at the Harrisburg paper to see the score, just in case Sue asked.

Sue asked, "So who won?"

"The Senators ... 8-3. Good game." Andy didn't know why it was so important that Sue not know that he had not known the score.

Once at his desk he shuffled through the latest batch of press releases—the season for fundraisers; they all want free publicity. That's okay, Andy thought, that's why people buy a weekly, to read about themselves and their neighbors.

Andy's office was always a bit out of control; that's the nature of the business, but he did try to keep his desk in some kind of order. He worked at sorting the mail, putting it in appropriate piles. A losing battle, but one, he thought, worth waging.

Sue was at the door. "Here's a note for you. From Jacob. He slid it through the slot sometime before seven."

Andy took the note. It was on that rough, large-lined paper he remembered from elementary school.

Mr. Simpson,
Excuse me, but I would like you to come to my trailer after work this afternoon.

Jacob Weaver

"Fine," Andy thought, "Like I have nothing better to do."
He had nothing better to do.
So that afternoon he drove up the long lane to Jacob's trailer, thinking of Sarah a hundred yards away in the farmhouse. The kids are in school. It's just the two of them—Jacob and Sarah—a hundred yards apart, that close and yet they never even talk. Even Beth calls in occasionally, he thought. But maybe not now, now that the loft is sold. That was their last tie. Not even kids. Halfway up the lane, he stopped and looked over the potato field, the flat green leaves beginning to unfold on their own individual mound of land. Jacob keeps a neat farm, he thought. Then as an afterthought: I wish my office looked like that. He parked his car and started walking slowly toward the trailer. It's the kids, he thought, their two kids. What's this doing to them? At least he and Beth never had kids to hurt, to confuse. They knew what they were doing there at least.

Andy was about to knock on the door when he heard something around back. He went there and found Jacob sitting on a chair on the small porch to the rear of the trailer, a basin on his knees. He looked up as Andy approached and nodded to him.

"Hi," Andy said. "What you got there?" He had decided to use the casual approach.

"Sugar peas," Jacob said. "They are starting to come in. I like them when they are new and tender, first fresh vegetables of the year. Taste good. See, you just clip off each end with your fingernail."

"I remember," Andy said, "I used to help my grandfather clean sugar peas. Grandma always made soup out of the first ones— milk, potatoes, whole sugar peas, lots of butter I remember. It was a treat."

Jacob stopped clipping and looked away.

"Sarah used to make them too," he said. "Still does I guess."

"Oh?" Andy wasn't sure he wanted to get into that right away. He was afraid Jacob might demand pity.

Instead, Andy offered to help and sat down on the step next to Jacob. He took a handful and began clipping off the ends, dropping the pods into the basin on Jacob's knees. They worked silently for several minutes, Andy enjoying the peace of the farm, the pace of life. Maybe this is why I came back, he thought.

"I am going to church on Sunday," Jacob said.

The suddenness of the statement brought Andy back.

"Oh?" he said.

"Yes." Jacob continued with the peas, not looking at Andy.

Finally, Andy felt forced to respond.

"Is that why you asked me to come out here? To tell me you're going to church on Sunday?"

Jacob smiled without looking at Andy and wiped his hands on his pants.

"Thought you might like to go along," he said and then looked up at Andy before adding, "Might be interesting for you."

"I don't know, "Andy said, "I haven't been to church for a long time."

He was going to add not since his wedding, but decided against it.

"You see," Andy continued, "I'm not a very church-going person. It's not that I'm an unbeliever or anything. It's just that I'm not sure."

Andy kept going with his apologies, but Jacob interrupted with a wave of his hand.

"That is fine," he said. "But that is not why I invited you. For you it is business."

Andy was intrigued. "What business?"

"Newspaper business. You can put it in your newspaper."

Andy had finished his handful of peas and didn't pick up

more. He looked at Jacob and said, "What? What can I put in the paper?"

"That I went to church on Sunday," Jacob said.

Andy began to see that something more was going on here. Jacob was still smiling and clipping peas, the basin half full.

"Which church?" Andy asked.

"Kreider's."

"Isn't that the church that excommunicated you?" Andy knew it was.

"That's right. And I am going there Sunday."

"Why?" Andy asked. "They won't talk to you, will they?"

Jacob put down the basin and stood up. Andy noticed for the first time just how powerful Jacob looked.

"I will talk to them," Jacob said, "and when the people hear me, they will know the truth, and the ban will be broken. I will have my family back."

"That simple?" Andy remained seated, watching Jacob, who was looking across the fields.

"Yes," Jacob said firmly. "The truth is always simple."

Andy knew one thing. The truth is never simple.

"Why do you want me to go along?" he asked Jacob.

Jacob turned to Andy, his eyes revealing an intense conviction.

"For the story." he said. "For your newspaper. If it is in the newspaper, no one can deny the truth."

Andy saw that Jacob had a faith in the printed word held by few people, mostly simple people. Then he told himself that Jacob had written a book. He knows about the printed word, and he is not a simple man. Andy began to get the feeling that Jacob could do anything he wished with him, manipulate him, use him. I'll have to be careful, he thought. After a sufficient pause, Andy told Jacob he would think about it, but Jacob would not let it slide.

"Ten o'clock," Jacob said. Be there, was the meaning.

Andy didn't leave immediately. There were still more sugar peas and they worked together to finish them, mostly in comfortable silence.

When they were finished, Andy stood and stretched. He felt good, at home almost. He looked at the house and, trying to be casual, said to Jacob, "Do you think Sarah's at home?"

"She is at home," Jacob said matter-of-factly.

Andy tried to give Jacob the impression he was just making small talk as he asked Jacob how he knew that.

"I saw her hanging up the wash, over there, in the backyard," he said.

Andy leaned over and saw the black and purple garments hanging from a line going from the house to the tall pole.

"What's she doing now?" he asked.

"Cleaning," Jacob answered almost automatically.

"How do you know that?"

"I know," Jacob said.

More silence.

Jacob sat back down on the porch and clasped his hands before him. He talked almost as though he were remembering. "Soon she will come out of the house over there and walk around to the front and down the lane to work. She won't say anything, won't even look over here. That is my hell."

Andy thought he was beginning to understand.

"Is that why you're sitting out here in back?" he said. "So you can see her when she comes out of the house?"

"No." Jacob did not elaborate.

They sat for a while longer, even though the peas were finished. Andy made some motions to go, and then, as if on cue, Sarah came out of the house, glanced over at them, and walked around the front of the trailer. Her white linen bonnet covered the bun at the back of her hair. A black smock covered a purple dress, which covered her legs almost to her ankles. High-topped black shoes covered the ankles.

Andy thought he had never before seen such elegance. Soon, she was gone, hidden by the trailer.

"She saw you here," Jacob said as he leaned back in his chair.

"I know," Andy said. "Do you think she minds that I'm here?"

"She minds."

Andy tried to change the subject and asked Jacob if he'll give Sarah some sugar peas.

"Yes." he said. "She is my wife. I must provide for her needs, for the children."

Andy then asked if she will accept the peas, and Jacob assured him she would.

"But she won't talk to you? Not even to say thank you?" Andy said.

Jacob said she will say nothing. Andy then asked if she will cook them for him.

"She would, but I told her no. I have a kitchen here. I do all my own cooking. It is painful to sit at a table and be ignored by those you love."

After a pause, Andy said he had to be going, and Jacob offered to pick him up Sunday.

"No," Andy said. "If I decide to go, I'll drive down myself. I don't know yet. We'll see."

But Andy already knew he would be there, even as he walked around the trailer to his car.

Friday afternoon came quickly, the end of the week. Sue had organized her desk and was walking out the door, when Andy, sitting at his desk, announced, "I'm going to church on Sunday."

Sue stopped. "But you don't go to church. I asked you before. I even offered to take you."

"Well, I'm going Sunday," he said, smiling, hoping to intrigue Sue.

"Kreider's?"

"Yeah, how did you know?"

Sue put her purse down and sat on the edge of the desk. She looked at Andy for a moment, turned halfway away, and then back.

"Do you know what you're doing?" she asked.

"Yes," he said, "I'm going to church on Sunday."

"Then do you know why you're doing it?"

Andy thought for a moment, swiveled away from Sue, and confessed, "No, I guess I don't know why. Journalistic curiosity, I suppose. It's my job."

"Are you sure? It's not a kind of voyeurism, is it?"

Andy was silent and then, turning back to Sue, said, "I don't think so. I care about these people."

"You do?" Sue was getting angry, protective. "Do you care enough to leave them alone? I don't think it's a good idea to intrude into anyone's business, but I'm certain it's not a good idea to intrude into the lives of people as private as these people are. They don't even like to have their pictures taken. Do you think they like the idea of having their private lives spread across a newspaper? They're not exactly my neighbors, but I still don't like to see them hurt."

"Look, Sue," Andy said, "I'm just going to church."

"Why?"

"Jacob asked me. That's why."

"Sure."

Sue turned to leave and again turned back and asked Andy why he thought Jacob wanted him to go along to church. Andy repeated Jacob's statement that it would be worth his while.

Sue's tone became more conciliatory, apparently believing that Andy was as disingenuous as he sounded.

"Andy," she said, "you should know that Jacob is known around here as a troublemaker. He's the only Mennonite I know who actually wants to be in the paper. He's using you."

"Maybe," Andy said. "But all I know is there's one hell of a story here, and I'm going to church on Sunday."

"See you Monday," Sue said and left, banging the door just a bit harder than necessary.

Andy stayed sitting for a while longer, playing with the papers on his desk, checking e-mail, thinking. Maybe Sue's right, he thought. What right do I have to go to a church I would never otherwise enter? Why am I even interested in these people? The reason, of course, he convinced himself again, is the story. But is that the only reason? Is there a personal reason for wanting to know these people, for wanting to know about them and what happens to them? They're different, but how different?

Andy spent the evening and most of Saturday working on his house. He enjoyed making minor repairs, trimming shrubbery, cutting grass, anything physical and outdoors. He found he didn't have to think much when he did that.

And then, it was Sunday morning, and Andy was trying to decide if he should wear a coat and tie to church. He knew the Mennonites were simple people, so out of deference to their simplicity, he wore no coat and kept his plain blue shirt open at the collar.

It was a fine morning for church, he thought, cool and bright, just the kind of morning he associated with his childhood and with the church he had attended every Sunday. He tolerated the church service as a kid but almost always enjoyed Sunday School, especially the free-flowing discussions the teacher got going. They talked about school and sports, just about everything but religion, except for the one time they got on the subject of Hell. What is Hell like, they asked their teacher, a kindly older man who never put any pressure on them. Do you know how you feel when you're sick and throwing up all the time, he said. Well, he went on, if you multiply that by a thousand and just keep throwing up forever, that's Hell. Andy had been sick the week before that discussion, so the analogy made an impression. Endless throwing up and clear cool mornings, Andy thought of one or the other when he thought of church, which he rarely did.

Which would it be today, he thought, as he headed down Route 15 and turned on to Kreider's Road at the sign that points to Kreider's Reformed Mennonite Church. He didn't know what to expect, but he did know it would be interesting.

Andy pulled up within sight of the church but far enough away that he could not be noticed, rolled down his window, and waited for Jacob to appear. The church was made of wood and painted white with a small bell tower at one end of the roof. It was a perfect rectangle with small windows along both sides and a door at the end facing him. He estimated it would not seat more than 100 people. While sitting there, he watched several families park their black cars and walk into the church, but he didn't see Jacob. At 10:00 patches of a hymn drifted toward him, and he wondered if Jacob had changed his mind.

"Mr. Simpson."

Andy looked up and saw Jacob standing beside his car.

"Are you ready?" Jacob said.

Andy didn't know how to respond.

"I suppose so," he said finally. "Do we just walk in or do we wait for an appropriate time or what?"

"I will know when to walk in," Jacob said, "You can come along and just sit on a bench at the back. There is a lot of space."

"Won't they notice I'm there?" Andy was concerned about the reaction of the people in the church to his presence.

"No, they will not notice you," Jacob said.

They walked together to the church and stood outside the open door, waiting, while the congregation finished the hymn. It sounded vaguely familiar to Andy, but he couldn't place it. Most hymns sound the same, he thought.

When the singing stopped, Jacob looked in the door. Andy stood beside it and listened. It sounded as though someone, a man, was making announcements, reporting on illnesses in the congregation.

"Follow me," Jacob said and walked through the door. Andy

slipped in behind him and sat on the first seat of the last bench. The interior was simple, a large open room with rows of small benches and a table at the far end. Jacob took a few steps up the aisle before people began to notice him, turning and whispering.

Andy recognized the man making the announcements as Bishop Souders. When the bishop saw Jacob, he stopped talking, and the members of the congregation also went silent. Jacob and the bishop looked at each other, neither saying anything. Then Jacob began.

"I have come for the truth," he said, his voice low but deliberate, "and I demand the truth of you, Bishop Souders."

The bishop did not flinch, but kept looking directly at Jacob. "You are welcome here, Jacob," he said, "if you accept the decisions of the church. Do you accept these decisions?"

"No," Jacob shouted. He raised his right arm, the veins in his neck tightened, and he roared at the congregation.

"Whatever God joins, let no man put asunder," he shouted, pointing directly at Bishop Souders. "The bonds of marriage are sacred. No man can break those bonds. No church can break those bonds."

Jacob began making his way down the aisle towards the bishop, shouting to the congregation on the right and left as he went, waving his arms, pointing at individuals. The members sat passively, looking down. No one looked directly at him.

"Paul said in Ephesians," Jacob shouted, "'Wives submit to your husbands.' This church is disobeying the teachings of Paul. This church is destroying my family, God's family. This church is making a living hell of life for me and for my family. It must stop. You must see the evil you are doing. You must return my wife and children to me. Paul said in Corinthians, 'The head of the woman is the man.' You are violating the teachings of the Bible."

Andy watched with fascination. Jacob simply filled the space completely, apparently intimidating everyone there, except possibly the bishop, who continued to stand his ground as Jacob, waving and shouting, came closer. Just before he reached the bishop, Jacob stopped and turned to a woman sitting in the second row of benches. Andy knew it was Sarah.

In a lowered voice Jacob said to her, "Sarah, I know you love me. I know you want our family together. Speak to me. Tell me what you want me to do. Tell me why we cannot be a family again. All I ask is that you tell me what I should do."

Sarah did not respond. She sat there silently and looked down at her lap. Jacob said nothing more, just looked at his wife.

"We do this out of love for you," the bishop said. "Jacob, can you not understand that you must come back to the church? Your soul is in danger. We want to help you see this."

Bishop Souders spoke softly and deliberately. Jacob turned slowly toward him.

The bishop continued, "In Titus, we read, 'A man that is a heretic reject.' If you preach heresy against the church, we must cast you off, we must excommunicate you. But if you renounce your heresy and obey the church, we welcome you back with love and forgiveness. Your wife will be your wife again."

Jacob exploded.

"My wife is your hostage. She will give herself to me if I reject what I believe. You are using her body as ransom. You tell me, if I give in to you, she will give me her body again."

Andy could see that the bishop was having difficulty controlling his anger. He stiffened, and his face grew red.

"Jacob," he said, but Jacob interrupted him.

"She did come to me one night since the ban was in effect, and in that act the ban was destroyed. She must admit that."

He turned again to Sarah.

"Do you deny that you gave me your body, Sarah? Do you deny that we have been husband and wife once since the ban?"

Sarah did not look up. She did not reply.

The bishop had regained his composure. He spoke with a calm, firm voice. "Paul also said in Romans, 'Mark them which cause divisions and offenses and avoid them.' We are obeying Paul when we reject you, Jacob."

Andy was fascinated by the argument. The Bible used against the Bible, each person choosing what served his purpose. Jacob was like an Old Testament prophet, Jeremiah perhaps, railing against the sinners, trying to force them by the sheer power of his words to capitulate. The bishop's power came from a calm assurance that he is speaking for God. And Sarah. Sarah sat silent, feeling who knows what, as her husband humiliated her in the name of his love for her. And somehow she remained above it all, aloof, reflecting dignity, untouched by the anger, the vindictiveness, the showmanship.

And it was showmanship. Andy was convinced that Jacob reveled somehow in the spectacle he himself created. Perhaps that's why he did it. Perhaps it's as simple as that. The man is an egomaniac. But Andy quickly rejected that possibility because there was more to Jacob than that. The Jeremiah was real and as far as Andy could tell, like Jeremiah, sincere.

The two men stood finally in silence, exhausted perhaps, their anger, their frustration voided. They simply looked at each other, as though neither knew what to do next. And then, slowly, one by one, the members of the congregation got up and walked out of the building, a somber procession as if in mourning, as if leaving a funeral. The bishop, Sarah, and Jacob remained.

Jacob's voice was softer now. "Sarah," he said, "what must I do?"

Sarah said nothing.

By now Andy was too embarrassed to stay any longer. He got up and walked out the door, leaving the three of them, returning to his car where he waited. A few minutes later Jacob left the church and walked slowly over to Andy.

"It is over," Jacob said, sounding defeated.

"Yes," Andy said.

"I am going home, to my home of hell."

"Did you get what you came for?" Andy asked.

"Yes," Jacob said, then turned and walked to his car. When Jacob had left, Andy turned on the engine and drove out of the stone-covered parking lot, down Kreider Road, and out onto Route 15. He was shaken by the morning's events, and never relaxed as he made his way back towards Carlisle. Like eternal throwing up, he thought.

Monday morning Sue came in the office, made some coffee, checked the mail, and began working on her computer, ignoring Andy. Andy sensed she was still angry. He came out of his office and said, "I went to church."

"So?" she said, without looking up.

Andy leaned against the doorway. "It was quite a show," he said.

"Really?"

Sue was sarcastic but also obviously interested. Andy continued trying to impress her, or perhaps himself, with his professional callousness.

"Yeah," he said, "Jacob reamed out the entire congregation. They never did finish the service. People just walked out."

"And you were there?"

"Yeah, I was there. I saw it all."

"And you'll write about it?" she said.

"I don't know. It wasn't pretty. I don't know how people can do that to each other in the name of religion."

"Did you ever hear of the Inquisition?" Sue asked.

"Yeah," Andy said, "that's what it was, I guess. An inquisition. Except I'm not sure who was burned at the stake."

"What are you going to do now?"

"I don't know," Andy said as he turned to go back in his office. "I think I'll try to get an interview with Sarah."

"Andy!"

Six

Another week went by, and another *Courier* came out, but without any reference to the incident at the church. Andy told himself it was part of a bigger story, that he could insert it in some story at a later date. But he had no idea what the bigger story might be. He had expected Jacob to come to see him and complain about the lack of coverage, but he had not come by. Meanwhile, Andy spent his days on the routine of the paper and his evenings trying to read or watch television or anything to take his mind off of Sarah and Jacob.

On Friday he went home for lunch, fixed himself a sandwich, and thought of Jacob, alone, perhaps having lunch, and Sarah, also alone. I don't have any choice, he thought, but they do. It's crazy. He thought about the disruption of the previous Sunday, the anger, the humiliation, but he also thought about the dignity that Sarah displayed. She doesn't deserve any of this, he thought, and yet it happens.

Andy didn't have to go back to the office. He had started taking Friday afternoons off, just to look around the area, do some shopping, relax at home, getting used to the idea of being on his own. But this Friday he was curious about Jacob's reaction to last Sunday and to the fact that he had not published anything. He thought about it for a while before finally deciding to go see Jacob, even though he knew the meeting might be a disaster.

He changed his mind several times in the next hour, but he

was curious, and so by two o'clock he was driving up the lane to the trailer and the house.

He noticed immediately that Jacob's car was not there. The lot next to the trailer where he usually parked was empty. Well, he thought, it looks like I came all the way down here for nothing. Jacob should at least have a telephone. Andy got out of the car and walked to the door of the trailer. He knocked. Nothing. He peeked in a window but saw nothing. He walked around to the back of the trailer, saw no one, and returned to the front. Jacob had a straight-backed, wooden rocking chair next to the front door, so Andy decided to sit a while. Maybe if I wait a few minutes, he thought, he'll be back. He might have just gone to the store.

Andy sat there, rocking slightly, enjoying the quiet, looking at the potato plants in the fields off to his right, growing a bit more each week. He looked at the farmhouse and again was impressed with how much it looked like his grandfather's house, down to the porch going all the way across the front of the house and even the darker paint of the shutters.

He thought of Sarah. Perhaps she's in the house. He tried to look around to the back of the house to see if she had hung out any clothes, but could see nothing. Not washing day, he thought. He knew he would like to talk with her, but he was not sure why. On the surface, he would like to get her side of the story, although he was sure she would never tell him that. On the next level down, perhaps, he just wanted to get to know this woman whom he admires. She endures more than he could imagine, and yet it just seems to wash over her. The pressure on her, within her, must be overwhelming. How does she manage? He was sure that was part of his reason for wanting to talk with her. Beneath that second level, however, he had no idea what his motives were.

After sitting there for several minutes, Andy decided to go over and knock on the door. I have nothing to lose, he thought, and besides she's probably not there. He told himself she is working at the market, but he had not seen her when he turned off Route 15.

He went up the three steps to the porch and hesitated. He could still leave, he told himself. He was sure she had not noticed him yet. But he decided to go through with it and knocked on the screen door. No answer. He opened the screen door and knocked again, this time on the inner door, a bit harder. A few moments later, the inner door opened a crack.

"Yes," a female voice said. It was Sarah.

"Hello, it's Andy Simpson."

"I know who you are, Mr. Simpson."

"I came to visit Jacob but he's not here. I thought I might talk with you. For just a moment. If it's okay."

Sarah did not reply immediately. Then she opened the door wider, wide enough for Andy to see her face.

"What do you want?" she asked. She was calm, but at the same time tentative, not letting go of the door.

"Just to talk," he said.

"I am sorry, Mr. Simpson. We have nothing to talk about. Goodbye."

She began to close the door, but Andy spoke quickly. "Please," he said. "Just a few minutes. I want to explain, to apologize. I'm sorry I came to the service on Sunday. I know it was wrong."

Andy kept talking, saying anything just to keep the door from closing, apologizing for interfering, for intruding into their lives, her life.

Sarah just stood there, looking at Andy, until she interrupted him, "You were there Sunday?"

Andy stopped talking, looked in Sarah's eyes, and said, "Yes, didn't you know?"

Sarah said she had not known, and then she asked quickly if he had put it in the paper.

Andy sputtered, "No, no. I didn't."

"Why not?"

Andy was surprised. He thought if anything she would simply be grateful. He didn't expect her question.

"I don't know." he said, "It's just that . . . if I would know more, from your side, I suppose I could be fair." And then he stopped, looked back at the trailer, turned to Sarah, and said, "Look, I'm sorry I'm here. It's an intrusion, I know. I really don't know what I'm doing here, but I know I don't want to hurt you. Just forget I came."

Andy began to walk across the porch, toward his car.

"Mr. Simpson," she said.

He stopped. "Yes?"

"You must be thirsty. Would you like some iced tea?" She smiled shyly.

Andy did want to stay and told Sarah he would like some iced tea.

She went back in the house. Andy was not sure just what to do so he sat on the wooden porch swing and waited. Soon Sarah came out with a glass of iced tea and offered it to him.

"Thank you," he said. "I'm very sorry. We don't need to talk. About anything really."

Andy was confused by the sudden shift. Sarah sat on a wooden chair near the steps, facing the swing. She looked at him.

"I was rude to you," she said.

"That's okay," Andy said, "I shouldn't have — "

"No," she interrupted, "it's your job."

Andy swung slightly and drank some of the iced tea. It was heavily sugared, not the sugarless, low-caloric type he had gotten used to in New York restaurants. He sat in silence for a while, then looked at Sarah. She looked up, saw him watching, and lowered her head again.

Andy decided to start the conversation, hoping it might go somewhere or at least provide a reason for his presence on the porch.

"I tried to see Jacob," he said, "but I guess he's not home."

"No," she said, "I saw him go out, but I do not know where he is."

She raised the pitcher of iced tea and motioned toward him. He smiled and shook his head.

"I'm fine," he said and then asked if she knew when he might be home. She said she did not know.

"Oh. That's fine," he said. "I didn't have any particular reason to see him. I can come back later."

Andy thought of asking Sarah to give Jacob a message, but then he realized that would not work.

"It's very pleasant here," he said. "Good iced tea."

He held the iced tea up. She smiled. He could think of nothing else to say. Here he had her. This is what he wanted, and he could not think of a question. He glanced at her. She had turned her head and was now looking down the lane. This close he could see that she was actually older than he thought she had looked from a distance. There was a bit more gray. There were more lines in the face. But she was still attractive, and her skin was almost translucent. Andy thought that he had never seen such purity, such innocence. And yet he also saw in Sarah complete confidence, an unwavering certainty as to who she is. Finally he just said what was on his mind.

"How can you live like this?" he asked.

Sarah turned back toward Andy, paused, and then spoke softly, almost as if she had expected the question.

"It is given to me, and I accept it," she said.

Andy was not sure how far to go.

"But you . . . love Jacob."

"Yes," she said, "and that is why I will do what I can to bring him back to the church."

"You must love him very much." Andy knew he had crossed the line and wished he could take that back.

Sarah said nothing. She turned again to the lane and looked down it, perhaps expecting Jacob's return, perhaps hoping for it, before turning back to Andy.

"Do you love someone, Mr. Simpson?" she said, again taking Andy off-guard.

"Yes. No. I mean I did. Once. I'm . . . we're divorced."

"I'm sorry," Sarah said. "It must be difficult."

"It is," Andy said.

Neither looked at the other. Andy wondered how she could think of his difficulties. They were nothing compared to hers.

Then Andy spoke. "Do you mind talking with me?"

"No," she said, but she did not look up at him.

"May I ask you something, Sarah?"

She did not reply.

Andy hoped her lack of response was not negative. He continued, "Do you think much about your life before you joined the church? About school and what you did then? About your friends then? I understand it was quite different."

She didn't ask how he knew her life had been different. He assumed she knew Jacob had told him.

"We do not join my church until we are adults," she said by way of explanation, "So our life before the church can be quite different. I do not think of it much. I still have friends, some of them the same as before."

Andy pursued this point. "I understand you joined the church because of Jacob," he said.

"Yes," she said, "Jacob led me to the church. I shall always be grateful for that. I hope to lead him back."

"But don't you ever wish you could do those normal things again?"

"This is normal," she said.

Andy couldn't answer that. Sarah changed the subject and asked if she might ask a question. Andy agreed, wondering what he could tell her. She stunned Andy by asking why he got a divorce. Andy asked her why she wanted to know.

"You loved a woman," she said. "You married her. And then you left her."

"Well, actually, it was her idea. It's just that two people, who are close at one time, can drift apart. Suddenly, they wake up and they have nothing in common. So they go their separate ways."

"It sounds easy."

"I guess it is," he said, although he knew it was anything but easy.

"But it should not be," Sarah said. "Jacob and I pledged we would be together until death."

"Well, Beth and I did too, but I guess we didn't really mean it or maybe we just changed our minds. You have to realize it was all very civilized. We both agreed, and we even still keep in contact."

"Is that civilized?" Sarah asked, apparently with complete innocence.

Andy was getting uncomfortable with the line of questioning. At the same time, it was becoming easy to talk with Sarah. He felt the need to talk to her about himself, however uncomfortable, perhaps because he knew she would not understand. Or perhaps she would. He also knew he should fight this need.

While he was considering which way to go, he noticed two children, a boy, dressed like Jacob, and a girl, dressed like Sarah, walking up the lane toward the house. School must be out, he thought. He guessed the boy was about twelve and the girl ten. They came up on the porch, and Sarah introduced them.

"This is Mr. Simpson," she said, "a newspaper man."

They smiled shyly and said hello.

"This is Isaac and Isabel," Sarah said.

"My name is Ike," the boy said and went into the house. Isabel smiled again and followed her brother.

"They're fine children," Andy said.

"Yes."

Andy decided this might be a good time to leave, and excused himself, saying he had business back in town. He hoped to leave before Jacob came back, but he asked Sarah if he could stop by again some time.

"You may," she said, "but why would you want to?"

Andy was again bumped off center by her directness. He tried to think what he should say, and then smiled at her for a moment.

"Maybe I'll think of something," he said, and turned away to his car. As he reached his car, he heard the screen door close.

Over the next several weeks, Andy began to do his vegetable and fruit shopping at Souders Market. He said hello to Sarah, picked out what he wanted, and tried to find a moment or two when she was free before he left. Each time they exchanged a few pleasantries.

During those weeks Jacob stopped in the office several times with new ideas for gaining publicity. He was thinking about a billboard, he said, and maybe some posters. He was considering putting posters up inside some of the other Reformed Mennonite churches in the area, and then one Friday morning he stopped in to tell Andy that he was going to Washington that afternoon. He hoped to see someone at the *Post* and would be staying overnight with a relative. He wanted to know if Andy could give him any advice when dealing with big-city newspaper people. Andy told him to do whatever he had done before, and then wished he could be there for the encounter.

That afternoon Andy thought he might go out to see Sarah. He could pretend that he went to see Jacob and since he wasn't there, maybe he and Sarah could talk. She obviously wouldn't know where he was and that he wouldn't be back. Then he thought maybe it wasn't such a good idea. Finally, he decided to go out after dinner.

When he pulled in next to the trailer, he noticed Sarah sitting on the porch swing. He waved to her and then went through the charade of calling on Jacob: knocking on the door, waiting, looking in a window, walking around back. Finally, he walked over to the farmhouse.

"Jacob isn't home?" he said.

"No. I do not know where he is. He left early afternoon."

Small talk continued, neither seeming to want to end it.

"Nice evening." Andy looked around the farm, still standing.

"Yes, it is," she said.

"Hot for the time of year."

"Yes, it is hot."

"Feels good sitting on the porch?" Andy realized what a

ridiculous question that was to ask her. Why else would she be sitting on the porch?

"Yes, it does," she replied kindly, tolerantly.

Andy was at the end of his small talk and thought he should leave. It had been a bad idea from the beginning, but as he was about to excuse himself Sarah surprised him again.

"Would you like to sit a bit?" she said, "The children are with their grandparents."

Andy was not sure why Sarah added that, but he thanked her. Sarah moved over on the swing, and Andy sat next to her. Sarah asked if he would like some iced tea. He said he would.

When she returned with the tea, a large tumbler filled with ice, she sat down again in the swing.

"I have thought about you," she said.

"You have?" Andy was pleased.

"Yes, I was wondering how you are doing."

"I'm fine," he said.

"I was thinking about you and your wife."

"My ex-wife," Andy said quickly, before he could think about it, and then he regretted having said it.

"Yes." Sarah said. "It seems so sad to me. It must be very difficult to live alone."

"Oh, I manage," Andy said. "I have a small house just on the outskirts of Carlisle."

"Do you miss her?" she asked.

"Sometimes," he said.

Andy found himself wanting to talk about Beth, but then thought this was perhaps not the appropriate time or place.

"Most of the time it's fine," he said, and then he added, "Are you lonely?"

"No," she said, "I have my children, and Jacob is just over there. I must avoid him, but I know he's there. And then I have my friends, the church. And I have God, but I suppose you would not understand that."

"Yes, I think I do," Andy said, "but I don't think of God as being, you know, sort of here."

"Then you are lonely," Sarah said. She spoke with compassion and assurance.

"Yes, I suppose so." Andy continued, trying to answer Sarah's earlier question. "I did enjoy—I suppose that's the word—having someone around, someone I knew would be there. But the divorce seemed so sensible at the time. Beth wanted to keep working in New York. I had had it with that life. I wanted something simpler, less pressure. We had no reason to stay together."

"But you loved her."

"Maybe. I don't know. You see, part of my problem I think is that I don't really know if I ever loved Beth." Andy instantly regretted saying that.

Sarah did not back off. She asked him why he married her if he were not sure he loved her.

"That too seemed like a good idea at the time," he said. "We were living . . . I mean we had been very close, so it just seemed natural to take the next step."

Sarah said, "Marriage is not a light matter," and Andy agreed, thinking, now, at least, he knows that.

The conversation dwindled as they sat quietly, the evening cooling off.

Andy interrupted the silence by a slight clearing of his throat and then asked a question without really knowing why he was asking it. "Sarah, do you know what love is?"

Sarah thought for a moment.

"I know love," she said confidently. "I know love for my God, for my family, for my friends."

"I really don't have any of those," Andy said, and then added, "Do you know love for Jacob?"

"Yes," she said without hesitating.

"You know love," he said, pressing the point, "but do you know what love is? Can you tell me what love is?"

"What did you feel when you were married? What did you want for your wife?"

Andy thought about that and realized that he had never actually thought about what he wanted for her. He also knew he had to say something.

"Happiness. I guess I wanted happiness for her," he said. "I hope I wanted what was best for her, but I don't know."

"How much did you want happiness for her?"

He was confused by the question, not even knowing what she meant. How do you quantify love, he thought.

Sarah continued, "What were you willing to sacrifice for her happiness?"

Andy was confused by the question. He knew he had not even thought about sacrificing anything for Beth's happiness. He knew, or thought, he had not been a bad husband. He kept telling himself that. Perhaps he had simply not loved her enough, or she him. They had always been so busy that he had had no time to think about it. They had never really talked about love. He was feeling uncomfortable, especially in the presence of what he was beginning to understand as wisdom. He thought Sarah might have answers he needed, but he too had questions of her.

"Sarah," he said, deciding to ask his most important question. "I don't understand why you choose to shun Jacob if you love him. Shouldn't you sacrifice your own convictions, even your faith in God, for someone you love?"

"You do not understand, Mr. Simpson," Sarah said, continuing her patient explanation. "I want for Jacob the greatest happiness anyone can know, and that is to come back to God and to His church. I am sacrificing my happiness because I want Jacob's happiness so much. I will do anything possible, I will sacrifice all that I have to bring Jacob to God. I will live apart from him for him. And I do that because I love him."

Andy was pushed to silence again. After a moment Sarah added, "I cannot tell you what love is, Mr. Simpson; I can only show you."

Andy wasn't sure if Sarah was referring to her own love for Jacob or his own lack of love. Either way he thought he knew what she was saying, but it didn't help because he still saw his own life as even more confused. Through it all, however, one thing stood out. Andy knew that he wanted someday to experience a love like this. As he thought about this love, Sarah quietly asked him if he were going to put this conversation in his newspaper. He assured her he would not. "That's not why I have been talking with you," he said.

"Then why have you been talking with me?" she asked.

"I don't know. Perhaps because I can talk with you. Do you mind?"

Sarah paused and then looked up at Andy.

"No," she said, "I do not mind."

Without thinking Andy reached across and put his hand on Sarah's hand, which was resting on her knee. She put her hand on his.

Sarah looked into Andy's eyes and said, "God loves you."

"Yes," Andy said, but it was not God's love he was thinking about at the moment.

Sarah continued to look into Andy's eyes, then dropped her own eyes and withdrew her hand. For the first time she seemed uncomfortable.

"Perhaps you should go, Mr. Simpson," she said.

"Yes," he said, and then, after a pause, he added, "Sarah, I should not have come. I'm afraid I'm only confusing you."

"I am not confused, Mr. Simpson," she said in a quiet voice. Andy knew she was not. He also knew he was.

Andy thanked her for the iced tea, excused himself, and left. As he walked across to his car, he heard the door to the house opening and closing. All the way back to Carlisle, he thought about her comment that she was not confused. If she's not, he thought, she's the only one.

❦ **Seven** ❧

Andy dug slowly. He loved the way the soft soil turned over on his shovel and fell in loose clumps to the ground. He had finally decided to put in a garden, and now, Saturday morning, he had the time. He knew it was too late for some vegetables, sugar peas, but he wanted to put in some tomatoes, some lettuce, some cucumbers, easy things. He felt the need to create life, but he also felt he did not have the time to nurture it too much.

Life in Carlisle is good, he thought. He liked the people he had come to know. Sue and her husband. Mary at the restaurant. Mildred who ran the small corner store where he usually got his food. He hated the supermarkets. He liked his neighbors, although they usually stayed to themselves. That's the nature of the people here, he knew, but that's the way he liked it. He stayed to himself as well. He liked the slower pace too. He could sit on his porch for hours, if he had hours, and no one would think it strange. They would nod to him as they walked by, perhaps stop and comment on the weather. "The paper wants rain tonight," they might say. He would nod in agreement.

Now he was digging in the earth, turning over spades full of rich loam, raking it into smooth soil, hoeing the rows, getting ready for planting. It was a good feeling, almost spiritual, and it kept him from thinking of Sarah. When a thought of her began to take shape, he dug harder. If only, he thought. Another time. Another place. Another life even. But not now, not here.

As he went down on both knees and began to put the tomato plants into their holes and smooth the dirt around them with his hands, he heard Jacob above him.

"That is good, Mr. Simpson," he said, "good straight rows."

Andy turned and looked up at Jacob. He was in his work clothes, bib overalls over a long light-blue shirt, heavy shoes.

"Hello, Jacob," he said. "I'm just trying to put in a few things."

"You seem to know what you are doing."

"I told you," Andy said, breaking up a large clump with his hands, "I spent time on my grandfather's farm when I was a kid. I always helped him with the vegetable garden."

Jacob knelt next to Andy and began to smooth out the soil around the tomatoes.

Andy leaned back on his knees and asked Jacob how his trip to Washington had gone. He asked specifically if he had seen anyone at the *Post*.

"No," Jacob said, "nobody important. I tried to. I told the lady at the desk my story. She called someone and then told me I should write to them. But I already did that and nobody wrote back."

"Look, Jacob," Andy said, "why do you want to put your story in a newspaper that far away? I don't think the people in your church read that paper."

"No," he said, "they do not."

"Then why bother with it?"

"It is a big newspaper, one of the biggest."

Andy asked him if he just wanted the attention. He had been hoping for a chance to frame the question.

"No," Jacob said, standing, "I just want justice. I want what is right to be done."

"Are you sure you know what's right, Jacob?"

"Yes. My family returned to me."

"So you can be head of the family?"

"Yes," he said, "That is the way it should be. That is what the Bible says."

Andy did not know where to go from there. Should he try to convince Jacob that marriage is a 50-50 arrangement? He knew he did not exactly qualify as an expert on the subject of marriage, but he knew something was wrong with Jacob's perception.

"Jacob," he said, "can I ask you something?"

"Yes. You may ask me anything. I do not have anything to hide."

Andy thought it over for a moment and then stood beside Jacob. He knew he might offend Jacob, but he had to ask anyway. "Have you ever considered what Sarah wants?" he asked.

"I know what Sarah wants," he said. "She wants me to obey the bishop. She wants me to come back to the church defeated."

"No," Andy said, "that's not what I mean. Have you ever considered what she wants out of your marriage? Have you ever tried to put yourself in her place, just to see what it feels like?"

Good advice, Andy thought. Maybe I should have tried something like that.

"What it feels like to be a woman?"

Jacob was clearly confused.

"No," Andy said, "what it feels like to be the other person in a relationship, what you appear to be to that other person."

Jacob thought for a moment.

"No," he said finally, "I do not think I ever did that. I do not know why I would. I guess I do not know what you are saying."

"That's okay, Jacob," Andy said, thinking perhaps he did not know what he was saying either. He then added, almost under his breath, "Maybe I'm just talking to myself."

Jacob looked over the garden, ignoring Andy's comment or perhaps not hearing it. "Are you planning to put in anything else?" he said. "It is small for a garden."

"I don't know," Andy said. "It's too late in the season for most things, isn't it?"

"For some things, but you can still put in some beans and peppers. You could can the beans."

"Maybe," Andy said, "I never tried canning."

"Women's work," Jacob said.

Andy knelt again and started to work the soil with a hand hoe, breaking some of the clumps of dirt into smaller clumps; Jacob straightening the tomato stalks. They talked some more about gardening, Jacob giving advice on when to sucker the tomato plants, how to string pole beans. In the midst of this, Andy mentioned that he had been out to see Sarah. Jacob asked if she had talked with him.

"Some," Andy said. "I stopped by to see you and you weren't there, so I went over and knocked on the door. We talked for a bit on the front porch. She gave me some iced tea."

"She makes good iced tea."

"It was good."

Jacob asked if she had said anything about him. Andy admitted that she had, and Jacob asked what she had said.

Andy replied without hesitation, "That she loves you."

"I know that. Did she say anything else?"

"Like what?" Andy was puzzled that Jacob was not moved by Sarah's statement.

"Did she say anything about coming back?"

"No," Andy said, "she didn't say anything about that. She just said she fears for your soul because you're outside the church."

Jacob was clearly becoming irritated. He stopped working and just sat on the ground saying nothing, pushing his hands into his thighs, rocking slightly. Andy thought it better to change the approach and said he had heard they had met while she was still in high school.

"Yes," Jacob said, "we met at a social. She was not a member of the church yet. I do not think she planned to be a member. She liked high school."

Andy asked if they had gone to the same school; Jacob said, yes, but that he had been there seven or eight years earlier. Andy decided to push the subject and asked Jacob what she was like then.

"What do you mean?" Jacob replied.

"In high school. When you met her. What kind of a girl was she?"

"She was good," Jacob said, "I saw that right away. And pretty."

"Was she quiet?"

"Quiet? No, I do not think so. I would not say she was quiet. She was popular, had lots of friends. She always seemed happy. She was a cheerleader, you know."

"Yes," Andy said. He remembered Jacob telling him about Sarah's past when they had first met. "Did you ever see her being a cheerleader?"

Jacob said he never went to things like that. Andy asked if his church prohibited attending such activities.

"We were not forbidden," he said. "We just did not do it."

"So then you got married?"

"No," Jacob said, "not right away. I knew right away I wanted her, but I was older and thought she would not want me. She asked about the church, and I told her all about it. I guess I was like her teacher. She got more and more interested, and finally, about a year out of high school, she joined. About a year after that we got married."

"Do you think she would have married you if she had not joined the church?"

"No, I do not think so."

"Did you bring her to the church so you could marry her?"

Jacob thought about that, letting the fine soil seep between his fingers.

"Maybe. I did want her real bad." Jacob held more soil for a moment and then dropped it.

"We were happy at first, for a long time. Then the bishop did something he should not have done. He gave sacrament to his parents when they were feuding."

"What do you mean feuding?"

"I would rather not say. That is enough. I should not have said that. Do not put it in your paper."

"Of course not," Andy said, and then filed it away in his mind, wondering momentarily if he would really use it.

Andy asked Jacob to sit for a while, and they walked over to the wooden picnic table Andy had purchased recently and placed on the grass just outside the kitchen door under a maple tree. Andy straddled the end of the bench; Jacob sat awkwardly on the other end.

After a moment of sitting in silence, Andy asked, "Don't you believe in forgiveness, Jacob?"

Jacob looked puzzled by the question and asked Andy what he meant.

"Forgiveness." Andy said. "If someone does something wrong and they're sorry for it."

"He has never repented," Jacob replied.

"No," Andy said, "not the bishop. I mean the parents."

"I forgive them."

"Isn't that what the bishop did? Forgive them?"

Andy thought he had Jacob there, but Jacob countered quickly.

"He hasn't the right to absolve them of their sins," he said.

Andy decided to change the direction of his questioning. "Would you like to be bishop, Jacob?"

"No," Jacob said and stood up to leave. Andy stood with Jacob, thinking the question offended him, or perhaps he simply wanted to avoid the subject.

"I'm sorry, Jacob," he said, "I shouldn't have said that. I didn't mean it the way it sounded. It's just that I'm a journalist. I ask questions for a living."

"If you are a journalist, you should be putting my story in your paper, the whole story."

"We'll talk about it," Andy said, wiping the sweat from his brow. He then asked Jacob to stay a while longer, making a peace offering.

"How about some iced tea?" Andy knew the tea would be anemic beside Sarah's; he felt Jacob might feel the same way, so he was surprised when Jacob said he would like some. "It is hot," he said.

"Fine," Andy said, "I'll go in and whip up some. Have a seat."

Jacob sat back down at the picnic table and wiped his face with his large, red handkerchief. Soon Andy returned with two glasses of iced tea.

"I'm sorry," he said, "but I only have this instant tea. I brought some sugar if you want to add it and a slice of lemon."

Jacob took the tea, sipped it, and then added three spoons of sugar. He stirred it for a while and then squeezed the lemon with his fingers and wiped his fingers on his bib overalls. He took a long swallow.

"It tastes good," he said. "Thanks."

Andy squeezed the lemon slice with his fingers and sipped at his sugarless tea.

Jacob began to tell Andy about his potatoes and how they're coming along, when they heard a voice coming from the side of the house.

"Hello. Anyone here?"

It was Beth. She came around the corner and stood looking at Andy and Jacob. Andy was stunned.

"Sorry," she said, "I was knocking on the front door but no one came. I thought maybe you were back here, so I came back and here you are. Hi."

She was clearly embarrassed.

"Hi," Andy said. "We were just taking a break. Jacob was helping with my garden. Here, sit down."

Andy stood to make room for Beth. She sat down across from Jacob. Andy sat next to Jacob.

"Oh, I'm sorry," Andy said, "I should introduce you. This is Jacob Weaver. A friend of mine."

"How do you do, Mr. Weaver," Beth said.

"Nice to meet you, ma'am."

Beth didn't let on that she knew about Jacob. Andy was grateful and relieved. He could also see that she was not comfortable being called "ma'am." That probably had never happened to her before.

Jacob, uncomfortable with the couple's obvious discomfort, excused himself, saying that he should get back to the farm.

"I should be out in the field on a day like this," he said.

Andy spoke to Beth, "Jacob farms potatoes. He has several big fields."

"Keeps me busy."

"It was nice to see you, Mr. Weaver," Beth said.

"Pleasure, ma'am."

He shook hands with both of them and invited Andy to come visit him at the farm. Then he was gone.

Beth smiled, nervously, then stopped and looked around. Andy watched her, wondering what brought her to Carlisle, but pleased that she had come.

"Is that his black car out front?" Beth said.

"Yes, they paint everything on the car black." He was relieved that the conversation had started.

"Oh."

Beth stood for a moment.

"I suppose you're wondering why I'm here," she said.

"No, that's okay," he said, "You don't need a reason. Did something go wrong with the sale of the loft?"

"No," she said, "that's fine. No problem there. I actually don't have a reason. I was sort of in the area. I'm driving to Pittsburgh for a meeting and thought I would stop. You're close to the turnpike. Do you mind?"

Andy said he didn't mind, but continued to wonder why she was really there. She had never even come with him when he had visited his relatives in the Sunbury area.

"It's beautiful here," she said. "I love the town."

"Yes," he said. "Not much like Manhattan, huh?"

"No, but it's charming." She looked around again, at the garden, at the house. "I like your house," she said.

"I'm just renting it," he said. "I might look around for a place to buy."

"So you think you'll stay?"

They both began to relax, now that the initial nervousness was gone.

"I think so," Andy said. "Long enough to get my money back anyway. The rates are good right now."

Andy didn't think Beth had come to talk about his house. Perhaps she was having second thoughts, but it's too late now. Maybe she was in some sort of personal trouble and has no one to talk to. She has plenty of people to talk to, he thought. I'm the one with no one to talk to. Maybe she's just curious. He didn't care. It was good to see her again.

"Would you like to see the place?" Andy said, not knowing what else to say.

He took her from room to room, each spartan. Andy explained that he got most of his furniture from a used furniture store.

"It's nice," she said, but Andy knew she was baffled by how little it took to satisfy him.

"How long do you have?" Andy asked. "Can you stay for dinner? There are some nice restaurants up in Harrisburg. You like Indian. There's a good Indian restaurant overlooking the river."

"No, I can't stay," she said. "I have to get on the road soon, but thanks for asking."

Andy invited Beth to sit on the front porch, explaining that it's a tradition to sit out on the porch.

"Won't people bother us out there?" she said.

"No, that's a tradition too. Tomorrow I'll just have to tell everyone who you are."

"What will you tell them?"

"The truth."

"Whatever that is, right?"

"Right. I'll figure something out."

They sat on an old, green metal swing that Andy had found in the basement. It swung on chains hanging from the ceiling of the porch, a bit squeaky and peeling but perfectly serviceable.

"Nice," she said.

"Yes, but I think it needs some oil."

Beth smiled again. Andy thought she must be wondering what he knows about oil.

"Are you still managing okay in New York?" Andy said.

"Yes. The job's going well. I have a new place, down in the Village."

"You look good." Andy wasn't sure if he should say that, given their circumstances.

"Thanks." He thought she looked pleased with the compliment.

"Your hair is very flattering. You changed it."

"Yes, a bit."

"I always liked the way your hair looked."

"Really?"

"Yes."

"You never told me that."

"Didn't I?"

"No. You never asked me how I was doing either. Are you turning over a new leaf?"

Andy laughed nervously.

"No," he said. "It's just that I haven't seen you for a while. I guess I've just never gotten the sense that it's over. We never fought about it or anything. There was no bitterness. It was more like I was going away for a while. Even the divorce doesn't seem real."

"You have the papers, Andy. It's real."

"I know."

Andy didn't know where he was going. He also didn't know what Beth was thinking.

"I think it's better this way," she said.

Which way, Andy thought, but he said nothing.

"I think we both have to accept that we share responsibility." Beth continued, "I was busy, always paying more attention to my job than to us. You never expressed yourself."

"What do you mean?"

"You never talked to me. You never told me what you thought. Like now. With my hair. That's a trivial thing, I know. What I mean is that you just kept clammed up. I never knew what you were thinking."

"Oh," he said.

"I'm sorry," she said, "I didn't come here to tell you that, or to criticize you. You're a good person. It's just that maybe we should have tried a little harder."

"Is that why you came today. To tell me that?"

"No. I don't know. What do you mean?"

"So we could try harder? Who knows?"

"No," she said. "Oh, Andy, I'm sorry. I didn't mean that. You weren't thinking that?"

"No," he said. "I just thought . . . I didn't know what to think. Why did you come? This is all pretty awkward since neither of us knows what the other is thinking."

"You're right," she said. "I guess I came to tell you something that you might not be at all interested in. You see, I started seeing this guy, this client. We've known each other for a while, but nothing happened until recently. You know. Now we're pretty involved, and I didn't want you to hear about it from someone else."

Andy could feel himself losing it. He knew he should remain detached, objective, but he couldn't.

"Who else would tell?" he said, turning away from her and then back again. "They're all your friends. You don't have to tell a divorced husband you're seeing someone, for God's sake. You're free. What are you doing, bragging?"

"No," Beth said, "it's nothing like that. I just thought . . . I don't know. I thought I was doing the right thing."

"Well, maybe you know what the right thing is, but I've

discovered since moving here that I don't have any idea what it is." Andy's anger and confusion were coming through.

"I guess I don't either." Beth said. "I should go."

"You don't have to go." Andy's confusion continued. "We can still talk. This does put an end to it, doesn't it? This is what the psychologists mean by closure, I guess, at least for you?"

Andy realized he looked absurd, wallowing in self-pity but unable to stop. Beth didn't respond. They sat quietly, rocking back and forth on the swing. Finally, Andy regained a degree of composure and said, "My grandfather had one of these swings on his porch. I spent whole evenings sitting there with him."

"I didn't know that," she said.

"Yes. I lived more with my grandfather than with my parents, especially in the summer."

"I know your parents are both gone. I suppose your grandfather too?"

"Yes. He died when I was in college. He was proud of me."

They kept swinging slightly as people walked by, noticing them but pretending not to.

"Did you talk much with him?" she asked.

"No," he said. "We just sat with each other and worked together. We sort of knew what we were thinking. Men didn't talk much in that society."

"Did you talk much with your parents, with your mother?"

They had never discussed his parents before. He was pleased to do it now.

"Almost never," he said, his voice taking on a far-away tone. "My dad worked all day and came home to eat, work in his den, and go to bed. Mom was always busy around the house, volunteering a lot, and all that. I had my school and my sports. I spent most of my spare time outside, a lot of time on the river. That's the way most kids around here were raised then. Still may be, for all I know."

"It's not bad," Beth said quietly, and then asked Andy if it feels good to be back.

"Yes," he said, "in a lot of ways it does. But in other ways it doesn't. I've been away, and now I've come back. I'm not the same. I don't understand lots of things."

Beth didn't respond right away. Then she said, "Like Jacob?"

"Yes, Jacob, and his life, his story. By the way, thanks for not giving away that I had told you about him."

"Sure. He seemed like a nice man. Pretty intense, though. He's handsome. Those blue eyes look right through you. Do you like him?"

"In some ways, for some things, I do," Andy said, "but I don't understand him."

"How about his wife?"

"I don't know if she understands him or not," Andy said.

"No, I mean do you understand her?"

Andy was beginning to get uncomfortable again.

"Oh. Even less. She loves him and yet lives apart. It makes no sense to me. They both inflict suffering on themselves and each other for what they say is a higher truth, a nobler cause, or something like that."

"Do you like her?"

Andy paused. Despite the intrusiveness of the question, he decided to respond as honestly as he could. What do I have to lose, he thought.

"To be honest, I do," he said. "She's as pure as anyone I've ever met."

"Nobody's that pure, Andy."

"Maybe not, but I admire her steadiness, and I enjoy talking to her."

"You've talked?" Beth seemed intrigued by the idea of Andy talking.

"Yeah, a couple of times."

"Alone?"

"What do you mean alone?" Andy asked.

"Just the two of you. No one else around. Alone."

"Well, yeah, we were alone. On the porch of her house. Nothing like what you're thinking. We just talked. It turns out she's pretty easy to talk to. She has that kind of sincere concern that good counselors can fake really well, but I don't think she's faking."

"You like talking with her?"

"Yeah, I suppose I do."

"You like being with her?"

"I don't know. What do you mean?"

Beth got up from the swing. She walked over to the porch railing, turned around, and asked Andy if he would mind her being blunt. Andy did not answer, did not look at her.

"Well then, I'll tell you," she started. "It sounds like you might be getting too involved in your story. You're a journalist, but she's married. If you insist on doing this story, you should remain outside it, objective. I know I'm telling you something you learned long ago, but maybe you need to be reminded."

Andy thought about this and asked Beth why she was telling him this. She said she was only thinking of him.

"Sure, as usual," Andy muttered.

"Andy! There's no need to be sarcastic," Beth countered.

Andy paused before responding. "Okay, maybe I am getting too involved with this story."

"Maybe you are," Beth said, "but with her, Andy, not the story."

Andy looked at his hands; he had been rubbing them together. He looked up at Beth and said, "I just want to see Sarah—and Jacob too—happy, both of them."

Beth asked if he had any idea what happiness is to them. He admitted he did not.

"Then it sounds like an uphill struggle," she said, "with lots of chances to cause harm."

"I suppose so. I know what you're saying. If it gets to that, or close to it, I'll stop."

"I hope so," Beth said and came back to sit on the swing. To Andy's relief, the discussion of Sarah was closed. They talked for a few more minutes, Andy telling her about Carlisle, about its history, about its role in the Civil War. Finally, Beth stood up and gathered her things. Andy stood also, not knowing what to say, wondering whether he should kiss her or shake her hand or what.

"I'm glad I stopped, Andy," she said as she turned to him.

"I'm glad you stopped too."

"I probably won't do it again," she said.

"I know," he said and then, nervous with the situation, asked, "What's the protocol in a situation like this?"

Beth smiled and kissed him on the cheek.

"Good luck," she said.

"Thanks."

She walked over to her car and unlocked the door. You're not in New York, Andy thought, as he smiled and waved to her. She gave him one last wave as she pulled out onto the street and headed for the turnpike. He still didn't know why she had come to Carlisle. He wondered why she had come all this way to tell him something she could have told him over the phone. He even suspected she was not really going to Pittsburgh. He wondered to himself if he cared.

Andy stood on the porch, finished his iced tea, and went back to his garden. The afternoon began to fade into evening.

Eight

Andy knew Beth gave good advice. She was street smart, a product of New York, and he knew he should take her advice seriously, even if he disagreed . . . especially if he disagreed. He thought about what she had said over the next few days, busy days early in the week, getting the paper out. He knew she was right. But then Friday afternoon came, and he ignored her advice and went to see Sarah. He wasn't sure why, except that he wanted to see her, even if it was just to chat at the vegetable stand.

As had become his routine, he bought a few things when he stopped at her market. She was there, of course, as he knew she would be, and she waited on him, standing shyly behind the wooden stand.

He asked her politely for three tomatoes. She picked out three and held them up. "These?" she said. Andy said they would be fine and asked her for some local celery. Sarah said they only had North Carolina celery today.

Honesty, Andy thought and asked for one stalk. She put those items together with some other things in a plastic bag.

He asked her how her children were.

"Fine," she said, "busy."

"What do they do now that school's out?" he asked.

"They have things to do," she said, "regular chores. They like to read, and they spend time with their friends."

She did not seem entirely comfortable talking with him about private matters in a public place. She straightened out a row of small baskets containing peaches, probably from Georgia, Andy thought.

"They sound like good kids," he said.

"Yes, they are," she said without looking up at him.

One of the other women called Sarah over and told her it was four o'clock and she could go now. Andy overheard her. When Sarah took off the apron she used at the market and went over to get a bag, probably vegetables for dinner, he thought, Andy asked her if she was going home.

"Yes," she said.

"I want to go see if Jacob is home," Andy said,. "Do you mind if I walk along?"

"But you have your car here."

"I can leave it here. I would like the walk. The exercise would be good for me."

He asked the woman in charge if he could leave his car there. She said yes, but looked at him in a strange way.

"May I walk with you?" he asked again.

Sarah nodded and began to walk up the road. Andy walked beside her, surprised at her willingness to walk with him.

"Would you like me to carry your bag?" he asked.

"No. It is not heavy. Thank you."

She looked either straight ahead or down as they walked, at first briskly, Andy struggling to keep up with Sarah, but then more slowly. At one point near the turn into their lane, Andy stopped. Sarah stopped too.

"It's so beautiful here," he said, "I can never get over these fields, with crops beginning to grow, green against brown, and the trees lining the fields, perfect rectangles, even the blue hills off in the distance. Do you ever think of how beautiful this is?"

"I think about it all the time, and I thank God for it. The beauty of the land is a great healer," she said. "It heals the soul."

"I know," Andy said. "I think it's beginning to do that for me. I feel better since coming back here, better about myself even."

"Then you are a religious person, Mr. Simpson."

"I don't think so. Could you call me Andy?"

"No," she said. "That would not be proper. I do not know you very well."

They remained standing at the turn in the road. Andy felt contentment, standing there with Sarah, looking over the countryside.

"Do you mind that I call you Sarah?" he asked.

"No," she said. "That is your way. It is not my way."

Sarah turned and began to walk up the dirt road to her house. Andy followed and caught up.

"How long have you lived here, in this house?"

"Since we were married," she said. "It belonged to Jacob's grandfather. He gave it to Jacob and lived with us until he died a few years ago."

They walked more slowly, Andy savoring the moment, hoping it would last. He hadn't felt this contentment since his childhood, at least since his own grandfather had died.

"Did you like him?" he asked.

"Yes, very much. He was a good man. A man of God."

"Did he die before this happened between you and Jacob?"

"Yes." She stopped and shifted the bag to the other arm before continuing.

"Do you think he would have understood?" Andy asked.

"I think so, but it would have pained him. I think he would have understood both of us."

"It sounds like he was a very wise man."

"Yes, he was," she said.

They walked, each in a rut in the road, past the row of trees that separated the road from the field, the spreading potato plants almost completely covering the soil. Andy hoped that Jacob would not be at home, or at least that he was out in the fields. He didn't know what reason he would give for coming out to see him. When they rounded the last turn to the house, he looked at the trailer and didn't see Jacob's car. Sarah saw the empty parking place also.

"I am afraid your walk has been in vain," she said.

"No," he said, "I enjoyed walking with you. Remember I needed the exercise. I sit at a desk most of the day."

Sarah stopped and smiled. Andy stood there.

"I was wondering," he said.

"What?" she said.

"It's awfully dusty walking up here. Do you have any of that iced tea?"

Sarah hesitated and then said, "Yes. Would you like some?"

"I would," he said.

He followed her to the house and sat in the swing on the porch until she returned with the tea, a glass for each of them.

"This is the best tea I've ever tasted," he said.

She smiled.

"Everyone around here makes tea like this," she said.

She sat facing him on a wooden chair, her hands in her lap, holding the glass. The sun shone on her through some trees, the light and shadow highlighting her features, making her skin even whiter, purer, and her hair and eyes even darker. Andy could watch her because she kept her eyes down. When she raised them to look at him, she did it slowly enough for him to avert his eyes. But she must have known he was watching her. He didn't want to leave.

"Your church is very simple," he said.

"Yes," she said.

"I think it's also very beautiful."

"You are welcome to attend a service," she said, adding, "You do not need to wait for an excuse and you do not need to be working."

He knew she was sincere, and he also knew that he had just been criticized. He felt shame for the first time with her, but didn't wish to try to explain or even to apologize. He knew what he had done was wrong. It was intrusive and boorish. But he also knew that journalists sometimes need to be intrusive and boorish.

"Perhaps some day I'll be there," he said, "but I doubt it. I don't think I'll ever be going back to a church again."

"You must have pain, Mr. Simpson," she said.

Andy thought about that. He did have pain but he didn't think he could tell her that. On the other hand, he also knew that if he did tell her about Beth, she might sympathize with him because of his ability to appear vulnerable and hurt. He could pretend to be sensitive. He had done it before, and it had always worked. Before he could say anything, however, Sarah spoke.

"I think about you often, Mr. Simpson," she said.

Andy shifted in the swing. "You do?" he said.

"Yes, about you and your wife."

"My ex-wife."

"Yes."

Andy said that Beth had come to see him last Saturday, thinking perhaps he could try sympathy after all, at least to see where it would take him, how she would react.

"She did?" she said, seeming to Andy interested, or perhaps just confused. And then she asked if she wanted to come back to him.

"No," Andy said. "She wanted to tell me that she had found someone else."

Andy knew that was unfair to Beth, to the truth, but he was interested in seeing what effect it would have on Sarah.

"I am afraid I do not understand the world," she said, looking down at the tea she held in her lap.

"No," Andy said, "I'm afraid I don't understand it very well either, especially my part of the world. I think I understand other parts of the world better."

"Have you been to other parts of the world?"

Andy began to answer and then realized that the sympathy angle was gone. Sarah had effectively blunted it without his even realizing it was happening.

"Well, yes," he said, "I have been to some other countries, but I was thinking about countries I've read about."

"What countries have you visited?" she asked, persisting for some reason in this line of questioning.

"Oh, let's see. A half dozen or so. I visited Europe during the summer between my junior and senior years in college. I also visited Asia as part of a Rotary fellowship. A group of us, young professionals they called us, went for six weeks. We visited Taiwan, Hong Kong, the Philippines, and China. We spent most of the time in China."

"China," Sarah said, "I have always been interested in China. We had a missionary there when I was a child. It was another church. We sent pennies to her to save the souls of the people there."

"Their souls are just fine the way they are," he said. He had never approved of know-it-all missionaries trying to impose their beliefs and culture on other people. Sarah did not see the sarcasm, however, and Andy was relieved.

"What is China like?" she asked. "I have read all the books I can find on it."

"The main thing," Andy said, "is all the people."

"Yes," she said, "over a billion. I cannot even imagine a number that high."

"It is amazing," he acknowledged. "And the second thing is the industry. Everyone seems to be working on something all the time. You don't see people sitting out on porches in the evening. They don't even have porches. They're always working on something. The sidewalks are filled with people selling things. Most families live in one or two rooms. A house like yours would have twenty Chinese living here."

"It must be wonderful to see such things," she said.

Andy sensed that Sarah longed for adventure, for expanding her life somehow. The books she read suggested that, but so did her questions, her curiosity. He also sensed a hopelessness in her, a realization, even a fear, that it would never happen, but he also knew she would never admit it, not even to herself.

"The children," she said. "What about the children? I read where they try to limit each family to one child."

"Well, that's true," Andy said, "Over-population is their biggest problem. They have to do something."

"Do they love their children?"

"As much as any people. More than many, I suppose. They seem to be always carrying and cuddling babies. And the children seemed happy, at least where we went, mostly in the cities but in a few villages as well." Andy enjoyed being the expert, especially to Sarah's eagerness.

"But it is different, is it not?" she said.

"Yes," Andy said. "As different as it can be. Walking around China is like walking on a different planet. Everything looks strange. But it's exciting too."

"Yes," she said, "I would like that. Here, we are all the same."

Andy was amused by her statement. He had to admit that he found her culture just as alien as he had found Chinese culture.

Their conversation was interrupted by the children returning, apparently from a neighboring farm. They said hello to Andy, the little girl smiling behind her brother. He could see Sarah's smile there. Sarah put her arms around them and told them to complete their chores. The children went around to the rear of the house. Sarah and Andy were alone again, but by then the spell was broken. Sarah's curiosity seemed to have been satisfied for now with what he had said so far about distant countries. Andy didn't want to leave, but he was not sure just how to continue the conversation. He tried another direction.

"Jacob said you enjoyed high school."

"Yes," she said, shifting again, her discomfort obvious. Nevertheless, she responded. "I did enjoy being there. I enjoyed learning and I had friends."

Andy asked what she did in school, what she did with her friends.

"Lots of things, she said. "We went to sports events, of course."

"Because you were a cheerleader?" Andy was still fascinated by what he saw as this incongruity.

"Yes, and because I enjoyed them," she said. "I played field hockey too. We also went to church activities. I was in another church then."

Andy asked if she had gone to dances at the school. She said she had. "I liked to dance," she added.

Andy could see her dancing, whirling and laughing. "Do you miss that?" he asked.

"The dancing?"

"The whole thing. Being able to do those things with friends."

"That was for my youth," she said. "I enjoyed doing all of it. Now I do things with other friends, mostly at the church. We are always doing something to help make money for the church, cooking, baking, sewing. I enjoy that."

Andy didn't know how far he could go with his personal questioning, but he was curious.

"What did you look like then?"

Sarah hesitated and then asked, "What do you mean?"

"I mean how did you wear your hair? How did you dress? Did you wear make-up?"

Sarah laughed softly. Andy thought she might be flattered by the question. At least she seemed to him pleased to be thinking about herself at that earlier time.

"No," she said, "I never wore make-up, but I did wear my hair very long and very straight. That was the fashion. Everybody did. I guess I wore the same clothes the other girls wore. We were all very aware of what we should wear. I enjoyed those times. That is what childhood is for, I suppose. To be free."

"Can't you be free now?" Andy asked.

"It is a different kind of freedom," she said. "It is a freedom to love my family, to love my church, to love my God. I have freedom to do all that. I do not need any other freedom."

Andy heard Sarah say these things she had said before, but he sensed a small desperation now in her voice, like she was trying to convince herself of this. She knew what she had had. She knew that she did not have it now, and that she would never have it again.

"So you'll never visit China?" he said.

"No," she said.

The sun began to slide down behind the trees that grew beside the road. Andy knew he should be going. Jacob would be back, and the children would be returning from their chores. As he began to rise, Sarah spoke quickly.

"You asked what I looked like," she said.

"Yes." Andy settled back into the swing.

"If you really want to know, I can show you my yearbook."

Andy was surprised by the offer. "Your high school yearbook? You still have it?"

"Yes, of course," she said.

She stood and told Andy to come with her. They went into the house, into the living room. Andy looked around, but it was almost too dark to see anything clearly. The furniture was brown and overstuffed, a rocking chair sitting in one corner, wooden with a needlepoint cushion, a floral design. The walls were papered, a simple straight-line design, the few pictures of a religious nature, a standard picture of Jesus featured most prominently over the mantle of a fireplace, apparently no longer used. The floor was stained mahogany with a few small area rugs.

Sarah asked Andy to sit, motioning to the sofa. Andy settled into it while Sarah went to a chest under a window and began to search for the book.

"Here it is," she said, "I knew I still had it. I have not looked at it in years."

She returned to Andy, turned on a floor light, and sat beside him on the sofa, opening the book on her lap. She paged through it until she stopped and stared.

"Here I am," she said, "I cannot believe that is me."

Her finger remained on the picture of a young girl, smiling

shyly. Her face was open, and her long hair hung down over her shoulders. Her blouse was pinned at the neck. She was strikingly pretty. Someone had written beside her picture, "Best of luck to a sweet girl. Don't forget to have fun." People used to write things like that all the time, Andy thought. He remembered someone had written something about the pen being mightier than the sword beside his picture.

"You were very pretty," he said, deciding not to add that she still was. "This must bring back happy memories."

Sarah did not answer. Andy looked at her, but she kept looking down, at the book.

"What is it, Sarah?" he said. "Are you all right?"

She nodded her head but did not say anything.

Andy knew she was crying. Finally, she looked up at him. He could see the tears beginning to slip down her cheeks.

"Sarah," he said, "it's okay."

She leaned her face into his shoulder and cried softly. He put his arm around her and held her, trying to comfort her, unsure of what to do but not wanting to let her go. She stayed there for several minutes.

And then she sat back in the sofa and tried to wipe the tears from her eyes with the back of her hand. He offered her a handkerchief, which she used to wipe the tears, and then returned it to him.

"I am sorry," she said, "I do not know why I did that. I never cry."

Andy wanted to help but had no idea what to do.

"Whenever I see pictures of myself at that age," he said finally, "I think how things might have been different. That's just a normal reaction, I think."

"No," she said, "I am happy with the way my life has turned out. I would not want it any other way. It is God's will. Even with Jacob. This has been my life."

She kept insisting, too much Andy thought.

My God, he thought to himself, how has she done it all these years? She must want out of this situation desperately, but she won't even allow herself to think about it. I can't imagine the pressure she's under.

By now Sarah had composed herself and was clearly embarrassed.

"Please forgive me, Mr. Simpson," she said.

She moved to the chair she had been originally sitting in.

"Sarah, don't be ashamed. This happens to all of us. It's good to let your feelings out. It's even good to cry sometimes."

This statement came from a man who could not remember when he had last cried. He knew he should leave, but was not sure how to do it.

"Are you all right now?" he asked.

She nodded.

"I should really go, but I'll stay if you need me to."

"No," she said. "The children will be coming in soon. I must make supper for us. Perhaps Jacob has returned."

Andy looked out the window and saw the parking place was still empty.

Sarah wiped her eyes with her hand and sat back in the sofa, presenting a more composed appearance.

"Please do not tell Jacob about this," she said.

"Of course not," he said.

Without knowing why, he reached out for her hands. She let him hold them, perhaps needing the comfort.

"If I can help, please let me know," he said.

She nodded and gently pulled her hands away.

Andy opened the door and walked out into the evening air. It felt good to him. As he walked back down toward the lane that led to the highway, he thought about what had just happened and wondered why the quiet, darkening evening felt so good to him. He thought he had seen past the image that Sarah, as a Reformed Mennonite, projected, perhaps even to the woman beneath, and he felt good about being able to do that, but at the same time he felt sad at what he had found there, feeling pain for her pain. As he made his turn onto the lane and as the evening grew rapidly to night, he thought of his own pain as well, perhaps, he thought, not so different from Sarah's pain. He realized that he too was unable to open up to others, even others close to him. He tried to remember when he had last told someone something really personal, but he could not remember. Strangely, he felt that Sarah might be that person someday, although he realized at the same time that it would never happen because it could never happen, should never happen.

The vegetable stand was dark, the wooden frame standing in the even darker shadows by the side of the road. As a car came by and threw the frame into relief, Andy thought it looked almost like a skeleton, or an x-ray. And yet, standing there in the dark by the side of the road in the cooling night air, Andy felt good. That night, however, he did not sleep well.

The next morning he was at his desk when Sue came in.

"Good morning," she said as she passed his office.

He didn't hear her. She came back, looked in the door, and said good morning again. Andy sat, still staring at his desk. Finally, Sue walked into his office and put her hand on the desk in front of him. Startled, Andy looked up.

"Good morning for the third time," Sue said. "What planet are you visiting this morning?"

"Planet?" Andy looked up, smiled slightly, and said almost under his breath, "No planet, just China."

Nine

Andy was troubled all week. He could not concentrate on his work, forgetting things he had never before forgotten. Sue told him the size of a hole she had left for a story, and he wrote one twice as long as she had said, so she just lopped off the last half and never told him. Thank God for the inverted pyramid, she said to herself. He also came close to missing his deadline on Thursday, something he had never done before. The meticulousness that usually drove Sue wild was gone. She worried about him, and Andy knew she was concerned, but there was nothing he could do.

Finally, Thursday afternoon, she confronted him. The fact that he was her boss was irrelevant in this office; Andy knew she worried about him as a friend.

"It's been a bad week," she said to him, standing before his desk.

He looked up and then down again.

"Oh, yeah, I guess it has been. I'm sorry. I know I made things a little difficult."

"A little? Anything you want to talk about?"

"No."

Andy never wanted to talk about anything, but Sue persisted. "Is it about Beth?"

"No," he said, and then added, "That's all over now, finally. She told me she's pretty serious about someone else. I think she was telling me not to be surprised if I hear she's getting married again."

"When did she tell you that?"

"A couple of weeks ago, Saturday a week."

"Did she call you before coming?"

"No," he said, "She stopped by, on her way to Pittsburgh or somewhere."

"Sorry. You never said anything."

"Why should I? You're not my mother," Andy said, regretting it instantly, and then quickly adding, "I'm sorry I said that, Sue. I know you mean well. It's just that I don't think you can help."

Sue ignored his comments and in her usual manner went straight to the issue.

"Is it Sarah then?" she asked.

Andy looked up, surprised. He thought about ignoring the question, thought about simply swiveling away from Sue, letting her know he was not happy with her interference, but he didn't. Instead he asked her why she asked about Sarah.

"Like I said, Andy, you're pretty transparent, and I'm a friend, so if I can help, if I can just listen, let me know."

Andy was always suspicious of people who claim to be good listeners. He always thought they were just busy bodies with nothing better to do, but he knew Sue wasn't like that.

"It's just that I'm worried about her," he said. "I've talked with her enough to know that she's under a terrific strain. I have no idea how she manages."

"Do you mean with Jacob?"

"No," he said, "it's not just that. It's her life, the way she has to suppress everything that's human, her emotions, her feelings, her hopes. It's all boiling there beneath the surface. I'm afraid for what might happen."

Sue pointed out that Andy was an expert on suppressing emotions.

"I know," he said. "Maybe that's why I understand her so well."

"Don't deceive yourself," Sue said. "There's no way you can know her well." Then she added, "How well do you know her?"

"What do you mean?"

"I mean how much have you talked to her?"

"A couple of times."

"Where?"

"At her farm."

"On the porch?"

"Yes. And inside too."

"You were alone with Sarah inside the house?" Andy realized Sue was beginning to sound like Beth.

"In the living room. She showed me her yearbook."

Sue was disturbed and without thinking dropped the listening pose.

"Her yearbook. My God, Andy, what the hell are you doing? She's married, and marriage is sacred to her people. Even if she's having trouble with her husband, you have no right to do that. No wonder she's having emotional problems. Have you ever thought you might be the cause?"

"I'm not the cause," Andy said calmly, but he was not sure.

"What do you think is the cause then?"

"Her church. Her religion. It controls her. It manipulates her. It puts her in a situation and then gives her no way out."

"You don't need a church for that," Sue said.

Andy knew Sue was talking about him, his life, and he also knew she had a point. Perhaps he and Sarah were too much alike to help each other. He wasn't sure. The rest of the conversation went nowhere, Andy refusing to allow Sue into his thoughts, ignoring her invitations to talk further about Sarah.

"You just don't understand," he said. "You don't know her."

The rest of the afternoon passed in silence, Andy looking over his stack of press releases and Sue working on next week's layout. At four o'clock Sue went out the door and then came back to Andy's office.

"Look," she said, "I'm sorry for butting in. Maybe it's hopeless."
"Maybe it is," Andy replied.
Andy was referring to Sarah, but he thought Sue was probably referring to him.

That evening Andy decided to go to the big mall near Harrisburg, something he rarely did, but he was unsettled, and, besides, he knew there was some sort of religious bookstore there. He thought he might be able to find out more about the Reformed Mennonites. Maybe, he thought, if he could understand the religion, he might be able to understand Sarah. At least it was something to do.

He had to walk a long distance across the parking lot from where he parked his car. The mall was packed, but the bookstore he wanted was located just inside the door he had entered. He took it as a good sign. He loved to browse through bookstores, especially used bookstores, but he also liked the mall ones, the discount and remainder stores that promised bargains. He wasn't sure about religious bookstores. Beth liked to spend hours browsing through boutiques and gift shops. When he had gone with her, which was rarely, he always went straight to the bookstores, spending hours standing and reading from the books, rarely actually buying them. He thought if he could just find the time, over several weeks, he could read an entire novel just standing in the aisle.

But this store bothered him. It was filled with religious books, something he expected of course, but which still overwhelmed him. There were bibles of every sort and self-help books through religion: happy marriage books, raising kids books, getting along with friends books, loving yourself books, dealing with money problems books, even divorce books, all promising answers in the Bible. He looked through several of these briefly, but found no answers to anything.

When a clerk asked if he could help, Andy said he was looking for a book on the Mennonites, the Reformed Mennonites, and the clerk walked along with him to the church history section.

The clerk said he had no books just on the Reformed Mennonites, adding they're a pretty small group, but he did point out a reference book on the Mennonites and suggested it might have something on the Reformed sect.

Andy thanked the clerk, feeling self-conscious, and then told him he's just doing some research for an article he's writing. The clerk nodded. Andy paged through the book, a large, heavy volume, and found what he was looking for. The sect was founded in 1812 by John Herr in Lancaster County, splintering off from the main Mennonite church. No one knew exactly why, but it apparently had something to do with Herr's disagreement over the direction of the church, which, according to Herr, was getting away from the teachings of its founder, Menno Simon. The founders of the Reformed Mennonite church had been dissenters who wanted to purify the Mennonite church of its wayward teachings and practices. Sounds familiar, he thought. They had nowhere to meet so they started their own church. There was only one true church and they were it, no matter how small.

Andy continued to read. Here it is, he said to himself. He read where the Reformed Mennonites practice the ordinance of banning, "the practice of excluding contact with members who have erred or who have otherwise lost the spiritual life." He noted that this included not just the minister's avoidance but avoidance by all members. The article cited Matthew 18: 15–17 as the Biblical source for this practice, but it did not include the quote. I suppose they think everyone has it memorized, he thought. He closed the book and went down the aisle to one of the bibles and looked it up. Verse 15 was straightforward enough: If someone wrongs you, tell him about it. Verse 16: If he does not listen to you, take a few friends as witnesses and repeat the accusation. Verse 17 read: "And if he shall neglect to hear them, tell it unto the church, let him be unto thee as an heathen man and a publican." Andy thought it was quite a leap from there to what was happening to Jacob, but he realized that the word of God is open to some interpretation.

Andy then returned to the reference book on the Mennonites and continued reading. The purpose of the practice of banning, the entry said, was not just to avoid contact with the impure but also to bring the wayward one back to the church. The article stressed that traditionally the practice of banning or shunning was done in the spirit of love. Some love, Andy thought. Finally, toward the end of the article, Andy read that the children of Reformed Mennonites who remain outside the church, a practice not discouraged, could live the normal lives of other children in the community, having the usual contacts, activities, and friendships that a child in the world might have. The article also noted the difficulties that many members experience when they join the church as adults, especially dealing with "the transformation from the freedom of childhood to the rigidities of church membership." Andy thought of Sarah. Then he read the last line, which reported that in 1965 there were only 600 Reformed Mennonites, mostly in Lancaster County and the surrounding counties, obviously including Cumberland. Andy wondered what the number is now.

The information did not help him accept what was happening to Sarah and her family, but it did make it all more real to him, and it gave him some historical perspective since the ideals and practices go back almost two hundred years. There must be something to it if it's been around that long, he thought. He could not just excuse them all as cranks. It's not easy, he thought, not even possible perhaps, for Sarah to walk away from it. He felt even sadder, even more helpless.

Andy returned the book to the shelf and walked quickly from the store, out into what he thought was the fresher air of the mall. He sat on a bench for a moment and then thought of going home, but he was not ready to be alone. Instead he decided to walk though the mall, something he didn't remember ever doing. He could never understand how people could spend hours there, most never even going into the stores, just walking and talking.

But this time he decided to wander, paying no attention to what was around him, vaguely unsettled, disturbed.

As he came into the center of the mall, he noticed a crowd gathered on the other side of the large fountain that formed the centerpiece, water cascading endlessly down a series of plastic planes. He walked around to the crowd and joined it, elbowing his way in for a better view.

He saw Jacob.

What's he doing here, he thought. Jacob was standing behind a card table in his bib overalls and a dark work shirt. He wore his straw hat, the flat one with the wide black band. He had hung posters down the front of the table and had other posters sitting on make-shift easels behind him. He was talking, but Andy couldn't make out what he was saying, although he could read the posters. One said, "Banned by the Church to a Life of Hell." Another said, "The Church Destroyed My Family." Others described the "Outrage" that was perpetrated on him in the name of religion. Andy moved closer and began to make out the large poster directly behind and above Jacob. It was in smaller, hand-printed letters, done with a black magic marker, key words underlined.

> THE REFORMED MENNONITE CHURCH WANTS ME TO SURRENDER MY SOUL. I MUST CHOOSE BETWEEN THE TRUTH AND MY FAMILY. IF I CHOOSE THE TRUTH, I LOSE MY FAMILY. IF I CHOOSE MY FAMILY, I LOSE MY SOUL. MY WIFE WILL SELL HER BODY FOR THE CHURCH. I AM CHOOSING FOR ALL MEN. SIGNED JACOB WEAVER.

Andy's first reaction was outrage. Why would he drag his wife into this so publicly? Why would he humiliate her with this nonsense about selling her body? He was about to leave, but Jacob began to raise his voice.

"Do you know what people do in the name of the church?" he shouted. "Those who have ambition for themselves, those who think only of themselves, those who think not of the truth, those who have the arrogance of the selfish will do anything to bend the will of the people to their will."

His cadences reminded Andy of some of the revival preachers he remembered hearing as a child.

"The evil one is Bishop Souders."

"My God," Andy thought, "he's naming names. He could be sued." But then he remembered having read in the bookstore that Reformed Mennonites do not engage in court disputes.

"Bishop Souders has taken my family from me. By his direction, my wife does not talk to me, does not eat with me, does not sleep with me."

Jacob had gathered a crowd. Many seemed bemused by the spectacle. Several, in fact, were taking photographs. He could imagine them back in New Jersey saying, "Wait till you see the pictures I got." He heard one man tell his wife that this beats anything on TV. A woman said, "The poor man. Why doesn't someone take care of him. He could hurt himself." Several drifted away as others came to take their place. Kids selling soft pretzels at a nearby stand tried to see, ignoring several potential customers.

Jacob continued, now standing on his chair, waving his arms.

"There is only one church," he was shouting, "the true church. Bishop Souders does not know the true church. He is a false prophet. He has lost his authority. You are looking at a dead man, a man in a living hell. In Ephesians, Paul said, 'Wives submit to your husbands,' but Bishop Souders has violated the word of God and has taken my wife and children from me."

By now Andy was becoming embarrassed by Jacob's bizarre behavior and feared that he might have suffered a breakdown. I could understand if a demented man was doing this, he thought, but I can't understand why a perfectly rational man would do it. To Andy's mind, this would accomplish nothing.

"I have written the truth of this," Jacob was saying. "It is here in my book. You can have the truth for just ten dollars."

He's hustling his book, Andy thought. That at least makes sense. As he stood there, several mall security people, two men and a woman in brown uniforms with official-looking patches on their shoulders, moved through the crowd toward Jacob. Andy could hear them explaining to Jacob that he did not have permission to be there, that he would have to apply for a permit through the regular channels.

At their request Jacob began to disassemble his materials, folding them neatly into a cardboard box he had brought. He then folded his card table. It looked to Andy as though Jacob knew the show was over and it was time to break down the set, something he had obviously done before, perhaps many times.

As the crowd began to drift away, Andy walked over to Jacob, who was putting a dozen or so copies of his book back in a canvas bag.

"Do you need some help?" Andy asked.

Jacob looked up, surprised.

"What are you doing here, Mr. Simpson?"

"Shopping," Andy said. He looked closely at Jacob to see if there were any signs of emotional instability. Jacob seemed perfectly composed.

"Do you do this often, Jacob?"

"Not often, but sometimes," he said. "Usually I do it outside a church, but I thought I would try it here in the mall. There are more people here, but I found out it is not legal so I will do it somewhere else next time."

"You do obey the law then?" Andy said.

"Of course," Jacob said, and then as he put his last book in his canvas bag, he added, "unless it violates the law of God."

"Can you see an occasion," Andy said, "when you might break the law of man in order to obey the law of God?" Andy was thinking of Antigone, the young woman in an ancient Greek play who chose death over obeying an unjust law. He also thought of Thoreau spending an unpleasant night in jail for the same reason. He knew Jacob's response as he phrased the question.

"Yes," Jacob said, "I can see many such occasions when I would obey God's law rather than man's."

"No matter what the consequences?" Andy asked.

"Of course," Jacob said.

Andy didn't ask for specific examples. Instead, he picked up some of Jacob's materials, his easels and a few posters, and helped him carry them out of the mall. He felt uncomfortable as people looked at them and nudged one another. Insanity by association Andy assumed they were thinking. Andy felt terribly out of place. On the other hand, Jacob looked like he had just finished a carpentry job on his farm.

As Andy was helping Jacob put his materials in the trunk and back seat of his car, he asked him why he had not contacted him ahead of time to let him know of his plans.

"This would have been an ideal incident to report," Andy said.

"I know," Jacob said, "but you do not seem interested. Besides it was in Harrisburg and not Carlisle."

"I'm still surprised you didn't try to get some PR for it."

"I did," Jacob said. "One of the Harrisburg TV stations was here."

Of course, Andy thought. As usual Jacob was a step ahead of him. He asked Jacob which station showed up.

"I do not know," Jacob said. "I asked all of them to come. I do not have a television set."

That night Andy flipped among the three Harrisburg stations. Finally, at the end of the Channel 27 newscast, Jacob was there, the subject of what they call "human interest." The anchor, smiling and obviously pleased with himself, reported: "A local man caused quite a stir this afternoon when he took over a corner of the Swatara Mall. Here's Randy Stewart reporting."

The story then went to a film of Jacob flinging his arms and silently shouting as a voice-over continued: "Mall goers were given an extra diversion today when Jacob Weaver, who lives on a farm near Carlisle, set up his own soap-box and began to berate his local church. He claims they are causing the separation of his family. A group of tourists from Massachusetts watched with fascination."

The film then switched to a shot of a husband and wife in their fifties: "We hoped to see some Amish when we came down here for vacation, but we never expected anything so exciting," the man said. "Nothing like this ever happens in Massachusetts." His wife stood beside him, smiling proudly.

The anchor returned, also smiling, and said, "Nothing like freedom of speech, is there? That's it from the News 27 team. For all of us, good night."

"Where the hell is Jacob going with this?" Andy said aloud and flipped off the set with his remote control.

The next morning Andy was at the office early. When Sue came in, she asked if he had seen the Channel 27 news last night. He said he had.

"What did you think?"

"I was there."

"At the mall?"

"Yes."

Sue asked him what he was doing at the mall and then asked if Jacob had told Andy he was going to put on his protest.

"No," Andy said, "I was just there."

"Shopping?"

"Well, not exactly. It was more like wandering until I accidentally saw him just as he was finishing. Being finished might be more accurate. The security guards made him leave."

"Do you think he's mentally competent?"

Andy assured her that Jacob seemed in control of his actions, even though the actions were somewhat bizarre.

"What's next?" she asked. "What's the next crazy thing he's going to do just to get some publicity?"

"I don't know," Andy said, "but I don't think he's done."

"He has a funny way of showing how much he loves her, doesn't he?" Sue was clearly losing patience with Jacob, and Andy thought probably with himself as well.

He thought also about how insulting this was to Sarah. If he pulls any more of that stuff, he thought, he would have to do something, but he had no idea what he would do or could do. Maybe he should have a serious talk with him. Maybe he should see a lawyer.

Sue continued, "Anyway, maybe he's learned his lesson."

"Maybe," Andy said, but he knew that Jacob was more interested in giving lessons than in receiving them, and he also knew that Jacob's lessons were not yet over.

Ten

The summer moved slowly for Andy. Although Monday to Thursday was a blur during the day with the business of getting the paper out, the evenings and weekends dragged. He took to covering more and more of the local government and school meetings, filling up as many nights as he could. When he had first taken the job, he had told the owners he would need many stringers to cover the local meetings since he was not given the money to hire full-time staff. They agreed. Now he was way under budget. He went to several Senators games and was beginning to be caught up in their season, as they had been in first place for the past month, but he always went alone and sat down the first base line, avoiding talking to people if possible.

He enjoyed his house and usually spent an hour or so, several late afternoons a week, working on his small garden, and then of course he did the trimming and cutting grass on Saturday. On Sunday, early, he usually did his shopping at the local open-twenty-four-hours supermarket and then relaxed the rest of the morning with the Sunday *Times*—he never got out of that habit, but now he read it on the front porch if the weather cooperated. In the afternoon he usually watched a ball game on TV, always the Phillies since that's all that was available in central Pennsylvania. And then, finally, the week was over. He grew less and less interested in what the Mets were doing, but promised himself to take a Sunday and drive up to see them. He told himself he missed the roar of the planes as they approached Kennedy. He did not go.

So his weeks filled up, but they also crept by. For one thing, he had not seen Jacob for almost three weeks. He expected him to stop by if only to ask if he had seen him on TV, but he never did. Perhaps he had given up. At dinner the other evening with Sue and her family—Andy's only social contact—Sue said she thought Jacob had finally learned his lesson and was too embarrassed to appear. Andy was not so sure. He had enjoyed the evening with Sue and with Ed, who always wanted to talk sports, and with her kids, who were usually well behaved, but Andy still felt he was intruding into something sacred. Sue and Ed communicated without even talking, and the kids seemed to know exactly how far to go before bringing down the wrath of their parents. Andy was outside all that. The next time he was invited, he found an excuse. At any rate, Sue assured Andy that Jacob had gone too far and he knew it. Andy hoped she was right.

Andy had also not seen Sarah recently. He decided not to go to her market on Fridays, telling himself he had no business making matters worse for her just because he had the normal journalist's curiosity. He convinced himself that this was his only interest in her, that and his sadness at finding another human being so lonely. He knew he could not help, so he forced himself to stay away.

He also thought of her almost all the time. Although he did not admit it, he knew he was taking those extra meetings just to get her off his mind. He woke up in the middle of the night thinking of her head on his shoulder, feeling the smoothness of her hair, and then hating himself for his weakness, for what might even be a kind of perversity. She's a holy person, he thought. Although he cared about what was happening to her, he convinced himself he could only make matters worse by seeing her. So he stayed away, even avoiding Route 15 when he could.

And then one Sunday morning in mid-summer, while Andy

was sitting on his porch reading an article about the Mets' Saturday night disaster, Jacob pulled his car in front of the house and got out.

"Good morning, Mr. Simpson," Jacob said as he walked toward the porch steps.

"Good morning, Jacob," Andy said. "What are you doing here on a Sunday morning?" He was genuinely puzzled as Jacob stopped at the steps and smiled slyly.

"My church ignores me, remember?" he said. "I usually read my bible by myself, but today I thought I might catch you home."

Andy put his paper on his lap and said, "Here's where you'll find me every Sunday morning, worshiping at the Church of *The New York Times*."

Jacob's smile faded. Andy thought perhaps that was just a bit blasphemous, but he had said it and had heard it said often enough that he never thought of it as offensive. Putting the newspaper on the table beside the swing, Andy invited Jacob to join him on the swing, but Jacob sat on the wicker chair Andy had found at a neighborhood garage sale. Jacob took off his hat and placed it on the floor beside him. Andy offered some iced tea, but Jacob declined, saying he was not thirsty. They sat for a moment, Jacob saying nothing, Andy beginning to feel awkward. "Looks like a nice day," Andy said. Jacob agreed.

"Good day to work on the potatoes," Andy offered.

"It is Sunday," Jacob said.

"Oh, right," Andy said, "I forgot. My grandfather never worked on Sunday either."

Andy was going to ask how Sarah was doing, but Jacob shifted his weight in the wicker chair, making it creak, and spoke up suddenly, saying he was there on business.

"Oh," Andy said, "on Sunday?" Again Andy wished he had thought first, but Jacob seemed to return a slight smile.

"Yes," he said, "an invitation."

Another publicity stunt, Andy thought. He wished he could

change the subject, but he knew he could not, so he asked Jacob what sort of invitation.

Jacob leaned forward, almost conspiratorially. The wicker creaked again. "I cannot tell you," he said softly. Andy's hopes rose, but then Jacob added, "but I can tell you when and where. Wednesday afternoon at four, out at Souders Market."

"Wednesday at four," Andy said. "Why?"

Jacob repeated his unwillingness to reveal details, but assured Andy it would be worth his while. Andy was concerned. He thought Jacob was responsible or at least he hoped so, but he also knew he was capable of fairly bizarre behavior if he thought it would further his cause, whatever his cause was. He asked Jacob who else would be there, and Jacob assured him it would be just the two of them.

"Is this something for the newspaper?" Andy asked, developing suspicion and interest simultaneously.

"You might say that."

Andy began to swing slightly, looking at Jacob and then out to the street, hoping to find something to change their focus. The street was empty. Typical Sunday morning, Andy thought. He then looked back at Jacob, who was sliding back into his chair.

"Jacob," Andy said, "you're not going to do something crazy, are you?"

"I am not crazy, Mr. Simpson."

"But people who are not crazy can do crazy things," Andy said, assuring Jacob that he had seen many examples in fifteen years of journalism.

"No," Jacob insisted, "it is not crazy."

"And you won't get in trouble?"

Jacob ignored the question and then excused himself, saying, "You will be there, yes?"

"I don't know, Jacob," Andy said. "I usually work late Wednesday because my deadline is Thursday noon. I'll see what I can do." But again, he knew nothing could keep him away.

Andy told himself he would never go out there if he were not a journalist. Although he was already deeper into this than he wanted to be, perhaps, he thought, he could just go and observe and decide what to do next. He then remembered that Sarah finished work at four o'clock, so it obviously had something to do with her, but even so, he decided he could just watch and be objective about the whole thing, whatever it turns out to be. Andy flipped open the *Times* and tried to care about the rest of the world.

For the next three days Andy resisted telling Sue about Wednesday afternoon. He knew what she would say, and he knew she would be right. He also knew he would ignore her advice. When he began to gather up his things about 3:30, Sue asked what was wrong.

"Nothing's wrong," he said, "I thought I would just leave a little early today."

"Early? We still have piles to do for tomorrow. When are you going to finish the rest of the stories and the layout?"

Andy was irritated because Sue was beginning to sound like she was the one in charge, and then he realized she was.

"I'll stop back later this evening," he said, "or maybe early tomorrow. I'll take care of it. We'll be okay."

"Are you okay?" she said. The tone of her voice had softened.

"Yeah," he said. "Don't worry. I just have something I have to do."

But, going down Route 15, Andy had second thoughts. He knew he had to be there, if only to make sure that Sarah was not in any danger. When he arrived at the market, he pulled off the road, across from the market, and waited. He was early and Jacob was not there yet. Soon Jacob pulled in a hundred yards ahead of him and got out of his car. Andy expected him to come back to see him, but instead he just stood there beside his car until four o'clock and then walked across the road toward the stand. Andy thought he might confront the bishop again.

Jacob approached the stand but stopped to talk with a

female instead. He then walked away with that person, and Andy could see now it was Sarah. They stood by the side of the road, Jacob talking, Sarah with her head down. Andy was about to go over to make sure nothing happened to Sarah, when Jacob grabbed her, lifted her off the ground, and carried her quickly across the road to his car. Stunned, Andy jumped from his car and began to run toward Jacob and Sarah, shouting at Jacob to stop. By the time he got to them, however, Jacob had pushed Sarah into his car and gotten in beside her. Andy tried to open the door, but Jacob had already locked it. Andy then began to pound on the window.

"Jacob, what are you doing?" he shouted, glaring at Jacob. "Get out of there. Let Sarah go. This is crazy. Are you crazy? You can't do this."

Finally, Andy stopped and leaned against the car, breathing more heavily than he had realized.

The people at the stand across the road, workers and customers, just stood and looked. Andy thought Jacob might leave so he went around to the front of the car to block his way, but when he looked in the car he could see that Jacob did not have his key in the ignition and apparently did not intend to go anywhere. He just sat there holding Sarah's arms down so she couldn't open the door. She did not resist, but she also did not look at Andy. She seemed sad or perhaps just embarrassed.

Andy calmed down and began to reason with Jacob. He asked him to crack the window so they could talk. Jacob wound it down two or three inches.

"What are you doing, Jacob?"

It seemed to Andy a reasonable question.

"I am keeping Sarah here until the police come," Jacob said calmly.

"Why?" Another reasonable, even obvious, question.

"It is my plan," Jacob said.

Andy looked at Sarah. Their eyes met.

"Are you okay, Sarah?" he said.

She nodded her head and turned away again. She didn't try to get loose. When Jacob finally released her arms, she just sat there, looking down at her lap. Jacob rolled the window down the rest of the way.

"Do you think anyone at the stand is going to call the police?" Jacob said. They were still just standing there looking across the road.

"I don't think so," Andy said. "They just look confused."

"I have kidnapped Sarah," he said. "They should call the police."

Andy was stunned that Jacob wanted to call the police.

"Why?" he repeated.

"Because I kidnapped her." Jacob was calm, matter-of-fact, almost business-like.

"No," Andy said, "why do you want the police to come?"

"So they can arrest me."

"But why do you want to be arrested?" Andy was insistent.

"I want the trial," he said.

Andy tried to comprehend what was happening. "You want to be arrested," he said, "and put on trial for kidnapping? You're not really kidnapping Sarah. She's your wife, and she's sitting here peacefully beside you."

"I forced her here and I am holding her here against her will. If I let her get out of the car, she will go to her house."

Andy decided to try another approach. "Sarah, are you being kidnapped?" he asked and then realized what an absurd situation this is, what an absurd question, calmly asking someone, also perfectly calm, if this is a kidnapping. Sarah did not respond.

Jacob returned to the business at hand and asked Andy how he can contact the police.

Andy thought for a moment. He had a cell phone in his car. Although he never used it, the owners of his company insisted he have it.

"I can call them from my cell," he said, "but are you sure that's what you want? I don't want to be the one to call the police."

"I would appreciate it if you would," Jacob said.

Andy stood there, looking at Jacob and Sarah, not knowing what to do, although he did know that a call to the police would set off an irreversible chain of events.

Finally, he said, "But why, Jacob? Why do you want to go to trial? It will be a mess and it will be costly."

"I want to talk with my wife," Jacob explained, his voice still calm, earnest. He explained, "If I am on trial, I can be my own lawyer and I know that I can ask her questions. She will be under oath and will have to answer me. I can think of no other way of talking with her."

My God, Andy thought, he's more desperate than I realized. Maybe he has gone over the edge. He stood a moment longer and then, knowing there was nothing he could do, he turned and walked back to his car. He dialed the police in Carlisle and was told the state police would have to handle it, so he dialed that number and told them of the kidnapping.

"No," he told the police, "no one's in any danger. . . . No hurry really. . . . I don't think you'll need sirens. . . . He's just waiting for you. . . . Yes, it's all pretty strange, a domestic thing, but everything's calm. Maybe you can straighten it out when you get here."

Andy walked back to Jacob's car.

"They're on their way," he said. "It shouldn't be more than a few minutes. They have a car up near the turnpike."

Jacob did not respond but just sat there, waiting. He did not try to talk with Sarah either, apparently knowing it would be futile. Andy stood by the window. He tried to talk with each of them, but neither would respond. Within minutes a Pennsylvania state police car pulled over, twenty yards from Andy's car, and two troopers got out. They motioned Andy over to them and asked if he had called them.

"Yes," Andy said, "Jacob asked me to call you."

"Jacob?"

"Yes. He's the one who's holding his wife. They're over there in the black car."

One trooper watched Jacob and Sarah while the other one asked for Andy's driver's license. Andy gave it to him. "You the person who runs the Carlisle newspaper?" he asked. Andy nodded his head and took his license back.

The troopers then walked over to Jacob's car. Andy followed, holding back a short distance but close enough to hear.

The troopers asked Jacob to get out of his car. He did. They got personal information from him, and then asked Sarah to step out. They all stood by the side of the road as cars slowed to look at them. The people at the stand across the road had grouped together and were also watching.

"You're his wife?" the one trooper asked.

"Yes," Sarah said, never looking at the officers.

"You claim he kidnapped you?"

Sarah did not respond, but Jacob did.

"I kidnapped her. I took her from the market over there where she works and I carried her to my car and made her sit here with me." And then he added quickly, "I locked the door."

The trooper doing the questioning looked at Jacob for a moment, looked at the open window, and then asked Jacob why? Good luck, Andy thought.

"So you would arrest me," Jacob said, as though the reason were perfectly obvious.

"Look, Mr. Weaver," the trooper said, "kidnapping is serious business. It's a felony. You could go to jail for a long time. Don't you want to talk this over with your wife first and let us know what you decide?"

The trooper took several steps away from the car, but Jacob was insistent. "She will not talk with me," he said. "You will have to arrest me."

The trooper walked over to Andy.

"What's going on here?" he said. "Is this some kind of newspaper stunt? You could get your ass in a lot of trouble, you know that?"

Suddenly Andy began to feel even more uncomfortable. "It's not a stunt," he said, "at least not one that I know about. Jacob asked me to come down here and watch while you arrest him. Maybe he wants a witness or something. I don't know."

Andy didn't volunteer any information about their friendship or the ongoing dispute with the church, but the trooper seemed to know something about it.

"Is this the guy on TV a couple weeks ago? Over at the mall?"

Andy said that it was. The trooper walked back to the car.

"Last chance, Mr. Weaver," he said.

Jacob did not respond, so the officer read him his rights and put handcuffs on him.

"Is that necessary?" Andy asked.

"Kidnapping's a felony," the trooper said. "It's automatic."

The three got in the police car, Jacob sitting in the back seat.

As they were beginning to pull out, Andy knocked on the window and asked where they were taking Jacob.

The trooper stopped the car and rolled down his window, obviously losing patience but still speaking calmly, professionally. "We usually take them to the District Justice in Carlisle for arraignment," he said. "Harvey Imhoff. He's in his office until six today."

Andy asked if he could come along. The trooper said it's open to the public. It was clear to Andy, however, that the trooper was not happy about Andy being there. Andy thought he might still suspect some sort of plot between him and Jacob.

When they pulled away, Andy returned to Sarah, who was beginning to walk back across the road.

"Sarah," he called.

She stopped. Andy caught up with her and asked her what was going on.

When Sarah did not respond, he asked if he could take her home. She said no.

"I'm sorry," Andy said, "I didn't have anything to do with this."

Sarah nodded and walked across the road into the group of people at the market stand. They closed around her.

Andy hurried to his car and drove well above the speed limit back to Carlisle. He knew Harvey Imhoff, a kindly, older man, but a man who took no nonsense in his office. The office was in Harvey's home, a side room with its own entrance.

When Andy arrived and entered the office, he realized he had almost caught up with the troopers, who looked at him and then at each other. He thought he might be in more trouble.

Harvey, seated at his desk and just beginning to fill in some papers, looked up at Andy.

"Mr. Simpson," he said, "you sure don't waste any time. You have a monitor or something?"

The trooper said that Andy had called in the crime.

"How'd you get there?" Harvey asked. He was an informal man, more interested in understanding the situation than in just going through the motions.

"Jacob invited me to be there," Andy said as he began to take a seat.

"Sort of makes you a witness, doesn't it?"

Andy paused halfway to his seat and then said quietly, "Yes, I suppose so."

"An accomplice?" Harvey offered.

"No," Andy answered quickly.

"Just kidding," Harvey said. "Always like to put the needle in the newspaper people."

Andy smiled and relaxed a bit.

Harvey took off his reading glasses and sat back in his chair, his hands on the desk.

"So, Jacob, Jacob Weaver." he said, "This is pretty serious stuff. You should try to settle your domestic disputes before they turn into something like this. It's always good for a man and wife to talk to each other. Communication is the key, you know."

Andy noticed one of the troopers rolling his eyes. Everyone knew that Harvey liked to sermonize whenever he got the chance, especially in his office.

"Looks like there's every cause to keep you for trial—bound over, you know, legal talk—so you gentlemen can take him over to the jail. I'll set the bail at $100,000."

"That's pretty high, isn't it, Harvey?" Andy said.

"No, that's about right for a felony. His lawyer might be able to get it down some. You can call your lawyer once you get to the jail, Mr. Weaver."

Jacob said he did not have a lawyer. Harvey said, "You will."

They left Harvey's office, and the troopers put Jacob, still cuffed, back in the car. Andy knew that the county jail was just outside town. He asked one of the troopers if he could go along.

"Afraid not," he said.

"But I'm also a friend of his," Andy insisted.

"You his lawyer?" the trooper asked, knowing the answer. Andy said no.

"Then you can't go in with us," he said, adding, "The jails are not open to the public, only during certain hours."

Andy watched as the car pulled away. Well, he's done it now, he thought. This time he's in trouble. And all because he wants to speak to Sarah and he wants Sarah to speak to him. Andy thought it was the most preposterous thing he had ever heard, but at the same time he knew that Jacob had carefully thought everything through and everything was going according to plan, Jacob's plan.

Eleven

As the police car went down Main Street and turned right onto Chestnut, Andy remained standing outside Harvey's office, not knowing what to do. It was still early, barely six o'clock. He wanted to go see Sarah but knew she would not want to see him, and besides, she's probably being consoled by church members. That's good, he thought.

At a loss for anything constructive to do, Andy decided to drive home. He pulled his car into the alley behind his house and then into the graveled area he used as a place to park. It had not cooled off much, so he got a beer and a glass and sat at the picnic table. He avoided his porch because he didn't want neighbors stopping by to talk. His thoughts stayed with Jacob. He could go to jail, he thought. Andy knew he would plead innocent so he can get his trial, but he's already admitted to a felony. Andy could not see how any jury would find Jacob innocent, and that means a jail term. It can't be worth it. But then Andy thought of Jacob's passion, his fervor, and knew that Jacob believed it was well worth it.

Jacob had given no reason for his behavior except to say that this was the only way he could talk with his wife. Is he really that desperate? Does he really love her that much? Is he willing to sacrifice his freedom for that love?

Andy thought of his own marriage, of what had passed for

love, of what he was willing to sacrifice, and then he forced himself to think of something else.

That something else was Sarah. He wanted to do something. He wanted somehow to ease the pain he knew she was feeling, but he knew he could do nothing. He wondered if she still wanted above all to bring Jacob back to the church. He wondered if she could still love him after what he had done to her. The public humiliation, the series of public humiliations, must be devastating. And she is so private. What does she tell the children? What can she tell the children? They go to the public school, so the other children will know about this. Andy knew that children could be mean at times.

Andy got up to get another beer, but decided not to. He walked to the living room, turned on his television set, and watched the news, although he knew there had not been enough time for the story to break. It will be on TV tonight and in the Harrisburg paper tomorrow morning, he thought. They always check the state police reports for interesting items. Andy knew they would find this interesting, especially after the mall episode. Everyone will be interested, he thought.

Finally, restless, not knowing what to do, Andy decided to go back to his office, walking the half mile or so. He had promised Sue he would catch up on the work. While walking, he found Carlisle peaceful, as always, but he knew that later some of the local kids will cruise familiar streets, looking for friends, also cruising. Andy was surprised when he came to Carlisle that this was the extent of the older peoples' complaints about the kids. If only the City had this problem, he often said to himself. He remembered telling the story to Beth one time, and her looking at him in disbelief. "You're kidding," she said. No, he assured her, that's what they complain about. Andy felt smug in the knowledge that he had at last told Beth something that astonished her.

Some of the stores were still open—it was Wednesday after all—but few people were on the sidewalks. Andy stopped to look in the window of Bissinger's Hardware Store. He liked to inspect the tools, most of which he had no idea how to use, but mostly he just liked the feel of the store. There had been a store like it in Sunbury when he was a kid, but that store had been changed into a TrueValue or something the last time he had been back. Here that way of life remained. Mr. Bissinger sat inside the door, surrounded by a wooden counter, rows of nuts and bolts flowing down one side of the narrow building, paint and paint thinner, brushes and pipes flowing down the other. Andy saw a pile of different-sized baskets in one corner and a stack of American flags in another, the small ones rolled neatly on a stick, good for the Fourth of July or the graves of veterans. Mr. Bissinger saw Andy and waved. Andy waved back and moved on.

He thought about stopping in at Harry's for dinner, but it was too early. He still had not adopted the local custom of eating at 5:30 or so. Besides, he could make himself something later at home, an omelet maybe. He kept walking, past the small park at the intersection, down Main Street, finally stopping in front of his office. Except for the small *Carlisle Courier* sign beside the door, no one would suspect this small, white, wooden-framed house was a newspaper office. Andy realized Sue might still be working, something she did when necessary, but he didn't want to talk to her just then, so he tried the door carefully to see if it was open. It was not. He took out his key, opened it, and walked in.

His desk was still piled with work for tomorrow's deadline. Sue had finished her work and had neatly placed information about the remaining space on his desk, complete with remaining column inches. Oh well, he thought, I might as well get to it.

Andy sat at his desk and began to rewrite, cut, and do headlines. He needed captions for a few photos and worked on them. He liked his captions to fill the space completely beneath the photos and he insisted that headlines fill their space too. He hated to see an inch of white space with what should be a three-column head. He knew only the *Times* worried much about that sort of thing anymore, but he expected that of himself. He found himself enjoying working in the quiet of the evening and decided to do it more often. Soon, it seemed, he had finished all the work he had left that afternoon and was ready to leave by nine o'clock, his desk beginning to resemble neatness. Sue will be pleased, he thought as he turned off the lights and walked out into the pleasant night air.

On his walk back home he thought of Jacob, sitting in jail. What must he be thinking? Were there other men in the cell with him? Andy knew they had some sort of holding cell where Jacob could be by himself, and he hoped that's where he was. Was he beginning to regret his actions? Would he change his mind tomorrow and try to say it was all a mistake? Would it be too late? And what about Sarah? Andy didn't want to think about Sarah.

When he got back home, he made himself a sandwich and tried to read but could not. He then turned on the television, keeping the sound down, waiting for the news and listening to the classical music on the local public radio station. Andy didn't know how exhausted he was and, slouching into the sofa, fell asleep. When he awoke, it was well after midnight, so he went to bed, grateful that he didn't have to watch how the local television stations handled the story.

Thursday morning found Andy sitting at his desk when Sue arrived. No hello. No small talk. Sue went straight to Andy.

"Did you see the Harrisburg paper this morning?" she said, holding up her copy for Andy to see.

He had.

"You knew about it, didn't you?" she asked, her voice reflecting a mixture of disappointment and exasperation.

Andy turned over some papers on his desk and swiveled to his computer.

"Good morning," he said.

"That's where you went after work, isn't it?" Sue was in her bulldog mode.

Andy did not answer.

"I couldn't believe it when I heard it last night," she said. "I was half asleep in bed and heard Jacob's name. They made it sound like a circus. Did you see that?" By now Sue was pacing the floor.

"No," Andy said as he swiveled toward Sue. "I'm afraid I fell asleep, but notice that I did come back last night and finished up all the work. Do I get any credit for that?"

Sue was getting increasingly upset. She stopped in front of Andy, stared at him, and then threw her eyes to the ceiling. "So," she said finally, "what's going to happen now? Why did he do it? Did he finally flip?"

Andy asked Sue to sit down. She did not. He said he had answers to none of those questions, but that he would try to find out. In fact, he told her, he was leaving shortly for the jail to see Jacob.

"Don't you want to do a story on it first?" Sue asked. "This might be one of our rare timely stories."

"No," Andy said, tapping a pencil on the palm of his hand. "I'll just include it in the police log. It seems to me that others will produce the spectacle."

Sue stood there unable to speak. Finally, she said, "You really are losing your objectivity over this one, aren't you? I hope the owners don't find out."

Andy knew they would, but he told himself he didn't want to put anything out until he knew what was going on. He also knew that was not the reason. He was just protecting someone. Jacob? Sarah? Or was he just cowardly?

"I can do an in-depth follow-up next week," he said.

Sue looked at him for a moment and then went to her desk where she began working on a new ad.

After checking his faxes and his e-mail, Andy left for the jail. Sue said goodbye without looking up.

The jail was new, built within the past five years. The old jail in town had recently been torn down to be replaced by a parking lot. Andy was relieved that Jacob didn't have to stay in an old jail. He had seen several old jails and knew they could be unpleasant. It can't be too bad for Jacob, he said to himself, but he worried about what he would find.

He walked into the office at the jail and told the secretary he was a friend of Jacob. She nodded and pointed to a seat. Andy sat down. Soon the warden came out to see him. He had met the warden in connection with several stories over the past few months, and the warden greeted him warmly, urging him to remain seated.

"Hello, Andy," he said. "Good to see you again. One of these times we should meet under better circumstances." The warden laughed. "That's what Charlie Lambert always says."

Andy knew Charlie Lambert was the one funeral director in town.

"Gordon," Andy said, and nodded. He was surprised that he was beginning to feel like a native, greeting someone with a first name and a nod. Andy said he was there to see Jacob, "a friend of mine."

Gordon led Andy back to his office, a small room with a clean desk and various workshop certificates on the wall. Andy noticed Gordon didn't have a computer. Good job to have, he thought. Gordon motioned for Andy to sit in the chair fronting the desk. He sat behind the desk and leaned back while he picked up the conversation. "Secretary doesn't have to know everything," he said. Then he leaned forward and asked Andy about Jacob.

"Is this all right?" he said. "I mean does he really know what he's doing?"

"He knows," Andy said.

"Then why's he doing it?"

"I guess that's what everyone's been asking, or will be," Andy said. "I don't really know. I just know he's in more trouble than he knows."

"Probably," Gordon said, "but he's no trouble here. He just sits in his cell. Doesn't say anything except thank you when we gave him breakfast. We put him in the holding cell for the night; we thought he might be out on bail today."

"I don't think so," Andy said. "He's not the type to dig up "$100,000."

"It'll be less than that. All his lawyer has to do is ask the District Justice. We all know he's not going anywhere."

Andy was reassured by Gordon's relaxed manner, but he also knew it would not be simple. "He's not likely to get a lawyer, especially a public defender," Andy said, explaining that Jacob will probably represent himself. He remembered that Jacob wanted to talk with Sarah.

"Really?" Gordon said, "Pretty strange. How about a bail bondsman? He can at least get out of jail."

"Forget that too," Andy said.

"Then he'll sit for a while," Gordon said. "Trial won't be for a couple months anyway."

Andy asked if he could see Jacob. Gordon agreed and got up to leave the room. Andy followed him out of his office, through a heavy door and down a corridor to the holding cell, beyond which, Andy knew, was the jail proper with its rows of cells. That could be Jacob's home for the next few months, Andy thought. They stood in front of the cell while Gordon got his keys out.

"Usually we would take you to a room we have for meetings with prisoners, but it's being cleaned this morning. Hope you don't mind," he said as he left, with the cell door open.

Jacob was sitting on a chair facing the window with its iron mesh. He turned to see who was there, and Andy asked him how he was doing.

"Fine, Mr. Simpson. The people here have been real nice to me," he said.

"Good," Andy said. He didn't know what else to say since Jacob seemed perfectly content to be where he was, a bit tired perhaps, but calm. Andy went into the cell and sat across from Jacob on the bed. The only other item in the cell was a toilet without a seat. Andy asked if he needed anything.

"No," he said, "I just had breakfast and they said I would get some clothes."

Jacob was still in the clothes he had worn the day before.

"Did you get some sleep last night?" Andy asked.

"Some."

Andy paused and then leaned toward Jacob. "Did you change your mind, Jacob?"

"About what?"

"About the kidnapping." Andy tried to think of some way Jacob could get out of this mess. "Maybe you could still say it was all a mistake. Sarah would agree."

"No. It wasn't a mistake," Jacob insisted. "This is all going the way I planned."

"Then you need a lawyer," Andy said. "Can I get one for you? Lou Frederick is a good one here in town. I can ask him."

"I'll be my own lawyer," he said.

When Andy pointed out that Jacob knew nothing about the law, he responded, "I've been reading about it the last few months. I know enough to ask questions."

Andy asked what kind of questions he had in mind.

"Questions to Sarah," he said simply.

Andy was concerned about the whole prosecution process, but he was more concerned, at the moment, about Jacob's immediate future and asked if anyone had told him what would happen next. He said no. Andy then asked him what had happened last night, after they brought him to the jail.

"They just took more information and told me I could call a lawyer. They took my fingerprints," he said, holding up one hand to show the black smudges on his fingertips.

"Didn't anyone ask you why you did it?" Andy asked.

"No," he said, "I guess they were just doing their job." And then he added, "Just like me."

Andy also asked if any newspaper people or TV people had talked with him yet. He said no.

"They will," Andy said.

"I know," Jacob said and then asked Andy if he wanted any information—an interview—for his paper.

"No," Andy said. "I'm here as your friend. I'm worried about you. I'm worried you don't know what you're getting into."

"I know," Jacob said, "but can we get an article in the paper about this?"

Andy assured Jacob there are already articles in the papers, and there will be more, but Jacob insisted that Andy do an article. "In time," Andy promised. Andy then asked him about bail, but Jacob would not discuss it.

"I'll just sit here," Jacob said. "It's part of my plan."

Andy heard the door at the end of the corridor open and knew that Gordon was coming. He stopped outside the cell and looked in at Jacob and then at Andy.

"Good news," he said, "Jacob can leave. Someone posted bail for him."

Jacob turned back to the window and said, "I'd rather stay."

"It's up to you," Gordon said.

Andy asked who paid the bail, and to his surprise Gordon said Jacob's wife had. When Andy looked at Gordon in astonishment, Gordon continued, "She went over to Harvey's this morning and gave him the deed to the farm. Harvey said it was fine. Don't think he's worried about Jacob going anywhere. The farm's worth lots more than $100,000. All Jacob has to do is sign as co-owner."

Jacob sat there unresponsive. Although Andy was not sure what to do, he did tell him he should sign it.

"I don't need to sign it," Jacob said. "If I don't sign it, I'll be able to stay in jail."

Gordon looked at Andy, shrugged his shoulders, and left. Andy decided to try another approach and said to Jacob, "Do you have any idea how much it costs to keep a prisoner in jail?"

Jacob did not answer.

"Do you know who has to pay for that?"

No answer.

"The citizens of this county," Andy said. "Your neighbors. Do you want them paying so you can stay here?" Andy knew this was a long shot, but to his surprise Jacob agreed to sign the paper.

Andy quickly called Gordon back to the cell and asked him if Sarah had done this by herself or if she had a lawyer.

"No lawyer," he said. "She had a half dozen or so Amish men with her."

"Mennonites," Andy said.

"Yeah, whatever."

When they stood outside the cell, Jacob seemed bewildered to find himself free. Gordon took him back to his office and gave him his personal belongings, his watch, wallet, keys. Jacob signed another paper saying he had received his belongings and was told his car was in the parking lot behind the jail.

Soon they were both standing outside the jail, not exactly sure what to do. It was only ten o'clock. Andy looked around as Jacob unlocked his car. Andy asked him what he was going to do now.

"Work in the field," he said.

Andy reminded him of the provisions of bail, that he had to stay in the county.

"I know," he said, "I'm not going anywhere, just back to the farm. Work to be done."

"Do you want me to go back with you?" Andy asked.

"No," Jacob said, "not unless you want to help out in the field."

They smiled at each other, as Jacob got into his car and turned the key. He pulled away, with just a slight wave of his hand, as if he were leaving the Grange with some fertilizer. Andy went back to his office.

"Your phone's been ringing all morning," Sue said as Andy came in the door. "The messages are on your desk. Everybody seems to know you have the inside track."

"What inside track?" Andy asked. He had been thinking of Jacob and had forgotten this had been a very public event.

"You know. Jacob?" Sue said. "Everybody wants to know what's going on with Jacob."

"So do I," Andy said, and he meant that seriously. "So who wants to know," he asked, "the Harrisburg papers?"

"Harrisburg, Philadelphia, Baltimore, New York."

New York, Andy thought. Maybe Beth will see it.

"It must have gotten on the newswire," he said aloud, to himself.

"It did," Sue said, getting up to refill her coffee. "It's on your screen if you want to read it."

Andy didn't want to read it.

Sue asked him how Jacob was doing. Andy said fine, although he really didn't know. Sue was not satisfied with that and asked him if he had seen Jacob this morning.

"Yeah, I saw him," Andy said. "He's out on bail."

"Really? How'd he get the money so soon?" she asked.

"Sarah," Andy said.

"Sarah, his wife?"

"How much is the bail?"

"$100,000."

"Wow," Sue said, suddenly even more attentive. She asked where Sarah got that kind of money, and Andy said she put up the farm.

"So why doesn't Sarah just withdraw the charges," Sue asked.

"I guess if Sarah doesn't want to press charges, he could go free, but she'll do what Jacob wants, and Jacob wants a trial. She knows if he's free this time, he'll just do something else, maybe worse."

"Bizarre," Sue said.

"Complicated," Andy said. Sue agreed.

"So, are you going to answer these calls?" she asked.

Andy said no; he didn't want to add to the circus.

"I have news for you, Andy," Sue said, "you are part of the circus. I don't mean to tell you I told —"

"Then don't," he said.

Andy spent the rest of the morning finishing the paper and then thought again about the phone calls. He decided to make one call, to a reporter he knew in Harrisburg. The other ones could wait.

"Dale? Andy Simpson returning your call. . . . Yeah. Sorry. I know you missed the afternoon deadline, but I can't add anything to what you have. . . . Sort of. I don't know if you could call me a friend. He stops in my office once in a while. . . . No, I didn't know he was going to do this. . . . Why? How the hell would I know? . . . He's out on bail now. . . . I think his wife. . . . Yeah. Bizarre. . . . I guess there'll be a trial. He seems to want one."

Andy was afraid he had gone too far. If Jacob wants to talk about why he wants a trial, that's his business.

He continued, "I don't know exactly why he wants a trial. . . . I saw him this morning. When he got out. . . . I don't know. He seemed fine, under the circumstances. . . . No, he didn't say anything. . . . Back to his farm. . . . Yes. He said he was going to work in his fields today. He grows potatoes. . . . No, I don't know what's going to happen next. . . . His wife? Yes, I met her. Briefly. . . . She's quiet, to herself. You know, like most of those people."

Andy was uncomfortable being interviewed. He had interviewed other people often enough to know what Dale was digging for. Some sort of angle. Something to set his story apart from the other stories. Andy could have given it to him, but he didn't want to. He also didn't want to get involved, especially in the trial. If Dale or any of the others want the story, they can go out to Jacob's farm and talk to him. Jacob would be happy to see them.

"Sorry, Dale, but that's all the time I have. I still have a few things to do before my deadline. . . . Noon. . . . Yes, today. . . . Yeah, I can talk with you later."

I wish journalists would mind their own business, he said to himself.

⊰ **Twelve** ⊱

Over the next several days Andy drifted, unsure what to do or think. On Saturday morning he went out to Jacob's farm and found him working in his fields, loosening the dirt in the potato rows with his tractor and harrow. Andy walked out to him, and Jacob stopped working for a few minutes, talking with Andy while still sitting on the tractor. When it became apparent, however, that Andy was just curious and had no additional information, Jacob excused himself and started up the tractor again, resuming his work, while Andy walked back through the field to his car. He stopped at the house to see if Sarah was at home; she was not. Andy was relieved since he had no idea what to say to her. He drove back to Carlisle.

In the afternoon Andy decided to get a few groceries out at the all-night market and saw Harvey Imhoff in the fresh vegetables section. He asked him if he knew any more about Jacob's case.

"Can't say," Harvey said, bagging several onions. "It's up to the judge, but I doubt that anything will be done for a while. Pretty cut and dried, I'd say. Be a jury trial. You'll be called as a witness. Did you know that?"

"No," Andy said, "I didn't think they would need me."

Andy certainly didn't want to get involved in a public way since he would have to report on the trial. He knew it would be at least awkward.

"You were there," Harvey said, placing the onions on the scale. "You saw it all. Probably call some of his Mennonite friends too. The ones across the road at the market stand."

"They're Sarah's friends," Andy said, perhaps too quickly he thought.

Harvey looked at Andy for a moment, apparently intrigued by his response, perhaps wondering how he knew that.

"Same thing," Harvey said finally, and then added, "I never could understand those people."

The phone calls from other newspapers had stopped by Friday afternoon, Andy convincing the reporters that he knew little if anything about the case, explaining that he had just moved from New York a short time before and therefore didn't know the culture, so at least he didn't have to contend with that anymore.

Andy dreaded Sunday. He got his copy of the *Times* and quickly scanned it to see if it had published anything on Jacob. He was relieved to see it had not. He thought of Beth, sitting on her bed, leafing through the pages of her copy. He wondered if she were alone and then felt a pang of jealousy. That's stupid, he said to himself. He told himself he just hopes she's happy. He knew she could be happy with someone else, but he still didn't like the idea of her with someone else. He read more of the paper than usual, even part of the business section, trying to squeeze out as much from it as possible, using up as much of the morning as he could. He knew the Phillies were home that afternoon, which meant he could not even watch them on TV with local blackouts, so he stretched out on the sofa and tried to read. When he could not concentrate on his book, he went out to the porch to sit for a while, lowering his head when people walked past, hoping they wouldn't stop to talk.

Finally, Andy decided to drive up to Harrisburg and over to the island where the Senators play. They were away for the weekend, but he had noticed a park there the last time he saw a game and decided to walk around the island. That will kill an hour or so, he thought.

The island was bigger than Andy realized. It had several other playing fields, a practice field for the Senators, and what looked like a soccer field. Along the water stretched a series of small booths, selling food and drinks, souvenirs, local crafts, and at the end of the island, the park that Andy remembered.

He sat on a bench under the shade of a large maple tree and watched the kids playing in the park. Fathers pushed daughters on the swings and tossed balls to sons and daughters. Mothers sat on other benches, talking, enjoying the moments free from tending the children. A few families had spread blankets out on the grass and were sitting or lying there, reading to children, playing games. It was idyllic small town once again, and Andy felt at home, even as a spectator.

He could not for long, however, keep Jacob and Sarah out of his mind. The happy families on the island reminded him of the complete rupture in that family, of the overwhelming sadness, of the pain. Soon he was unable to watch the scene any longer and walked back to his car. The evening still lay before him. He thought of driving up to Sunbury but decided against it, although he had not been back there since coming to Carlisle. He had thought he would go shortly after moving, but he had not. He wasn't sure why, although now he thought it might be another way to take his mind off Jacob and Sarah. And he tried desperately not to be reminded of Sarah.

Finally, Andy returned to Carlisle and stopped at his office. He had things to do, he told himself, and this would give him a start on the week. As he entered the door, he looked around to make sure no one was watching him. Once inside he spent several hours moving from task to task, accomplishing nothing. Finally, he went home.

By Thursday Andy had produced another edition, but he could think of nothing but Sarah. He had no idea what was happening to her, and this tormented him. He usually spent Thursday afternoon planning next week's issue, conferring with Sue about layout and how much space he might anticipate having. Instead he told Sue he was not feeling well and went out to find Sarah. He felt Sue watching him as he left.

Andy drove down Route 15 and, for the first time in weeks, pulled into the small parking lot beside Souders Market stand. He didn't see Sarah, although he knew she should be working; she worked every weekday afternoon. He walked around the rows of vegetables and fruit, pretending to be interested in them. As he was about to leave, someone, a woman, spoke to him.

"Are you Mr. Simpson?" she said.

When Andy turned to look at her, she looked familiar, although all the women looked familiar to him with their long, dark dresses and white aprons, and with their hair pulled back under their white bonnets.

"I'm Esther," she said.

"Yes," Andy said, "I recognize you." At least he remembered that Sarah had a sister.

She asked quietly if he were looking for Sarah. Andy took a few steps toward her and said he was, although he was not sure that was the proper response. Esther said she was not at the stand. Andy paused, considering his options, looking around to see if anyone was close enough to hear this. Finally, he asked if Esther could tell him where Sarah was.

Esther said, "She is very disturbed by everything that has been happening. She has not been here all week."

Andy was upset, but he wasn't sure how to proceed because he didn't know how much to tell Esther or how much she knew about him and his involvement with Sarah. Finally, he told her he wanted to see Sarah because he works for a newspaper, and then added, "and because she's my friend."

"Friend?" Esther clearly knew nothing of Andy beyond his work at the newspaper.

Andy decided to go forward, thinking he had nothing to lose

anyway. "I've gotten to know her," he said, "and Jacob too, and I want to help—both of them. Jacob doesn't want to talk about it now. Besides, he seems pretty much in control of himself. But I don't know about Sarah. If I could just talk to her for a few minutes, I would feel better."

Esther lowered her head. Andy wondered if she was trying to decide or was just embarrassed. After a moment, she looked up at him and said, "I am afraid we are more concerned about how Sarah feels. I think you might upset her more. She wants solitude now."

Andy was beginning to panic. Esther turned and began to go back to the stand. He knew he was losing Sarah. He quickly asked, "Do you know where she is? Is she nearby? Is she at home? "

"No," Esther said, "she is not at home."

"It's okay," Andy said, "I've been there before. She hasn't minded."

Esther paused. Andy thought she might be changing her mind. He tried to think what he might say that would convince her to tell him Sarah's whereabouts. He waited.

No," she said, "I cannot tell you where she is. I am sorry, but I am thinking of Sarah."

"I promise not to upset her," Andy said, attempting to convey control. "I won't mention the newspaper, and I won't use anything in it. I just want to know that she can handle this. I want to offer my help. I might be able to make it all easier for her."

Esther said nothing and then turned away again, quickly this time, returning to her people. Andy was distraught. He could see Esther talking to one of the older women. For a moment, he thought she might be discussing him, but then he realized they were simply talking about the yellow squash someone had piled up on one of the stands.

As he was concentrating on Esther and the woman, however, he heard someone, a woman, talking near him, behind another of the counters. He heard Sarah's name mentioned and shifted his focus, trying to hear what she was saying, but all he could hear was something about a church. Andy went back to his car and thought about what he had heard. She might be at the church, he thought. It made sense that she would seek out the church for peace. He knew the church was several miles from there—he remembered it from Jacob's tirade—and so he drove directly there, parking his car at the far end of the lot. There were no other cars there, which made him think he might have misunderstood. He walked to the church and turned the latch. It was open. He looked in but saw nothing. If Sarah had been here, she had left. He was about to leave but decided instead to go through the door, to enter the solitude of the church. The quiet of the interior drew him forward, and as he walked down the aisle, he saw a movement at the end of the front pew. It was Sarah, sitting quietly, her head down. Andy assumed she was praying.

He took another step and the floor creaked. Damn, Andy said to himself. Sarah turned immediately toward him, startled.

"Mr. Simpson, what are you doing here?"

Now that he was there, facing Sarah, Andy didn't know what to say.

"Sarah. How are you?" he said and then realized what a lame question that was.

"I am fine," she said, lowering her head.

Andy took a few more steps and stopped at the aisle end of the pew. He noticed her starched, white bonnet and her hands folded in her lap.

"No," he said. "I know you're fine." He couldn't stop there. "I really am concerned about you. How are you handling the whole situation?"

"You mean with Jacob?" She looked up at him.

Andy nodded.

"That is fine too," she said, and then she added after a pause, "It is not. I do not know what to do."

Her voice broke slightly. Andy walked to her and sat down beside her in the pew. He asked if he could do anything.

"Thank you, but no," she said. "I do not know what will happen. I have been trying to pray, but I do not know what to pray for. I prayed for Jacob."

"How can you pray for Jacob?" Andy asked. "Do you even know what he wants?"

Sarah looked down and said, "I pray for him, not for what he wants. I pray that he will come back to the church, to God."

"Back to you?"

"No, not that," she said, "I pray for what is best for him."

Andy was becoming impatient with Sarah's selflessness. He knew what she was saying but thought she should think of herself as well.

"Do you ever pray for yourself, Sarah?" he asked her.

"For myself?" she said and then added, her head still bowed, "I pray that I do God's will."

Andy stood and looked down at Sarah, hoping she would look up at him. She did not. Finally, he said, "That's not what I mean. Do you ever pray for something that you want or need?"

She said she needed nothing.

Andy forgot about tactics. He sat back down beside her and looked directly at her. "Could I pray for you?" he asked softly. "Would you mind if I did that?"

Sarah looked at him, surprised. "I did not think you believed in prayer."

"I don't know," Andy said, "I think I do." He ran his hand through his hair and said, "Yes, I would like to pray for you."

"Mr. Simpson."

"Andy. Could you call me Andy?"

She smiled slightly.

"Andy," she said and then remained silent for a moment as if she were ashamed of saying it. Finally, she said, "Do you know why I am here?"

Andy didn't know the answer to that question, but he tried to put himself in her place. "To gain strength from your beliefs," he said.

"No," she said, "just the opposite. I am here in this church, my church, because I am not sure about my beliefs. I try to live the way I think God wants me to live, but all of this happens. So many people are unhappy, and it is my fault."

"It's not your fault," Andy said.

Sarah was insistent. "Some of it is my fault," she said. "If my beliefs cause this much pain, I wonder if my beliefs are wrong. Do you have any idea what this is doing to my children? They saw some of the other children from their school this morning, and they made fun of them, calling them names. They came home crying. I cannot imagine what will happen when school begins again. I can endure this, but I do not know if they can. Something is wrong, and I do not understand what it is. I am afraid my faith is not as strong as I thought it was. I am afraid of losing everything."

Andy didn't know how to reassure her. How could he convince someone to retain faith when he had so little, when he had thought about it so little? He could tell her to be strong, but he knew he was weak. He was confused because he had been taking strength from her, and now she seemed fragile. Words would not do it, he knew. And yet words were all he had. He found it ironic that just when he was beginning to understand himself more, at least to confront himself with more honesty, she was beginning to waver, and she was the reason he was becoming stronger. He could only sit and watch her, her head again bowed. They sat in silence. He knew she was crying.

He offered her a handkerchief. She took it and wiped her eyes. When she handed it back to him, she turned her body to him and raised her head, looking him in his eyes.

"Andy," she said.

Andy could not respond. He didn't trust his voice.

"Help me. Please."

For the second time she buried her head in his shoulder. Andy held her, stroking her hair, and realized he too was crying. He didn't know, could not remember when he had last cried. He felt close to her, part of her, for the first time, and he knew he would do whatever was necessary for her happiness, for his happiness. They sat there together, holding each other, and Andy realized she was not withdrawing from him. He loathed what he wanted to do, what he was about to do, but he could not stop. He put his lips to hers and kissed her. At first she was impassive, but she did not pull back. He cupped her head in his hands and kissed her again. She responded, coming alive with a passion that astonished Andy. He finally pulled back, and they looked at each other. She put her head on his shoulder and then pressed her cheek against his. Soon they kissed once again, long and probing, and held each other for several more minutes in the darkening church, never quite relaxing, both beginning to come back to where they were, to what they had done, both feeling the awkwardness, as if they didn't know what to do next. Sarah pulled away first and sat upright beside him.

"Forgive me," she said. "I do not know why I did that. It is just that it has been so long."

At first Andy thought she meant it had been so long since she had joined the church. He thought perhaps he had taken her back to the days of high school, to the days of freedom. But then he realized she meant it had been so long since she had made love, had felt passion. The force of her kiss was physical as well as emotional. He remembered Jacob's claim that she came to him naked in the night, and he now knew it was possible. He also knew at some point he could make love to her, and the thought of doing that with her bordered on sacrilege to him. It also excited him.

"I shouldn't have done that," he said. "I'm sorry."

She did not respond.

Andy began to feel remorse. Why had he kissed her? Was it simply because he could? That's the reason he had always given before. They sat silently.

"You're a strong woman," Andy said finally.

She shook her head.

"This is a difficult time for you," he said. "You're being tested."

Andy thought of his own test, if it could be called that, and how he had failed it. Beth had said she thought they should separate. He agreed. That was it. What business had he to offer advice to this woman, especially the platitudes that came to mind?

"Was it wrong for me to kiss you?" he asked.

"Yes," she said, "and it was wrong for me to kiss you. It is wrong for me to feel the way I feel now."

"How do you feel?"

"I do not know, but I do know it is wrong."

"Are you sorry you feel this way?"

For a second time she shook her head.

"It's not possible to control how you feel," Andy said, "only to control what you do and what you say." He was speaking to himself.

"How do you feel, Andy?" She said these words deliberately, quietly.

"About you?"

"Yes."

Andy decided to be honest, to be as honest as he could be. "You are the most remarkable woman I've ever met," he said. "I'm very confused. I know that I should not have done that. I should not care for you the way I do. You're a married woman, and marriage is sacred to you. It should be sacred to me, too, but it hasn't been. You do love Jacob, don't you?"

She nodded and looked away.

"Then" Andy said, "what we did was wrong. I was wrong."

Andy looked at her.

"Is it possible to love two people?" she asked.

Andy could feel the emotion of the question, the desperation, the uncertainty, but he did not know how to respond. Was she saying she loved him? Was it just the confusion of the moment? He knew she was inexperienced, and he didn't want to take advantage of that.

"I think it is, Sarah," he said, "but I think the love would be different. I think only one love can be total, and I think that's the love you have for Jacob."

Andy knew he was arguing against what he wanted most, but Sarah meant too much to him to do anything else. Somehow he had to help her through this chaos in her life, even if it meant, as it would, losing her.

"Perhaps so," she said. "Perhaps I should love Jacob so much that he will return to me and the church."

Andy knew that if Jacob returned, it would be to Sarah and not the church.

Sarah continued, "Perhaps I should love Jacob so much that I can forget."

Andy was not sure where Sarah was going with this.

"Perhaps," he said lamely.

Sarah reached for her bag lying beside her in the pew and said it was time for her to go. Andy insisted that he should leave so she could be alone again.

"No," she said. "I am ready."

Before going, however, she reached for his hand and told him not to be sad. Andy was moved by this selfless gesture, but he also realized that she had now reasserted her control. Andy asked if he could see her again, not in the house, just on the porch. She shook her head.

"Why not?" he asked. He was feeling desperation now. I know I have no right to say this, but I will anyway. "Sarah, I think I —"

"I know," she interrupted, "that's why we should not."

"Oh," Andy said, and then asked, "Can I at least take you back to your house? How did you get here?"

"I walked," she said, "and I'll walk home. I need the walk."

They walked together back the aisle of the church and out into the late afternoon sunlight.

"You know where I am if you need me," Andy said.

She nodded.

Andy got into his car and drove off, leaving Sarah in the

parking lot. Rather than going straight to Carlisle, however, he drove randomly on the side roads that wound in and out of the hills and along the river.

By the time he got back to his office, Sue had gone. He sat at his desk and thought about Sarah. He stayed there a long time, more than an hour, and then, as if coming out of a dream, he suddenly sat up straight. He realized he had been praying for her.

Thirteen

During the next several weeks Andy grew more restless, feeling a growing hunger, new to him, to talk with someone about what was happening to him. He felt guilty for what he had done and for thinking so much of Sarah and what she must be doing and feeling at each moment. He found himself drifting off to her in the middle of a story, and woke up at least once a night thinking of her. He didn't see how he could continue, but he knew of nothing else to do.

Andy had made no close friends in the short time he had been in Carlisle. In fact, as he thought about it, he had no close friends anywhere and didn't remember knowing anyone he could have talked to in New York about this. Sue was the person closest to him now, but he knew she would be simply baffled; and besides, such a revelation might make it difficult for her to work with him. Beth was out of the question. Even when he and Beth were still married, he had not discussed his feelings with her. He would have never talked with Beth about anything really personal, which was, he was beginning to realize, part of the problem.

Andy thought of therapy. He knew there were counselors in Harrisburg, and it made perfect sense to seek one out, but he could not bring himself to do it, despite the fact that almost everyone he knew in New York had been in therapy at least once. Beth, in fact, told him she had been in therapy for a while before they met. She said a therapist is just someone you pay to be a friend and listen to your problems. Since he had no friends, that's what he should do, he thought. But still he couldn't do it. The idea of telling a perfect stranger what a bastard he was did not appeal to him. And besides, what could a therapist tell him that he didn't already know? He should stop thinking about her. He should let her go. He should get to know who he really is. Well, he thought, what if I don't want to know who I really am? No, a therapist was out of the question.

Andy also began to think more about Sunbury during this time, feeling a need to visit, to go back to where he had been a child. He realized his thoughts now centered on either Sarah or Sunbury, but he didn't know why. What did one have to do with the other? One was then; the other is now. Were thoughts of his childhood an escape from the pain of the present? Or did the answer to his current confusion lie somehow in the past, in Sunbury? Andy didn't know, but he did know that when he was not worrying about Sarah, he was thinking of the Sunbury of his childhood.

Although he could remember many events from his childhood, most connected either with school or athletics, he could recall no real conversations with either of his parents. His father had been a successful businessman, working with a large investment firm, running their office in Sunbury. His mother seemed to be always volunteering for something, rarely at home in the evenings. An only child, he remembered wishing his mother could help him with his homework or his father would come to a Little League game. They rarely did, and he grew up without much contact with either of them and with almost no affection from them. Strange as it seemed to him now, he could not remember a single instance when either of his parents had actually kissed him. And yet he thought he had loved his parents, and he was sure they had loved him.

His memory of his mother was dimmest because she died of cancer when he was thirteen and she was thirty-five. His most vivid memory, and that vanishing more each year, was of her in bed, incredibly thin, unwilling to talk. His father spent time with her, telling her the news, but she appeared not to listen. And then she died and was buried in the cemetery, which looked down on the town from a hill. Andy remembered being able to see out to the Susquehanna as the coffin, bearing a rose he had dropped on it, was lowered into the ground. The plot had been bought by Andy's grandfather, his mother's father, and his mother was buried next to her mother.

 Six years later his father died, of a heart attack while hunting in Alaska. He had never remarried, but he did spend more and more time away from home on business or on hunting trips with his friends. When his father was buried beside his mother, Andy looked out again at the Susquehanna, but this time his grandfather, who was standing beside him, put his arm around him, something his father had never done.

 Andy did love his grandfather. He knew that. He had spent summers with him during his teenage years and grew to love the farm just outside Sunbury. He helped with the work, mostly cultivating and harvesting some of the early wheat—"winter wheat," his grandfather called it. He milked the cows and tended the chickens. The chickens were his special responsibility, and he took his work seriously. His grandfather told him often that he had never seen such a clean chicken coop. Although he and his grandfather spent time together, working and sitting on the porch in the evening, they never really talked either. His grandfather was of German stock, and German men kept to themselves, rarely if ever showing emotion. Andy thought that was why he treasured that moment at his father's funeral when his grandfather put his arm around him.

 After high school Andy had gone away to college because it was expected of him. He chose a small school sixty miles away, but he came home only for Thanksgiving and Christmas that first year, spending Easter vacation with some friends in Florida. He got a job the following summer, working at a state park north of Sunbury, mostly cleaning up the mess left by campers, and then in October of his sophomore year his father died, and early in his senior year his grandfather also died. Someone found him slumped over in the chicken coop, his hand still full of feed. Andy took a day from school and attended the funeral. He knew no one else there. He finished his degree, falling in and out of love several times but nothing serious, just learning the game, coming out with a major in English. He loved reading and writing, even the interminable series of papers he had to write as an English major. He also wrote some poetry and tried some fiction, but he found by his junior year that his strength was in journalism. He had worked on the school paper and had been encouraged by some of his teachers, so he edited the paper during his senior year.

As graduation approached he thought about trying for a job with a newspaper, but was encouraged by his journalism teacher to take a master's degree at a good school. They chose Columbia University, and suddenly Andy found himself in the middle of a city, living in an apartment far from the campus, taking courses, and doing an internship at a small newspaper on Long Island. He learned to use the subway and trains, grew to like bagels and lox, attended some plays and concerts, so when he finished his degree and got an offer from the newspaper where he had done his internship, he decided to accept it and stay living in the City.

Gradually, he became part of a group of young professionals, all more sophisticated than he but fun. He enjoyed their parties, and at one of them he met Beth, the most sophisticated of them all. She had grown up there and knew Manhattan like he knew Sunbury. Andy found her completely fascinating. She seemed to respond to his innocence, so he began to play on that, flattering her and appealing to her at the same time. Somehow, at some point he moved in with her, keeping his own place for several months and finally letting it go. He didn't remember a time when they actually discussed their living together. It just happened. One time he stayed overnight, something he had done before, but that time he never left. She was comfortable with the arrangement; so was he, although he thought at times of what his grandfather might have said. Then they married. And divorced.

Now he was thinking of going back to Sunbury. How strange, he thought. He didn't know a person living there.

Putting his reservations aside, one warm Saturday in late August, Andy drove the sixty miles and fifteen years to Sunbury, crossing the Susquehanna River where the East and West Branches meet, over the old iron bridge he remembered, down into the center of town. Sunbury is an old town that never grew, everything red brick. Like many small towns in eastern Pennsylvania, it just added developments, groups of houses attached to the town like Post-it notes. Hello, town, Andy imagined one saying, I won't be home for dinner. There's something in the fridge for you.

Andy parked in front of a mini-market. He couldn't remember what had been there before, even though during high school he used to hang out in front of this place with friends. Most of the buildings were the same, but names and fronts had changed. The traffic seemed far worse than he remembered, trucks rumbling through the town on their way to the interstate a few miles north. He found it all vaguely unsettling.

He then drove out to where he had lived with his parents. He had known only that one house, 102 Mulberry Street, at the corner of Mulberry and Twelfth. He found it easily, and it seemed the same to him, the trees around it bigger, the shrubbery different, but the house—as he remembered it—had the same white wooden siding and the same box-like windows arranged symmetrically, two on each side of the main door. He walked around to the rear of the house and saw that a screened-in patio had been added and a sandbox with a swing set placed under the willow tree he used to climb. He spent hours in that tree, reading or just thinking about things. Kids, he thought. He hoped they were happy.

"Andy," he heard his mother call. "Andy!" she shouted, "I know you're up there. I'm going down to the Woman's Club meeting. We have our bake sale on Saturday. Do you need anything?"

"No, Mom."

"Goodbye, Sweetie."

"Goodbye, Mom."

He hated being called Sweetie, but she didn't know that. Shortly after that she came down with cancer. He never found out what kind, but she wasted away for a year before she died. It's a blessing, her friends said. She was such a fine woman, giving so much of herself. When the preacher talked about her at the funeral, Andy didn't recognize his mother. He had no idea what other people thought about her since he thought about her almost not at all. His father sat alone, next to him, saying nothing, looking straight ahead. He didn't see his father mourn, but he knew he was sad. Since his father shed no tears, neither did he.

Andy tried to remember what the inside of the house looked like. He could picture the fireplace in the living room, the large dark dining room suite they used for formal dinners, although he rarely ate there. He remembered when they replaced the orange Formica countertops in the kitchen with a more sedate brown. And he remembered his own room, the walls plastered with pictures of baseball players clipped from newspapers. He dreamed of being a major league player some day and saw his own picture up there, finishing a swing and looking at the ball arcing over the outfield fence or backhanding a ball deep in the hole at shortstop. At that age it was still possible to dream things like that. He never told his parents of his dream, and they never knew how good he was. Since he came home with good grades on his report cards and never got into trouble, they were satisfied. At least he thought they were happy with him. He wondered now, standing in front of the house, what they really thought of him. The realization that he would never know struck him deeply at that moment.

Andy then he drove out to his grandfather's farm and found it covered with small houses set on small lots, each identical to the other except for a shutter design here or a bay window there. He looked at the slope of the land, trying to find the highest point, the point where his grandfather's farmhouse had stood, but he could not. His grandfather was not there. Andy wished he had not come back to the farm.

He got in his car and started back through town to the bridge and the ride home, but decided instead to go up the hill, to the cemetery and to the graves. He vaguely remembered where his parents and grandparents were buried, and once in the general area, he found the location easily by moving toward the vantage point from which he could see the Susquehanna River. The view was the same, but the graves were strangely different. The grass had grown across all four so that except for the identical markers they were imperceptible from the rest of the lawn. It's been that long, Andy thought. If someone would take away the markers, as someone will some day, no one will ever again know they are there. Soon he will be there, he thought, or somewhere like it. He had never really thought that thought before, but he was now older than his mother was when she died and approaching his father's age. He sensed he was more than halfway through his own life and was suddenly overwhelmed by this total separation from his past. He didn't know it then and he didn't know it now. It was gone. He thought of his life as failure and of a future that looked equally bleak. He looked out at the river of his youth, and for the second time that summer he cried. Grandpa would be embarrassed, he thought.

"It's tough to lose your parents," he heard someone say beside him. He was a man about Andy's age, perhaps a few years older, graying hair, paunchy, a kind face.

"I was just visiting with my parents over there," he said, pointing to a plot of graves twenty-five yards away, "and saw you were having some trouble. It means you cared a lot about them."

"Yes," Andy said. "Thanks." He turned away and walked back to his car. He had hoped while there in the cemetery to draw up more memories of his grandfather, but he never had the opportunity.

Perhaps the memories he had were enough. Those memories of his grandfather were like the river, always there when he looked for them. He drove back to Carlisle, the road hugging the river for thirty miles or so. He felt good about the river and the road.

He felt good about the day too. For most of it he didn't think of Sarah at all and now that he was back, sitting on his porch, he thought of her as a future that would never happen, a side future, almost like a parallel plane of existence, one he could see but not enter. The real future, his future, was a blank before him, dim at best. Maybe that's what all futures are, he thought. Somehow they take shape.

He walked through the house to get a beer, planning to sit at the picnic table rather than on the porch so his neighbors would not see him drinking during the day, and saw the light blinking on his answering machine. He pushed the Play button.

"Hi, Andy. Uh, it's me . . . Beth. I probably shouldn't call. I hope you don't mind. But I just heard about Jacob. Someone told me. I know it's none of my business, but I just wanted to know if you're all right, if I can do anything. I can't imagine what. But I know you care about Jacob and his wife—Sarah— probably more than you should. I'm sorry. I shouldn't have said that. You should care about them as much as you like. I guess you can't just turn caring off and on. I thought you could. . . . Look, this is not going very well. If I knew how to erase this message I probably would. I should just butt out, but I know you're vulnerable now. Do I sound like a shrink? Sorry. It's been crazy here lately. Mel. . . . Never mind. Look, I just wanted to say—so I might as well say it—if you need someone to talk to about this, give me a call. I know it's ironic of me to offer that now, but if it helps, that's okay. Give me a call . . . or not. Whatever's best. I'll . . . see you. Oh, it's Saturday, 1:37. Afternoon. Bye."

My God, Andy thought, that was Beth. He turned off the tape but didn't erase it, just in case he wanted to listen to it again, got his beer from the refrigerator, and walked out the back door to the picnic table. The late afternoon was still warm as he settled down with his beer.

A few minutes later Sue came around the corner of the house and said hello.

Andy looked at her, unable to hide his surprise.

"Hi," he said. "What brings you out on a Saturday?"

"I was just getting some groceries," she said, "and stopped to see if you were here. I had called this morning, but you didn't answer."

"No," Andy said, "I was out most of the day, just doing some sightseeing. Why didn't you leave a message?"

"I hate those things," Sue said. "Besides, it wasn't like it was an emergency or something. How can you do sightseeing when you grew up in this area? You didn't go out to see Sarah, did you?"

"No," he said, "of course not. But thanks for your concern."

Sue looked at her sunglasses, slowly turning them in her hand, and then she put them in her hair.

"Sorry. I guess I do sound like your mother, don't I?"

"Not at all," Andy said, and he meant it.

Sue got to the point, her real reason for stopping by. "Well," she said, "what I wanted to tell you is that I heard the judge set the trial date. September 23, a Tuesday."

"That gives us plenty of time," Andy said.

"For what?"

"For . . . I don't know. I just mean I'm glad we finally have a date. They can all begin to prepare for it. I mean psychologically. We can get this whole thing over with. Of course, that also means the kids will be back in school then. The other kids will make life hell for them."

Andy paused and said nothing. Then he noticed Sue again.

"I'm sorry. Would you like a beer?" He held his own glass up to her.

"No," she said, "I really have to get back home."

"Sure?"

Sue paused then said, "Well, what the hell. Gary has the kids at the playground. I guess I can let go one time at least. Sure, I would love to have a beer with you."

"Glass?"

Sue looked at Andy's glass and said, "A glass? Why not."

Andy went into the kitchen and came back with a glass and a bottle.

"You'll never guess where I went this afternoon," he said.

"Sunbury?"

Andy put the bottle and glass on the table, in front of Sue. "My God," he said, "how did you know that?"

"I knew you would have to go back sometime. It's unnatural that you would be here this long without going back. You said you were gone for the day. It was easy."

Andy sat down at the picnic table, across from Sue.

"You ever think of being a detective?" he said.

"No," Sue said, "but I always know it's the butler in the living room with the knife."

"I'm sure," Andy said, smiling. He tapped the top of his glass with his finger, not knowing what to say next.

"So what did you find in Sunbury?" Sue asked. "Was it worth going back to?"

"I think so." Andy leaned forward, his elbows resting on the table. "I really didn't find much. My grandfather's farm—you remember, I told you about him—it's gone. Some tacky development. My house was still there, but it's lived in now. It looks nice. I went up to the cemetery to visit the graves. The first time since my grandfather died. You know, it looks natural there somehow, like they've always been there. That sounds strange, but do you know what I mean? It's all neat. Lots of other graves have followed theirs up the hill. I don't know. It seemed all right somehow, almost like they really belonged there. My grandfather had bought the plot, room for six graves, before I was born. I guess I'm supposed to be in one of them. Maybe Beth was supposed to be in the other.

It's not a bad thought. Except for Beth. In a sense, she's escaping the grave. Not a bad thought either. Sorry. I don't want to sound ghoulish. I'll change the subject."

"That's okay," Sue said and took a swallow. "Tastes good."

"I always said I wanted to be cremated," Andy said. He didn't want to let go. "So I don't think I'll end up there. Did I ever tell you what I want them to do with my ashes? Well, I don't expect to have any descendants or anything like that to argue over this, so I decided to be cremated and have my ashes spread over the third base area of some ball park after it's rained. Sort of help out, you know. Get the game started again. Maybe the Senators' field, if I'm still in the area. I thought of Shea Stadium when I was in New York, but I figured I didn't have much of a chance there. Maybe Harrisburg would be better."

"That's a pretty morbid thought."

"I don't think so. It's sort of a celebration. Of the game. Of life. Even dead, you're part of the game. I remember Whitman said at the end of *Leaves of Grass*, 'If you want me, look for me under your boot soles.' I might say, 'If you want me, look for me under your spikes.' I could have those words put up on a plaque in the locker room."

"Weird." Sue laughed and pushed her hair back.

"Yes," Andy said. "You didn't know I had a weird side, did you?"

"I suspected it," Sue said and then turned serious. "You know, this is the longest I have ever heard you talk. It's usually one or two words."

"I know," he said, "but I just feel like it now. You just happen to be here. Sorry."

"Not at all," Sue said. "I'm honored. Fascinated."

"Another beer?"

"Why not? Gary can get the kids sandwiches."

Andy and Sue sat at the picnic table for several more hours, Andy telling her more about his visit to Sunbury, about what he thought it meant to him. "I think I found what I need," he said, "what I've lacked. I don't think I can do anything about it, but at least I'm getting there." Sue listened, responding with a word or two when it was appropriate, knowing not to say much, knowing it's Andy's business and not hers. Finally, Andy became silent, looking at his beer, enclosed in his own thoughts, and Sue made a move to leave.

"I really must be going," she said. "Gary will kill me."

Sue stood up, and then Andy stood.

"Tell him it was my fault. Tell him I wouldn't let you go."

"Like you kidnapped me, right?"

He wasn't sure if Sue knew what she had just said. He changed the subject.

"Thanks for listening," he said. "You know, I never thanked anyone before for listening to me. That must mean something."

"It does," Sue said. "Think about it."

With that she carried her glass and bottle back into the kitchen, put them in the sink, and went through the front door to her car.

"See you Monday," she said, as she got in the car.

"Right," Andy said. "See you Monday."

The car disappeared around the corner; Sue was gone. Andy turned and walked around the house to the picnic table. He sat there alone as the warm summer afternoon turned to evening, too quickly, he thought. He spent the time thinking of his visit to Sunbury and of the trial to come. He thought too of the connection between them, if a connection existed. He was not sure. It will be a long month, he thought, and he wished it would never come.

Fourteen

The day of the trial arrived soon enough, an unusually hot, late September day, flies still buzzing as if they would live forever.

Andy arrived at the courthouse early, very early, more than an hour before the trial was scheduled to begin. He told himself that it was his job to be there; he was a reporter. But he was simply nervous—nervous about what might happen to Jacob, nervous about the effect on Sarah, nervous about the possibility of testifying. Several days earlier the district attorney, Dan Kurtz, an earnest young man with a recent election victory, had confirmed Harvey Imhoff's statement that Andy might be called.

The bailiff was sitting outside the courtroom, talking with the cleaning lady, as Andy started to enter the room.

"Sorry, mister, you can't go in. The metal detector isn't here yet."

"Metal detector?" Andy said. "This isn't exactly the mafia. What's the metal detector for?"

"Beats me. The judge said to check everybody. Just like an airport. Anybody has metal on them, the beeper goes off. Say, ain't you the newspaper man, from the *Courier*?"

"Yeah, sure. Andy Simpson." So much for anonymity, he thought.

"Okay, I guess you can go in, but you'll have to come back

out when the metal detector gets here, so you can go through it. Orders. Okay?"

"Right," Andy said, "thanks."

Andy sat in the back of the courtroom, which was surprisingly large and impressive with its dark wood paneling, heavy carpeting, light gray walls, and subdued indirect lighting. Even though he had been covering the news in Carlisle for a number of months and had often been in the courthouse, this was his first visit to the courtroom. Not bad for a small county seat, he thought.

As he looked around the room, he saw directly ahead, near the far wall, the small desk for the court stenographer and to the left of that the raised judge's bench. Immediately to the judge's left was the witness stand. The juror's box curved from the witness box along the wall on the left, almost to the half-dozen rows for the spectators. Comfortable looking seats, Andy thought, padded, unlike the spectators' benches, which were unpadded church pews. The two tables for the prosecution and defense teams were lined up in front of the church pews, the prosecution closest to the jury box.

Sitting there Andy remembered his conversation with District Attorney Kurtz a few days earlier. They had met at the local Y late in the afternoon. The D.A. had just finished running on the indoor track. At least once a week Andy played basketball with some of the young businessmen and several high school teachers. They had just finished showering and were drying off.

"Lots of publicity in this one, huh?" Kurtz said. "Sell lots of newspapers. It might put us on the map, you know."

"Maybe," Andy said, but he was not much interested in being put on the map. He was enjoying sitting on the bench in front of his locker, feeling the pleasant tiredness of basketball, his towel wrapped around his waist.

"So, you been covering this thing since it started," Kurtz said.

Andy said he supposed so, trying to sound casual.

"You think he's guilty?"

"I don't know," Andy said. "It's not as simple as that. Guilty. Innocent. I don't know." Andy got up to get his comb from the locker.

"Sounds simple to me," Kurtz said. "He took her, put her in the car, and kept her there. That's kidnapping, maybe assault."

"But his motives are important," Andy said as he bent his knees slightly to see himself in the mirror. He began to comb his hair.

"Not to me," Kurtz said and then added as he brushed his hair, sweeping it back. "You do the crime, you do the time. I'm going after him, set an example."

"Who for?" Andy said. "All those vicious, terroristic Mennonites out there? Are you going for a prison sentence here?"

"You're damn right," Kurtz said. "This is my first real trial, and I want to get off on the right foot. Hit the ground running, you know. The next election's only three years off. I like the job."

Kurtz was even younger than Andy and looked much younger. Andy got the feeling he would like to look older.

He asked Andy if he was a friend of the accused. Andy said yes, he thought he could call Jacob his friend.

"Okay, fair enough, but will you be objective on the stand if I call you?" Kurtz asked.

"Do you mean will I be honest?" Andy felt himself getting impatient. He wasn't the one on trial.

"Objective," Kurtz said. "I know how newspaper people can work things around with words. I just want to be sure you'll answer straightforward if I call you."

"Nothing is straightforward about this case," Andy said. "Do you realize a man kidnapped his wife so he could talk with her? That's how much he loves her. Can you understand that?"

"We'll keep it simple," Kurtz said. He ignored Andy's questions, or perhaps they simply didn't register. "Maybe we won't need your testimony," he added. "We'll see. Just be around."

Andy assured him that he would be in the courtroom during the entire trial. "It's my job," he said.

"Mine, too," Kurtz said. "Let's do it right."

They returned to the safe subject of exercise.

After that meeting, Andy worried even more for Jacob. Kurtz obviously wants a medal, he thought, and now he was sitting here in the courtroom as various court officials came and went, straightening chairs, putting out water, making sure everything was ready.

Soon Jacob will have his wish, Andy thought. He will be able to talk directly with Sarah and ask her the questions he has wanted to ask for years. Whether or not she will answer is another question.

Shortly before the trial was to begin at 9:00 a.m., Kurtz entered the courtroom followed by the stenographer. Andy saw Kurtz looking at him and nodded. Andy nodded back. Neither smiled. The bailiff then entered, saw Andy, and came to ask him to go out and come back in through the metal detector. Andy went out in the hall where he saw Jacob getting ready to go into the courtroom. He had on a black coat, his straw hat in his hand. Church clothes, Andy thought.

"Jacob, how are you doing?" Andy asked.

"Fine, Mr. Simpson."

Andy saw he was alone.

"So you haven't changed your mind about being your own attorney?" Andy asked.

"No," Jacob said. "I pretty much know what I want to say and what I want to happen. I have been reading."

Sounds like a lawyer to me, Andy thought.

"Come on, Jacob. I'll go in with you."

They went through the metal detector and into the courtroom.

"You're over there, at that table, Jacob," Andy said.

Jacob looked around the room and then said, "Yes. I know."

Jacob went over to the table and put some papers and a bible down. The judge had already entered and was talking with the bailiff and stenographer in front of the bench. Andy had met the judge, Robert Landis, and knew him to be a practical, no-nonsense sort of person. Andy took his former seat in the back row and waited while various people milled around. He knew that jury selection would come first and hoped it would not take too much time.

Soon the bailiff left and returned with several dozen members of the jury pool, who sat in the rows in front of Andy. Before jury selection began, the judge asked Jacob to stand.

"Mr. Weaver," he said, "I understand you're going to serve as your own attorney."

"Yes, sir."

"It's a bit unusual but perfectly legal under the law. Are you sure you understand the consequences of your decision? You're depriving yourself of expert legal counsel. If you wish, I can appoint an attorney for you. It won't cost you anything."

"Thank you, your honor," Jacob said, "but I have sufficient money to hire my own lawyer. I choose to represent myself."

"That's your right, Mr. Weaver."

The judge paused, leafed through some papers, and then looked back at Jacob.

"Mr. Weaver, have you ever heard the expression, 'Anyone who represents himself has a fool for a lawyer?'"

"Yes, sir. I have."

"What do you have to say about that?"

Jacob's stern expression did not change.

"I prefer a fool I know," he said, "to one I do not know, your honor."

Light laughter rippled through the jury pool, and the judge smiled slightly.

Judge Landis then asked, "Will the prosecution and defense please approach the bench?"

Jacob and Kurtz huddled with the judge for a few minutes before they returned to their desks.

"Let's get on with the selection," the judge said.

The bailiff stood up holding a small wooden box and called out the number and name of the first prospective juror. The man, slight, dark hair, in his middle thirties, took his seat in the jury box.

Kurtz began, asking the name and occupation of the prospective juror. After a few more perfunctory questions, he asked if the juror was a member of the Mennonite Church.

"No."

"Are you Amish?"

"No."

"Brethren?"

"No."

"Have you ever heard of Jacob Weaver?"

"No."

"Do you know anything about the Reformed Mennonites?"

"I know some Mennonites. I don't know what kind."

"Would you say that your religion is an important part of your life?"

"Well, I suppose so. I don't think I'm a fanatic or anything."

"Do you think you could render an impartial judgment in a case concerning religion?"

"I believe so."

"Thank you. Pass to the defense, your honor."

Jacob looked up at the defendant.

"Are you an honest man?"

"Yes."

"Your Honor, the juror is acceptable to the defense."

"Acceptable to the State, your honor."

And so it went through the next thirteen jury interviews, Kurtz challenging two men who said they were Mennonites, although not Reformed Mennonites. Kurtz asked the same questions, trying to uncover anyone who might be sympathetic to Jacob, and Jacob asked his one question, accepting each juror in turn, five men and seven women. They finished in twenty minutes. Judge Landis mumbled something about a new record and dismissed the other prospective jurors. It was as though Jacob didn't care who was on the jury. Andy knew that he cared about stating his case for all to hear, but he also knew that his only concern was to talk with Sarah. Who listened in on that conversation was irrelevant. The judge asked the jury not to discuss the case with anyone and announced that the trial would begin at 1:30 that afternoon.

Andy left the courthouse alone and went back to his office to see if he had any urgent business. He knew he would be working nights this week, at least until Thursday, to put out the next edition, but he thought he should check in anyway. Although it was only 10:30, he picked up a meatloaf sandwich and a Coke at Harry's on the way.

Sue was at her desk, working up some ads.

"How's the trial going?" she asked, putting her work aside. "Did they pick any jurors yet?"

"They have a jury," Andy said. "Record speed."

"Is that good or bad?"

"I don't think it matters, at least not to Jacob," Andy said. "He just wants to get to the point where he can put his wife on the stand and talk to her."

Instead of going into his office, Andy sat in a chair near Sue.

"Andy, do you think he's really stable enough to do this?" Sue asked. Andy had told her he was not having a lawyer.

"He's the most stable person I know," Andy said. "In fact, other than that boulder holding up the Civil War statue in the square, he's the most stable thing I know. He'll get it done."

Sue asked if he would go to jail. Andy said probably.

"Will it be worth it?" she asked.

Andy assured her it would be worth it to Jacob, but Sue pressed on, wanting to know what Andy thought Sarah might say on the stand, or if she would even say anything. Andy said he didn't know.

Sue stood and looked out her window.

"You're worried about her, aren't you?" Sue asked.

"I'm worried about both of them."

Sue turned to look at Andy.

"But especially her?"

"I suppose so," Andy said. "She seems more vulnerable than Jacob."

"Andy."

"What?"

"She's married."

Andy paused and then said, "I know."

Andy returned to his desk and spent the next hour going through his mail and checking the e-mail, trying to concentrate on the next issue, deciding what stories, besides the obvious one, he'll carry. He then went for a long walk around town, came back, ate his lunch, and by 1:15 he was back in the courtroom, waiting for the jury to enter. Kurtz was already there; Jacob came in soon after and nodded to Andy, and finally, at exactly 1:30, the jury filed in and took their seats along the wall to the left of Andy. By then a dozen or so spectators had entered the courtroom, none, so far as Andy could tell, Mennonites. The bailiff stood and called out, "All rise. The court is now in session, the Honorable Robert Landis presiding." Judge Landis entered from a rear door, sat down at the bench, and immediately addressed the jury.

"Ladies and gentlemen. First, I want to thank you for your willingness to serve on this jury. You are an important part of the democratic process in this country, and you have an important task before you. I ask you to take it seriously and not to discuss anything pertaining to this case with anyone, not even your family members. The case before you is unusual, but the law in this matter is simple. The defendant, Jacob Weaver, is accused of kidnapping and simple assault. The State contends that he forcefully abducted his wife from her place of employment, Souders Market on Route 15—you probably know the place—and kept her against her will for several hours before she was released by two police officers. The law is straightforward on this. If you find the defendant, beyond a shadow of a doubt, guilty as charged, then you must return that verdict. As this case proceeds, you will discover a number of extenuating circumstances, some related to the defendant's religion. You must consider all of these circumstances, and you must decide if any are relevant to the legality of the case, and I stress legality because we are concerned here with the law and with a possible transgression of the law. Remember that you are bound by that law, and you must not allow your sympathies to sway you in the understanding of the charge, in the weighing of the evidence, and in the decision you will arrive at."

As Andy listened to the charge to the jury, he realized that the judge was trying to avoid a circus here. The Associated Press reporter from Harrisburg was sitting at the other end of the back row waiting for something unusual to happen, something that would get his story on the wire. Andy hoped it would not come to that, but he was sure it would.

"Is the prosecution ready?" Judge Landis asked, looking at the district attorney.

"Yes, your Honor."

Kurtz approached the jury, and placed his yellow legal pad on the small table in front of the jury box. His demeanor was serious. He paused before beginning, obviously to underscore the gravity of the situation or perhaps, Andy thought, to compensate for his youthful appearance. He then looked up and down the box at each juror individually. Finally, he said good afternoon. Several members of the jury mumbled good afternoon. Throughout his opening remarks Kurtz did not move from the small table before him.

"Ladies and gentlemen of the jury. As Judge Landis has said to you, you have a serious, even sacred duty to perform here. You must render a judgment on a citizen's act, and I emphasize act because you are not to render the judgment on his intention, on his reasoning, or on his sincerity, but solely on the act which he performed. The charge is simple, and the evidence is clear. The State contends that the defendant, Jacob Weaver, drove, with purpose in mind, to Souders Market and forced Sarah Weaver, the defendant's estranged wife, against her will, into his car. Furthermore, he kept her there, again with force, and again against her will, until she was freed by two police officers. You will hear from witnesses who were present at the market, you will hear from the police officers who rescued Mrs. Weaver, and you will hear from Mrs. Weaver herself, and on the basis of that testimony, you will have no choice but to find the defendant guilty of the charges. Those charges are kidnapping and simple assault.

"The defense, represented by Mr. Weaver himself as you know, will contend that he simply wanted to talk with his estranged wife. That may well be the case, but taking someone against her will and keeping her for two hours against her will is a crime, pure and simple, no matter what the motive. We may sympathize with Mr. Weaver's desire to be reunited with his estranged wife, but the State contends that kidnapping is no way to achieve that end. The State is convinced that when you hear all the evidence, you will find the defendant guilty of all charges. Thank you."

Kurtz took one last long look at the jury and returned to his desk.

Not bad, Andy thought. He looks like a kid up there, but he got the jury's attention, and they're going to take him seriously. His strategy is to hammer away at the law.

Judge Landis nodded to Jacob, who was watching him intently, and told him he could present his case.

Jacob walked to the jury box without a tablet. He was wearing the simple clothing he always wore, black pants, with suspenders, and purple shirt. He had taken off his black coat. His large shock of white hair seemed to gleam in the courtroom as he looked, unsmilingly, at each juror, his steel-blue eyes fixing them.

"Ladies and gentlemen," he began. "I am not a lawyer, and I will not pretend to be one. I have a simple story to tell, and I think

I can tell it better than any lawyer. All I ask is that you give me a chance to tell my story, and then you can render whatever decision seems best to you. I'll abide by that decision."

Jacob too did not move from his initial position before the jury. He continued.

"You have heard the allegation that I took my estranged wife against her will. First of all, you must understand that my wife is not estranged. Neither of us has chosen to be separate; we love each other. It is the Reformed Mennonite Church that has separated us. The practice is called shunning, and it is a diabolical practice designed to destroy the family. It is that which is on trial here, the church."

Andy watched Kurtz squirm and try to get the judge's attention. Finally, Judge Landis interrupted.

"Mr. Weaver, I am going to allow you considerable latitude here, but I ask you in your opening comments to restrict yourself to the charge against you, at least as much as possible."

"I apologize to the State, your Honor," Jacob said. "Ladies and gentlemen of the jury, I have been charged with assault, but I never hurt my wife; I never intended to hurt her. I just wanted to talk with her. I know that if I have the opportunity to talk with her, I can convince her to come back to me, to break the bondage to the church, to the bishop of that church, and to return to me as my wife. If I took her against her will, it was because it was my only option."

Jacob's voice began to rise, but he kept complete control of himself, his emotion clearly boiling beneath the surface.

"I love my wife," he continued, "and I know it is not her fault that she obeys the bishop and not me. She believes in the bishop and the church, and she obeys them—even the evil practice of shunning. Shunning, ladies and gentlemen, means that no members of the church, even wife and children, can have intercourse with the one shunned, regardless of their own desires. Do you realize what it is like to live in a house with people you love and have them ignore you completely? It is a living hell, ladies and gentlemen. Imagine that in your own family. What would you do to get your wife or husband, to get your children back?"

"Mr. Weaver." Judge Landis interrupted again.

"Yes, your Honor. I understand, but I think why I did this is important here. I must explain the background of my crime, my alleged crime."

Kurtz was halfway out of his chair when Judge Landis motioned him back.

"Very well, Mr. Weaver," he said, "but try to present your case with less theatrics. Just state the facts as best you understand them."

"Thank you, your Honor," Jacob said and then turned back to the jury.

"Ladies and Gentlemen," he continued, "you have heard the charges. They are serious charges, kidnapping and simple assault, but they are not simple charges. I, the defendant in this case, acted out of self-defense."

Kurtz was again halfway out of his chair. The judge waved him down.

Jacob continued, "I have been assaulted and battered by my church. My wife has been kidnapped by my church. My life is held hostage by my church and by the bishop, who controls the mind of my wife. I have an obligation to do anything I can, short of causing harm to another to rectify that situation, and I did no harm to my wife. It is true she came with me against her will, but remember it was not her will which fought against me; it was the will of the church, the will of the bishop. I did not kidnap; I did not assault; I did not perpetrate a crime. I am the victim of a heinous crime, a crime against my very immortal soul."

Andy looked down the row at the AP reporter, who was writing furiously in his notebook. He's taking down every word, Andy thought.

After "soul," Jacob lowered his head and stayed in that position for several seconds before lifting it once more and looking at the jury with those steel-blue eyes.

"My wife did not talk with me in my car," he said slowly. "I used no force except the force of truth, and she did not talk with me. Now I hope to use the force of the law. Here, in this room, she will have to talk with me. Know this, please, ladies and gentlemen of the jury. I love my wife, and my wife loves me. Nothing, no church, no state, can break that bond."

Jacob stood still for a few more seconds, his head down, and then turned and walked slowly back to his desk. Andy felt absolute silence for the first time in his life.

When Jacob had seated himself, Judge Landis announced there would be a fifteen-minute recess. Andy remained in his seat while others around him stood, talked, left and returned. He talked to no one.

When court resumed, Kurtz called the first witness, Officer Fred Miller, one of the two officers who had arrested Jacob. Kurtz questioned him concerning the details of the arrest. Miller responded factually, telling what had happened.

When Kurtz finished, Judge Landis asked Jacob if he wished to cross-examine. Jacob said he did and walked slowly to the witness box.

Jacob began by asking Officer Miller if he had cooperated with him in every way requested. Miller said he had. Jacob then asked if there is evidence that he had harmed his wife in any way. Miller said there was no evidence of this. Jacob thanked Miller and told the judge he had no further questions.

Judge Landis excused Miller and then addressed the court: "The court is adjourned until 9:00 tomorrow morning. Again I urge all those involved with this case, and particularly the jury, to refrain from discussing anything that goes on here with anyone." He tapped his gavel.

The bailiff stood and said, "All rise."

Once the judge had left the room, people left quickly. Andy

was the last to leave. He knew he should go back to his office to work. It was only 3:00 and he could get some things done before dinner, but he knew he wouldn't do that. He also knew he didn't want to have to explain all this to Sue. He wanted to be by himself this afternoon and evening. Tomorrow would bring the rest of the witnesses, including Sarah. He wondered if she would testify. He thought she might be able to claim some sort of religious immunity or simply accept a contempt of court charge. Either way, he knew she would suffer. Whatever Jacob was up to, and he was not sure, it would not be good for Sarah. Andy considered going to Jacob and asking him to change his mind about cross-examining her, but he knew that was the only reason for the trial, the only reason for kidnapping Sarah in the first place. Jacob knew that Sarah would not talk with him in the car, but he thought she might talk under oath. He bet his future, perhaps his freedom, on that, and he would not change his mind now. Whatever tomorrow would bring had already been determined. Andy didn't sleep well that night.

⇜ **Fifteen** ⇝

Beth was standing on the steps of the courthouse when Andy arrived the next morning at 8:30. She wore a tan pantsuit, a matching scarf hanging loosely around her neck, and sunglasses in her hair.

Andy wondered why she was there. Concern? Curiosity? He wasn't sure.

"Hi," she said. "Do you mind?"

To Andy's mind Beth had an elliptical quality. Shouldn't she have said something else first, he thought.

"Mind? What do you mean?"

"That I'm here," she said, holding out her hands, gesturing to the surroundings.

"No. Of course not." Andy was not sure where to go with this? "Why should I mind?" he said. "I mean, it's okay. Anyone can come. How did you know?"

"I called Sue. Yesterday. Didn't she say anything? I knew it was starting about now, so I called. Happened to hit it right. She said it started yesterday."

When Andy asked if Sue had said anything about the trial, about how it was going, Beth replied, "It's all very peculiar."

"What? The trial?" Andy asked, again getting that elliptical feeling.

"No. Well, maybe that too. I mean it's peculiar, I suppose, that I'm here."

"How are you?" he said, giving up.

Beth said she was fine; he said he was fine too, and then added almost as an afterthought, "I suppose I'm okay."

They continued standing on the courthouse steps, Andy not looking directly at Beth but not wanting to go inside. To Andy, Beth appeared sure, poised, her usual confidence setting the tone, at least for her. The sun came out and she lowered her sunglasses. Andy squinted at the steps. She asked if he was concerned.

"Concerned?" Andy said.

"About Jacob. You must be concerned about Jacob. How did he do yesterday?"

"Do?" Andy was not sure what to say.

"Yes," Beth said. "How is he handling the trial?"

"Oh, right," he said, and then added, "You won't believe this. You know, he's his own lawyer."

"I know."

"How do you know?" Andy was at sea again.

"Sue told me."

"Oh. Did Sue tell you anything else?"

"About the trial?"

Andy nodded.

"No. She just said you were over here. I knew that, of course."

"So you came out of curiosity?" Andy asked.

"Curiosity?"

"To see the trial. To see how Jacob was going to do."

Beth looked away. The discussion was over. It had never really begun.

"Yes. Curiosity," she said.

The day was already hot. Various people, workers at the courthouse as well as spectators at the trial, were beginning to gather, some standing around talking, smoking, others going in the building, past Andy and Beth. Andy was about to suggest that they go in when he saw Sarah walking toward the steps, accompanied by her sister and the bishop. He knew they would be called today, but he assumed they would wait until later to come, perhaps this afternoon, and he thought they would enter through the rear.

"Sarah," Andy called just loud enough for her to hear him.

She stopped, said something to the bishop, and then walked over to Andy.

"Good morning, Mr. Simpson."

Andy was astonished, first that he had called to her and second that she had come over to him. She was here before him, and now he didn't know what to say to her.

"I . . . I'm glad to see you."

Sarah stood there, eyes down.

Andy continued, "I mean I hope this . . . Are you well?"

Andy wondered why he said that. He never asks anyone if they're well. It's not a phrase he would use.

"Yes, thank you," she said.

"Good." He looked around, not knowing what to say next. "Hot."

"Yes," she said, "it will be very warm today."

"Yes. Well," he mumbled. "Oh, I'm sorry. I should introduce you. To each other. Beth, this is Sarah."

Sarah raised her eyes and looked at Beth.

"I know," Beth said. "How are you? Really. How are you doing?"

Sarah relaxed, a slight smile flickered.

"I am fine," she said. "Thank you, Mrs. Simpson."

"Actually, I'm not . . . you know."

"I am sorry," Sarah said.

"No, that's okay," Beth said.

Andy wondered why she said it's okay. He also wondered why Sarah seemed more at ease at this moment with Beth than with him.

"I must go," Sarah said to Andy and walked over to the bishop and her sister. Together the three of them walked into the courthouse. Andy watched her and then said to Beth that perhaps they should also go in.

Beth said, "Andy?"

Andy turned to Beth and looked at her directly for the first time.

"What?" he said.

Beth paused and then said, "Nothing. Maybe I should go back to New York."

Andy was surprised to realize that he wanted her to stay. "No," he said, "you don't need to leave. You can stay for the trial. Today might be interesting for you. It will probably end today. Except for the jury deliberations. The verdict might come tomorrow. Can you stay over?"

Beth said she had taken two days and planned to stay at one of the motels in the area. Andy thought of suggesting that she stay at his place, in the spare bedroom, and then realized she would never do that. After all, he thought, we're not married. Instead he suggested again that they go in.

When they entered the courtroom, Andy took the same seat he had taken yesterday, the end of the last row. When he sat down, he saw that Beth had not followed him in and was sitting at the other end of the row before him. He motioned for her to join him, but she smiled and shook her head. Sarah and the bishop were sitting in the middle of the second row. They all rose as Judge Landis entered the room.

The next hour was taken up with the prosecution calling several witnesses who were at the farmer's market when the abduction took place. They all testified that Jacob had taken Sarah against her will and kept her in his car. Jacob didn't cross-examine. Finally, the prosecution called Bishop Souders, who agreed with the testimony of the other witnesses. Jacob said he would like to cross-examine the witness. He got up from his chair and stood as close to the bishop as he could. He looked him directly in the eyes and said with a strong voice, "Bishop Souders, why are you persecuting me?"

The D.A. jumped from his chair with an objection.

"Objection sustained," Judge Landis said. "Mr. Weaver, I said yesterday I would give you some leeway, but I cannot allow this line of questioning. Please restrict yourself to the charge against you."

"Yes, your honor." Jacob continued and backed off from the bishop. He's performing, Andy thought.

Jacob continued, "Bishop Souders, you said that you saw me physically force my wife into my car."

"Yes," Bishop Souders said, and Andy realized that the bishop was not intimidated.

"Would you say that I harmed my wife?" Jacob asked.

"Yes, I think you caused great emotional harm to Sarah."

"Physical harm?" Jacob asked, moving back to the bishop.

Souders relaxed into his chair and thought for a moment. Finally he said, "I cannot say that. I was not close enough, but I do think that Sarah struggled against you."

Jacob turned his back on the bishop and faced the jury.

"Bishop Souders," he said softly, "are you aware of a practice in your church called shunning?"

The bishop nodded and said he was.

Jacob pursued him. "Are you aware that I have been shunned by my church?"

"That is true, Jacob," the bishop said, "but you know that we have done that out of love, out of love for you."

Jacob turned to the bishop, and Andy noticed the veins hardening in Jacob's neck. Jacob raised his voice, "How can you say love when you have separated me from my family and caused me to endure a living hell on earth?"

By now Jacob was almost shouting. The D.A. rose out of his seat, his hands outstretched toward the judge. "Your Honor," he said, "the defense is leading the witness away from the issue."

"I'm going to overrule the objection this time," Judge Landis said.

The D.A. continued to stand for a moment and then sat down in obvious disgust.

"I'm going to let the witness answer the question," the judge explained, "because motivation is important to the case, particularly to the severity of the assault charge. Bishop Souders, please continue with your explanation of the practice of shunning, and Mr. Weaver, please do not interrupt."

"We are very concerned with Jacob's soul, your honor," Bishop Souders continued. "His soul is in mortal danger because he does not obey the teachings of his church. We wish more than anything to bring him back to the church. Shunning, or the ban, is a device which can make him realize the error of his ways and can help him return to the church. We know this causes pain, but the pain of hell is infinitely greater. As soon as Jacob shows obedience to the church, the ban will be lifted and we will welcome him back in our arms with full brotherhood."

Jacob began to speak.

"Please do not interrupt, Mr. Weaver," the judge said, the palm of his right hand toward Jacob.

Bishop Souders continued, "We believe that only by giving up the self to the church, to God, can a person attain everlasting life. There is no greater obligation on the part of the church than to guide a person toward that salvation. The ban helps us do that. I know that for many people the path to truth lies through the individual will. We believe, however, that the path to truth lies through obedience, through giving up the self. Whatever we have done to Jacob, for Jacob, we have done only through love for him. Our greatest prayer is for him to come back to his church. We pray every day for that."

Bishop Souders stopped, and Judge Landis motioned that it was Jacob's turn now.

"Bishop Souders," Jacob began, "you say that you are dividing my family out of love for me."

"No, Jacob." Bishop Souders said, pointing to Jacob. "You have divided your family by not obeying your church."

"But the ban is enforced by the church."

"That is true, Jacob."

"Could you tell the court what actions brought about the ban?"

"Your disobedience of your church."

"You mean my disobedience of you as bishop?"

"No, Jacob. The church."

"Is it not because I criticized your parents that you had me shunned?"

"No, Jacob, that is not true. My parents have no part in this."

"Is it not because I objected to your parents' receiving the sacrament? And did I not object because they had forfeited their right to the sacrament?"

Bishop Souders stood, but Judge Landis asked him to sit down. He sat and then said to Jacob in stentorian tones, "Paul said in Romans, 'Mark them which cause divisions and offenses and avoid them.' He also said, 'Withdraw yourself from every brother that walketh disorderly.'"

"Then," Jacob said, "love has nothing to do with it. You shun me because I have not obeyed you."

Andy realized that Jacob saw an opening here. He could use the issue of the individual conscience versus the power of the church and place himself in the long line of conscientious dissenters. The bishop seemed to take the bait.

"No," he said, "we shun you because you do not obey the church."

Jacob bore in, "And you, Bishop Souders, are the church."

But the bishop remained calm. "No, Jacob, I too obey the church."

Jacob lowered his head and almost whispered, "And you have gotten your revenge of me."

He's playing this for every ounce of emotion, Andy thought, but then he heard Souders say, equally softly and with apparent sincerity, "I love you, Jacob. I fear for your soul."

Jacob raised his eyes to the bishop and they looked at each other for several moments. Jacob then told the judge he had no further questions and sat down. Judge Landis adjourned the trial and asked everyone to reassemble at 1:30 that afternoon.

Andy gathered his papers and stood up to look for Beth, but she had already gone. He went back to his office and played with his papers until it was time to go back to the courthouse.

When Andy returned to the courthouse, early he thought, he waited a few minutes for Beth, hoping to see her when she returned, but she didn't. He thought she might have decided to go back to New York. When he got inside the courtroom, however, he saw Beth sitting in the same seat as before, and he also saw that Sarah and the bishop had taken their seats as well.

When court resumed, Judge Landis asked the prosecutor if he had any other witnesses to call. He said he did not. The judge then told Jacob he could proceed with witnesses, and Jacob called Andy, who had thought he was home free when the prosecutor didn't call him. He now wondered what Jacob would ask him.

Andy took his seat in the witness stand, and Jacob walked slowly to him.

"Thank you for coming here, Mr. Simpson." he said. "I know this is inconvenient for you since you also have to write the story, but I would like to ask you a few questions. How long have you known me?"

Andy said he had known Jacob since last spring, and, answering Jacob further, said he thinks of Jacob as a friend.

"Thank you, Mr. Simpson," Jacob said, "but I need to ask you further questions. Do you mind?"

Andy didn't know how to respond so he simply nodded his head. Jacob then turned to the court stenographer and told her to note assent. My God, Andy thought, either he did his homework or he has a TV hidden away somewhere in his trailer.

Jacob began his questions. "Have I ever done anything to harm another human being, so far as you know?"

"Not that I know," Andy said and then added that he had not known Jacob very long.

"That's fine," Jacob said. "You were with me when I detained Sarah in my car, were you not?"

"Yes," Andy said. "I had gone with you to the market at your invitation."

"And you called the police, did you not?"

"Yes, I did."

"Who told you to call the police?"

Andy said Jacob had.

Jacob then asked Andy if he would say that he had brought Sarah to his car and kept her there against her will. Andy said that she clearly did not want to be there. Jacob then asked if at any time he thought he would harm Sarah.

The D.A. objected, saying Jacob was asking Andy to speculate on something he could not possibly know, Jacob's real intention. The judge sustained the objection.

Jacob then asked Andy if he had harmed Sarah while they were in the car. Andy said no.

"Mr. Simpson," Jacob said, "do you know why I kept Sarah in my car?"

"Speculation again, your Honor."

Judge Landis sustained the objection. Jacob didn't miss a beat and asked Andy if he, Jacob, had told Andy why he had kept Sarah in his car and Andy said yes.

"What did I tell you?" Jacob asked.

"You said you wanted to talk with her."

"Did she talk with me while you were there?"

"No, she did not," Andy said and then added, although he wasn't sure why, "at least not that I heard."

Jacob then asked if he had told Andy when he hoped to talk with Sarah. Again, the D.A. objected to the irrelevancy of the questioning, but Judge Landis allowed Jacob to continue, "but only for a few minutes."

Andy responded. "Yes, you did tell me when you hoped to talk with Sarah. You said you expected to talk with her at the trial, this trial. You said you expected her to talk with you since she would be under oath."

Andy glanced over at Sarah, but she was looking down. Andy was excused and went back to his seat. When Judge Landis asked if Jacob had any more witnesses to call, Jacob said he would like to have Sarah Weaver take the stand. Andy was convinced that Sarah would not take the stand, but she did, slowly and deliberately, looking at no one. When she was seated, Jacob walked over to her and said hello. Sarah did not respond, did not look up.

"Sarah," Jacob said kindly, gently.

Again no response.

"Sarah, do you love me?" Jacob asked.

The D.A. jumped to his feet. "Objection. Irrelevant." He started to ask how long the court would put up with this, but Judge Landis raised his hand to stop him and then sat silently for a moment before asking both the D.A. and Jacob to approach the bench. They huddled briefly, the D.A. obviously not happy when he returned to his seat.

Judge Landis explained, "I agree that the question is highly unusual coming from a defense attorney to a witness, but Mr. Weaver is not the usual defense attorney and this is not a usual trial. I'm going to continue to allow considerable leeway here in hopes of getting at motivation. You may answer the question, Mrs. Weaver."

Sarah did not respond.

Jacob said again, "Sarah, I asked you a simple question. Do you love me?"

Sarah looked up at Jacob, directly into his eyes and said, "I love God."

"But Sarah, it is possible to love God and a mortal person. Do you love me?"

Sarah lowered her eyes and responded only with her love of God. Jacob did not press the question further. Instead he asked her if he had harmed her when he kept her in the car, continuing in a lowered voice. Sarah said no. Jacob then asked if he had ever physically harmed her. Again Sarah said no. Jacob moved away from Sarah, closer to the jury, and asked Sarah if she could describe their relationship before the ban went into effect.

Almost inaudibly she said, "We were married."

"We still are married, Sarah," Jacob said, "but could you describe the nature of our relationship? Was it a good marriage, would you say?"

For the first time Sarah deliberated her answer. "It was a good marriage." she said. "We had our home and our children and our church. We shared these things as husband and wife."

"Did you love me then?" Jacob asked, moving back to Sarah. She said yes, she did love him then.

"Do you love me now?" he asked.

Sarah returned to her previous reticence, saying only that she loved God. Jacob left that line of questioning and asked Sarah what the ban means to her. She said she must have no contact whatsoever with anyone under the ban.

"With your husband?" Jacob asked.

"Yes."

"But you are having contact now. You are talking with your husband."

Without pausing Sarah said, "I am talking with his defense attorney."

Jacob stopped, clearly not anticipating this. He did not look at Sarah again. Instead he pursued the nature of the ban.

"Sarah," he said, "are you allowed to be in the same room with me?"

"Yes."

"But not to talk with me or to touch me?"

"No."

"Are you allowed to sleep in the same bed with me?"

"Yes."

"But not to touch me?"

"No."

Andy could tell that Sarah was becoming increasingly uncomfortable. She smoothed her dress, looked quickly around the room, and then looked down again at her hands, turning them in her lap. Andy hoped that Jacob would back off now that he had made clear the seriousness of the ban, but he did not. Instead he asked Sarah if it is true that the ban is no longer in effect if it is broken. She agreed. Jacob then went into the territory Andy hoped he would avoid.

"Is it not true, Sarah," he asked, "that one time during the ban, the ban was violated?"

Sarah didn't respond. Andy shifted in his seat. He looked at Beth, who was completely focused on Sarah. Jacob looked at the jury, then at Sarah.

"Is it not true, Sarah," Jacob continued, "that one time you did touch me in our bed? That one time you came to me and offered your naked body to me and in that act the ban was broken?"

Sarah did not respond, and Andy experienced absolute silence for the second time.

Jacob was undeterred, unstoppable. Even the D.A. was quiet. "Is it not true, Sarah," Jacob said, "that Bishop Souders told you to come to me, to use your body as a bribe for me to return to the church?"

Again no response.

"Sarah," Jacob continued in the silent courtroom, "I am asking you, and you are under oath to God, did we not make love and break the ban that one night?"

Sarah looked again into Jacob's eyes, defiant, her eyes a match for his.

"No," she said.

"Sarah, you are under oath."

"We did not make love," she said.

"What do you call it then?" Jacob said. "You came to me in the middle of the night and offered up your body. What do you call it?"

"I call it rape," Sarah said quietly.

Jacob stood there, stunned, and looked at Sarah. She looked down. Finally, Jacob looked down, shuffled his feet, and looked back at Sarah.

"Sarah," he said quietly, "how are the children?"

Without getting up, the D.A. said, almost under his breath, "Your Honor, I'm sorry, but I must object."

The judge looked at Sarah and then back at Jacob and said, "I know. I'm sorry too. Sustained."

Jacob waited for a moment, looked at Sarah, and then back at the floor before slowly moving back to his desk and slumping in his seat.

"Do you wish to question the witness?" Judge Landis asked the D.A.

"No, your Honor."

"You may step down," Judge Landis said to Sarah, who went back to sit with the bishop.

Judge Landis asked if Jacob had any further witnesses. He said no. The judge then declared a fifteen-minute recess before hearing the closing arguments.

People began to mill about, some leaving the room. Sarah left quickly with the bishop and her sister; Jacob exited through another door. Andy sat there, wondering where all this would go. How can anything be salvaged from this mess, he thought. As he was trying to decide what to do for the next fifteen minutes, someone slid in beside him. It was Beth.

"My God," she said.

"I know," Andy said.

"How does she do it? How does she sit there so calm?"

"She's not calm," Andy said.

"Why do they do this to Jacob, to them? This ban thing. It's inhumane."

"No," Andy said, "you heard the bishop. They do this because they love him. They want him to return to obedience, to the church.

It's his only hope for salvation. They're serious about that. I believe them."

Beth asked him if he means he believes the doctrine. Andy said no, of course not, but he added that it doesn't matter what he believes; it's what they believe that's important. Beth then asked him if he believes that Sarah does love Jacob. He said he was sure she does, a difficult admission for him. He sensed that Beth understood the difficulty. He then asked Beth if she believes that Sarah really did come to Jacob in the middle of the night. Without hesitation Beth said she thought that was possible, that she probably did. Andy, not wanting to know, asked why.

"She's a human being." Beth said. "She has needs. Sex is pretty powerful."

"I suppose so," Andy said, knowing she was right.

Beth continued, "I can't even begin to imagine what pressure that woman is under. Everyone wants her to be something else. What is she? What is she under all of this, under the clothing, under the church, under the ban, under the, what, I don't know, under the whole perverse culture?"

"Who's to say it's perverse?" Andy said. "It's no more perverse than the games people play in New York or Carlisle. It's just their way of playing their games. Do you think we didn't play games?"

Beth sat back in the bench, releasing some of the pressure, relieved to be talking about them.

"We did. I know," she said, and then she added, "But you know, Andy . . ."

Andy looked at her.

". . . we're not playing games now," she said.

The people began to return to their places and Beth went back to her end of the row. Andy wondered why she didn't stay with him. He would have liked to ask her what she meant by that. But it was too late. They stood as Judge Landis returned to the bench. He asked the D.A. if he was ready with his summation. He said he was and approached the jury.

"Ladies and gentlemen," he began, "you have been witness to a most unusual situation. You have seen a family torn apart by good intentions on all sides. There is no villain in this tragedy, just the tragedy itself. My heart, as yours, goes out to Jacob and to Sarah, to the other members of their family, and to the members of their church. It is not our job to understand, only to have sympathy. We would be less than human if we did not feel for Jacob and for what he has endured. But I must remind you, as jurors, as representatives of this county, that you have been asked to decide the guilt or innocence of Jacob Weaver regarding a specific crime which the state has shown was committed, committed with forethought and with deliberation. The facts are indisputable. During one afternoon last summer, Jacob Weaver took with force and against her will, Sarah Weaver, to his car parked across the road from Souders Market, and kept her there for two hours until the police came to free her. That is kidnapping, pure and simple, and the state contends that the act also constitutes simple assault due to the force involved. You must put aside not only your concern for the people involved here, but you must also put aside the reasons for Jacob Weaver's actions. The simple fact is that Jacob Weaver did kidnap Sarah Weaver, and on the basis of that and that alone, you must find the defendant guilty as charged."

The D.A. sat down. Judge Landis then told Jacob he could address the jury. Jacob sat there.

"Mr. Weaver," the judge said.

Jacob looked up at the judge and then over at the jury. He slowly stood and walked to the jury box.

"Ladies and gentlemen," he began, "I did not kidnap my wife. I love her, and, as you must know, she loves me. I simply wanted to talk with her, which is why I took her to my car. We just sat there. She did not say anything. You have heard here today the total conversation I have had with my wife since the ban began. I suppose you could find me guilty, but I do not think I am guilty of anything except wanting my wife and my family returned to me. Is that a crime? I want to be able to watch my children grow into adults, to be with them as they discover their way into adulthood. Is that a crime? Perhaps so. I do not know anymore. If you believe any of this is a crime, then find me guilty. If you believe I kidnapped my wife, then you must find me guilty."

Jacob turned away, and Andy thought he was finished, but once again he realized he had underestimated Jacob, who turned back to the jury and began again, seeming to gain energy as he went on.

"But let me say what is in my heart, ladies and gentlemen. The real crime here is not what I have done. It is what has been done to me. The church is on trial here. Paul says, 'What God has joined, let no man put asunder.' I believe that, ladies and gentlemen. The church has sundered this marriage which was created in the eyes of God. That is not just a crime, it is a sin against God. Such people do not need to concern themselves with my soul. You have seen how they can turn a wife against her husband. You have heard the word 'rape' used by my wife against me. That is the church speaking, not my wife. I would say to you, ladies and gentlemen, that it is not I who have raped. It is the church which has raped me. They have raped me of my family, and in doing so they have created a living hell on earth for me. That is where I live today, ladies and gentlemen. Do you think that I care whether or not you find me innocent or guilty? After what I have endured, do you think I care what this court decides? But, ladies and gentlemen, you do have a duty to perform, and I respect that. Look into my eyes and then look into your hearts. Vote on what you decide there. Thank you."

Jacob looked at the jury one last time and then returned to his desk and sat down. Andy thought he had done well. A bit emotional, more theatrical than he would have liked, but Andy knew that that said more about him than about Jacob.

Judge Landis began with his charge to the jury, "Ladies and gentlemen, it's been a long day, and you are tired. I would ask, however, that you return to the jury room and try to arrive at a decision this afternoon. You have heard a great deal today, much of it possibly upsetting to you. As jurors, however, you must decide the guilt or innocence of Jacob Weaver solely on the basis of the law and the evidence. Kidnapping is forceful abduction and retention of another individual against that person's will. You must decide whether or not that happened. The law is simple in this regard. In your opinion, was the evidence sufficient to find the defendant guilty of that crime? Do not be distracted. Deliberate on the facts. If you have questions or need additional information, ask the bailiff and we'll accommodate you."

The people stood as the jury left the courtroom and the judge returned to his chambers.

Andy made his way to the courtroom lobby where he saw Beth waiting. He also saw Sarah, her sister, and the bishop leaving the building. Beth walked over to him.

"Andy," Beth said, "do you think Jacob would ever like to run for public office?"

"He's pretty persuasive, isn't he?"

"Well," Beth said, "he's pretty dramatic anyway, especially with his black clothing and those eyes."

Andy asked Beth what she thought the verdict will be.

"I think they'll find him guilty," she said. "He took her. He even admitted that. I don't see any other verdict."

Andy asked if she felt sorry for him, pointing out, fairly enough he thought, that Jacob suffered too.

"No, I feel sorry for Sarah," she said. "He's caused her just as much pain as the church has."

"But he's in pain too," Andy said.

"Yes," Beth said, "but at least he can make some decisions for himself. He's a man in this macho society, just like the bishop. She just does what everyone tells her to do, and when they say different things, she's caught in the middle."

Andy offered to go down the street to get some coffee at a restaurant, but Beth insisted that she go for it.

"It's your story," she said. "You don't want to miss the verdict if it comes quickly. You should stay here."

When she returned with the coffee, Andy told her the jury had not decided immediately so the judge told them to go home for the night and to report back the next morning at 9:30. He asked her if she planned on coming back tomorrow.

"I don't know," she said. "I should get back to work. We'll see. Probably. I've come this far. I want to see how it all comes out. Maybe I'll give it one more day."

"Did you find a place last night?" he asked.

"Yes, just outside of town."

He asked her if it is comfortable. She nodded. He asked if she would like to have dinner with him.

"I don't think that's such a good idea, Andy."

"I suppose not," he said.

⋖ **Sixteen** ⋗

Andy had never seen anything like that before. He knew that Jacob was willing to sacrifice everything, including his own freedom, for Sarah, but he had not realized before just how much Sarah was willing to sacrifice for Jacob. As he saw it, she was exchanging her own happiness for the hope of saving Jacob's soul. Of course, Andy knew that no such thing as a soul exists, which, to his eyes, makes the whole thing slightly absurd, even absurdly tragic, and he also knew that Sarah was sacrificing her love on the altar of an illusion and would probably live out the rest of her life under that misconception. But Andy was also able to put himself in Sarah's position, at least enough to understand why she acted and reacted as she did. Given her premise that God exists and that a person can come to God only through obedience to God as understood through the church, her church, she must do all she can do to save the soul and therefore the immortal life of the man she loves, even if it means never again being with that man. Andy was beginning to understand that kind of love, and he was also beginning to understand the failure of his own marriage, a marriage that simply folded through lack of attention. Sarah could make this sacrifice, while he simply said, okay, let's separate. That solves that problem. Was he willing to sacrifice anything for her? Again, he had not even considered sacrifice . . . giving . . . offering. Did he even know what love was then? No, he was sure he had not known. Did he know what love is now? He wasn't sure, but he thought he might be beginning to understand.

Andy didn't sleep well that night, thinking of the trial and the verdict. The jury had to find Jacob guilty. There was no question of that. The question was what sentence would the judge impose. The D.A. would push for a prison sentence. Would the judge agree? Perhaps. So as the dawn began to filter through his room, Andy got up, took his time shaving, showering, and dressing, and went out for something to eat, to Harry's Restaurant, of course. He sat there at the counter, stirring his coffee and thinking of Sarah, as he had done every day for the past several months. Did he love Sarah? Maybe, but where could that lead? Did he love her enough not to tell her? He didn't know.

Andy walked back to his office, down Main Street, watching the shops getting ready for the day. He had left word at the courthouse the day before to be called when the jury had made its decision. It was supposed to resume deliberations at 9:30; it was now 9:15, so he figured he had at least several hours before he would be called. Andy went to his office and began to review his notes and to work on the story, but shortly before 10:00 the call came. He had five minutes to get to the courthouse. Andy knew that a quick verdict usually means trouble for the defendant.

He hurried into the courtroom and saw Jacob sitting at the defense table, the D.A., Sarah with the bishop and her sister, and Beth sitting this time at the end of the row. He walked back the row and sat next to Beth.

"Do you mind?" he asked her.

"Oh. Yes, sure. I mean no, it's okay."

Before he could say anything else, the bailiff had everyone rise as Judge Landis entered from his chamber. After everyone sat down, Judge Landis asked Jacob to rise and then asked the jury foreman if they had reached a decision. The foreman, a middle-aged man with graying hair, short and heavy, said they had. The bailiff took the note from the foreman and returned to his position at the judge's right.

"What is the jury's decision?" the judge asked.

The bailiff read from the paper: "In the case of the *Commonwealth v. Jacob Weaver*, we find the defendant, Jacob Weaver, not guilty of both charges."

Beth grabbed Andy's hand.

"My God. How?" she said.

Suddenly the room was filled with talking. The judge banged his gavel and asked for quiet.

"The court is still in session. Please remain seated and quiet," he said loudly. When quiet returned, Judge Landis turned to the jury.

"Ladies and gentlemen. I want to thank you for your service to this county and for your time and effort. Jury duty is never pleasant, but it is essential to the way our country works. It's not a perfect system, but I believe it's the best we have. Usually, when the evidence is all laid out before us, we agree on the outcome. Occasionally, however, we disagree. I must say, however, in this case I am completely baffled by your verdict. If ever the evidence pointed conclusively to a guilty verdict, this has to be the one. Even the defendant admitted that he had taken his wife against her will and kept her for an extended period of time, also against her will. The charge of aggravated assault might be questionable, but the charge of abduction was never in question. I am surprised by your verdict, but it is your verdict, and it will stand. Mr. Weaver, you are free to go. The court is adjourned."

Again, the bailiff asked everyone to rise, and Judge Landis returned to his chambers. The D.A. was clearly upset, although Andy didn't know if he were more upset over the verdict or the effect it would have on his political career. He jammed his papers into his briefcase and left quickly. Bishop Souders went over to Jacob and said something, but Jacob did not reply or even look at him. The bishop then returned to Sarah and her sister, and all three of them left the courtroom. Andy watched.

"Andy." It was Beth. Andy turned to her.

"Oh," he said, "Beth. Look, can you wait here for just a minute? I have to go talk with Jacob."

She nodded.

By then several reporters from area newspapers and the AP reporter were already surrounding Jacob. Andy hurried over.

One of the reporters asked Jacob's reaction to the verdict.

"The verdict does not interest me," he said.

Another reporter asked if he would persist in his efforts to get his wife back.

"I do not know," Jacob said. "I do not know what else to do."

A third reporter asked what it feels like to be a free man.

Jacob jumped at this question. He turned to the reporter and said, "Free? Do you call this free?" Jacob was waving his right arm around the room. "Do you think I care about being free from walls and bars when my life is still kept in prison by the church? No wall is as rigid as a belief. No warden is as strong as the bishop. There is no greater prison than being in a hell on earth, and that is what I am in."

Andy saw the reporters writing furiously. Great quotes, he thought.

Finally, one of the reporters looked up and asked him what he was going to do now.

"Now?" Jacob said. "Now? What can I do?" His arms dropped to his side. "I am going back to my farm. It is soon time to dig up my potatoes. I can only grow potatoes. I cannot grow my family."

Andy knew that would be the lead in every paper carrying the story. Potatoes. He also knew that across the county, and probably beyond, there would be a swell of sympathy for Jacob. And, finally, he knew that none of this would budge the bishop and Sarah. Jacob had lost.

Jacob pushed his way through the courtroom, toward the exit.

Andy called Jacob's name, following him out to the hallway.

Jacob stopped but didn't turn around. Andy asked him what he planned to do now. Jacob didn't answer. Again, Andy asked for his plans. Again no response.

"Can I help?" Andy asked "Can I come with you? Are you going back to your farm?"

Jacob said he was going back to his farm. He looked at Andy and then at the other journalists beginning to come over to him.

"Maybe later," he said to Andy, "maybe you can come later," and he walked into the lobby and out of the building.

Andy stood there as the hallway emptied. It's over, he thought, and he wasn't sure how to feel. Nothing was resolved.

"Andy." Beth was standing beside him.

"Andy," she said again, "are you okay?"

He realized that Beth was beside him. He looked at her, and she asked him what he was going to do now.

"Now." he said. "I guess I better get back to my office. I have my own potatoes to dig up." He moved toward the door.

"I'm leaving," Beth said. "My car is just outside. I'm packed. I guess this is goodbye."

"Do you have to leave now?"

She nodded.

Andy suddenly realized what was happening. "Beth," he said, "I really need someone to talk to. Could you do this for me? Just stay for a bit while we get some coffee?"

"I'm sorry, Andy," she said. "I told my boss I would leave as soon as the verdict came in. I can be back in Manhattan by early afternoon. Look, you have some thinking to do here. If you still want to talk, give me a call in a week or two, or come up to see me. We can talk then."

Andy agreed.

"Andy," Beth said.

"What?"

"That's the first time you ever asked to talk with me."

"Beth."

"What?"

"It's the first time I ever asked to talk with anyone."

Andy went back to his office and finished the story. When he was done, he sat in his office and looked out on Main Street, not quite sure what to do next. He wanted to see Sarah, but didn't know how or even if it was a good idea. He wanted to see Jacob, but Jacob had not wanted to see him. And now Beth was on her way back to New York.

Andy finished putting the paper together and spent Friday and Saturday mostly sitting on his porch, reading and thinking about the accounts of the trial and of what all this meant. On one hand, Jacob was the victim of a heartless institution, the monolithic Reformed Mennonite autocracy. On the other hand, Sarah was a pawn, an innocent victim caught in the middle of this archetypal struggle between the little guy and a bureaucracy bent on protecting itself at any cost. Andy knew the split was not that simple, but he also knew he didn't know exactly what to think of all this. In his own article he had tried to be fair, to represent the complexity of the situation in a way the ordinary reader could understand. His was the only story that didn't include potatoes in the lead. But he also knew that he too had missed the point because he didn't know what the point was. What could be the point when everyone was hurt, when everyone was a victim?

By Sunday afternoon Andy knew he had to go see Jacob. Somehow he had to begin to understand why Jacob did this and who Jacob really was and what he thought of him and why. He thought if he could understand Jacob better, he might be able to begin to understand himself, but he also knew he was further away from understanding Jacob now than he had been when Jacob had first entered his office earlier in the year. Perhaps, he thought, he was also further away from understanding himself. He hoped not. Regardless of the futility, however, Andy had to see Jacob.

And so Andy drove down Route 15 one more time late Sunday

afternoon, past the ageless mountains, past TMI, beyond those mountains, and turned onto the road leading to Jacob and Sarah's farm. The weather was still hot, unusually so for late September. When Andy pulled into the front yard, he saw Jacob sitting on the porch of his trailer, reading. Andy got out of his car and saw that Jacob was ignoring him. As he walked over to the porch, he realized that Jacob was reading his bible. He looked at Jacob and then at the bible. "Ephesians?" he asked.

Jacob gave the faintest trace of a smile.

"Is that a welcome?" Andy asked.

Jacob said he was always welcome. Andy sat on the edge of the porch, not knowing exactly what to say next, so he asked Jacob if he had seen the newspapers. He said he had not.

"Jacob," Andy said, "I want to talk with you, as a friend. I'm not here to help you. I'm here to have you help me. I'm confused by a lot of things. Can we go for a walk?"

Andy and Jacob walked out behind the trailer, back along the rows of potatoes, and stopped under a tree. Jacob had his bible with him. They talked, looking at the potatoes and not at each other.

"They look like they're about ready," Andy said, pointing to the potatoes, now covering most of the ground, hiding the mounds.

"Yes," he said, "but it is Sunday."

Andy knew what he meant.

They said little after that, until, finally, Andy asked if Sarah was at home.

Jacob said he thought she and the children were with her sister. Andy asked if he thought she would return to the house.

"Yes," he said, "she will be back there. It is where she belongs. She knows that."

They continued to walk, around the rear of the property, along a stream lined on the near side with trees that separated Jacob's property from the neighboring farm. They went as far as they could, to the end of Jacob's property, to where they could see the mountains again, and stopped before beginning their return. Andy leaned against the fence, while Jacob stood erect, staring out at the mountains in the distance as Andy talked with him.

"You might have to give in if you're going to get her back," Andy said.

"I will not give in," he said. "I am right. I am on God's side." He held up the bible.

Andy asked about Sarah, if Jacob thought she was wrong. Jacob did not hesitate. "Yes," he said, firmly.

Andy decided to go in another direction. He turned to Jacob and leaned his back against the fence. "If you love her as you say you do," he said, "shouldn't you put her happiness before yours? Shouldn't you be asking what she wants, what she needs? Shouldn't you be asking what you can do to make her happy?"

Jacob's jaw set even harder, and his eyes flashed. "She can be happy only if she comes back to me and restores our family. Our family is sacred." There was no doubt in his voice.

Andy, however, for the first time, was not intimidated. "And you are the head of it?" he asked.

Jacob said yes, that it had to be that way. Paul again.

"This must all be very embarrassing for you," Andy said, and then, again not intimidated, asked, "Do you see this as a failure, as your failure?"

Jacob turned to Andy and fixed his eyes on him.

"You do not understand," he said. "My wife left me because I am strong. Your wife left you because you are not strong."

It was the first time Jacob had referred to Beth, or even to any aspect of Andy's personal life. He was stunned.

Jacob turned back to the mountains, looking at them in the distance, and said, "I am sorry. I should not have said that. I just want you to see why you cannot understand why I must do what I am doing."

Andy took a few steps from Jacob and then turned and came back. He looked directly at Jacob, who continued to look in the distance. Andy was angry.

"What does strength have to do with it, Jacob?" Andy said, "If you love her, what does strength have to do with it? Are you sure you are doing this because of the Bible, or are you using the Bible as a crutch for your own weakness? Remember that the meek will inherit the earth, and maybe that inheritance includes Sarah too."

Andy knew he should not have said that. In a battle of the Bible, Jacob would destroy him. He was surprised that Jacob did not strike back.

"Why do you say I am weak?" Jacob asked.

"What?"

"Weak. Why do you say I am weak?"

"I don't know. I don't think I said that exactly. You're probably the strongest person I know."

Jacob said nothing. Andy thought again of the mountains over toward the Susquehanna. Millions of years ago they had been as high as the Rockies today, but over the millennia they were worn down by erosion. He remembered again his grandfather telling him that fact as they stood watching those same mountains from the other side. Back then he could not understand how something that solid, that stable, that fixed, could be worn down like that. It just made no sense to him. It still made no sense, although he now understood that it could happen, the wearing down part at least. He turned back to Jacob.

"Maybe you need to see Sarah differently."

"Differently?"

"Yes. Maybe you need to see her as a woman and not as a possession."

As soon as Andy said that, he realized the hypocrisy. Who was he to lecture anyone on sensitivity? He had never seen Beth as a possession, he thought, and then he realized that he had never seen Beth as anything. He had never really seen Beth. But that was his problem. Maybe, he thought, he could help Jacob even if he could not help himself.

"Possession," Jacob said. "I do not see Sarah as a possession. I see her as a wife."

"A wife who must obey you?"

"Yes. The Bible says she must obey me."

"Are you sure it's not Jacob who says that?"

"I say it because the Bible says it."

"But what can you give Sarah?"

"I give her a home, a family. I can protect her."

"And love?"

"Yes, I can give her love. I have told everyone, even in court."

"But have you told her?"

"Yes, of course. You heard me tell her that. Everyone did."

"But did you ever tell her that when you were alone with her? Did you ever see her as a woman? Did you ever put her first? Did you ever try to understand what her needs are, what you could do for her, for her needs? Did you even try to understand that she has needs?"

Jacob didn't answer. He seemed not to comprehend. And then Andy said, under his breath, "Neither did I."

They walked back to the trailer in silence, around the other side of the farm, along a row of elm trees, capturing the shade on this hot late September afternoon.

When they had returned to the trailer, Jacob asked Andy if he would like to sit for a while. Andy said no, that he had to get back to town, even though he did not. He dreaded the thought of spending Sunday evening alone in his house. They stood beside Andy's car, neither saying anything.

As Andy began to get in his car, Jacob said, "Thank you, Mr. Simpson. You have helped me and I appreciate it."

"What do you mean, helped?" Andy asked. "I'm afraid I've been of no help at all. I don't think you understood anything I've said."

Jacob insisted that Andy had helped because he had gotten his story in the newspaper. So that's what Jacob was really after. Only that. Andy understood. When he asked Jacob when all this would end, he was stunned to hear Jacob's answer. "When Sarah comes back to me," he said. Andy was sure she wouldn't, but he said nothing. He offered Jacob his hand. They shook.

Andy drove back to town, and when he pulled in behind his house, he saw Sue sitting at his picnic table. She said she just happened to be in the neighborhood. The usual chitchat: You been waiting long? Just a few minutes. How've you been? Fine. Andy knew Sue was worried about him. She knew of his concern for Jacob and of his special concern for Sarah, but, as usual, he didn't want to talk about it. He would rather that it all just go away, that Sue would leave. He wondered if she knew that's what he wanted, but she gave no indication of leaving. He sat down across from Sue. She asked how Jacob was doing.

Who knows?" Andy said. "He seems to like martyrdom. I can't figure him out. Would you like a beer or something?"

"No, thanks."

"I tried to get him to open up, to tell me what he really feels, but it's difficult for some people to do that."

"Tell me about it," Sue said.

Andy knew what she meant, but he also realized she was as concerned for him as he was for Jacob. Friendship, Andy thought. It does get complicated. Sue asked about Sarah, and Andy thought of the dreary future she was facing. For probably the rest of her life she'll be caught between an obsessive husband and an unforgiving church. Some choice. And what happens when the kids are grown? Will she really be alone? Will Jacob be there, somewhere, lurking in the background, reminding her constantly of her pain, embarrassing her with his publicity stunts? Will her church make up for all that? Some future, he thought.

"Andy," Sue said.

"What?" Andy came out of his thoughts but did not look at Sue.

"There's nothing you can do," Sue said.

"I know, and that's what really hurts. She's trapped."

But Andy wondered if she was really trapped. Maybe this is

what she wants, at least enough to put up with all the pain, with the loss of love, and he wondered if he was talking about Jacob or himself. What had he done to Beth? What had he been doing to Sarah? What had he been doing by doing nothing?

"I don't know, Sue," he said. "I don't know anything anymore."

"Some people say that's the beginning of wisdom."

"Some people," Andy said, " have never met Jacob and Sarah."

Sue asked Andy about his future, something he had not thought about before, so he told her he would be in the office the next day, knowing that she didn't mean that. He knew that whatever happened, his future did not include Sarah, and that was too painful to talk about.

"You'll get over it," Sue said.

"I know," Andy said, and he was sure he would.

"And you'll be different," she said.

Andy realized that's what he hoped for, perhaps that's all he could hope for. It didn't solve any problems now, but at least it gave him a kind of a future.

Sue watched him, not saying anything, just sitting at the table. His mind was blank.

Finally, Sue stood and made motions to leave, gathering her keys from the table, looking around. She looked at Andy again, until he noticed her standing and looked up at her.

"Are you going to be okay?" Sue asked.

Andy came back from his thoughts and took a deep breath.

"Yeah, thanks for coming by," he said.

Sue said something about it being time to butt out, reached down, and squeezed his arm.

"See you in the morning," she said.

"Yeah," he said.

Later that night Andy lay in bed, unable to sleep. It was a mistake to come back, he said to himself. I should have stayed in New York. At least there I wouldn't have known anyone.

Seventeen

Several weeks went by as Andy resumed his routine with the newspaper. The comfortable normalcy of the small town returned, and Andy began to feel better or at least to feel that there might be some future for him there. He stopped going to Souders Market, instead buying what he needed at the supermarket on the edge of town. Jacob had not stopped by since before the trial, and Andy doubted that he would ever see him again. It seemed like a new beginning, of sorts, perhaps.

And then one Thursday afternoon Andy told Sue he would not be in the next day. He said he had to make a trip to New York.

"Business?" she asked.

"Maybe," he said.

"Not mine though."

Andy just smiled.

He had called Beth the night before. He was not sure why, and she seemed even more confused. He asked if he could come up to see her, reminding her of her earlier offer. He wanted to talk. About what, she asked. He didn't know. Sure, she said.

And so he had plans to meet her for lunch at Ama's, a Mexican restaurant on 50th Street. It's probably another of my mistakes, he thought, but what's one more?

Andy decided to drive to Lancaster, where he could get a train to Philadelphia and then New York. He knew it would be cheaper to drive directly to the City, even if he had to pay Manhattan's extravagant parking costs, but the train took him through eastern Lancaster County, which would allow him to look once more at the Pennsylvania Dutch country he had not seen since he and Beth were there together more than a year before. It's been a tough year, he thought. Shortly after the train had left the Lancaster station, Andy watched the neat farms floating by and saw a buggy or two along the roads. He thought again of the dead Amish woman, and that image returned him to thoughts of his life with Beth near the end of their marriage. They had had nothing to say to each other then. He wondered what they might say to each other now. He wished he had driven to New York. He wished he had decided not to go to New York.

Andy walked out of Penn Station into the confusion of the city, lunch-time crowds pushing him, horns, people shouting. He had never gotten used to the humanity of it all. Since he had plenty of time, he decided to walk up Seventh Avenue to Times Square, and then over 42nd to Fifth, and up Fifth to 50th. He knew the restaurant was just around the corner. So many people and no one seemed to know anyone else. He decided this was another planet and he was an alien.

Even with the walk, he arrived at Ama's before Beth, so he sat at the bar and ordered a beer, a Dos Equis. As he sipped his beer, his doubts returned. Bad idea, he thought, but it was too late now. He at least had to wait until Beth arrived. He could then quickly excuse himself, saying his appointment was moved up or he wasn't feeling well or something. Over his thoughts he could hear the sharp New York accent, clipping off the words, a jumble of sounds all somehow working. People were understanding each other. A miracle, he thought. How do they do it?

He felt a tap on his shoulder and turned suddenly. It was Beth.

"Sorry. Am I late?" she said.

"No," he said. "It's just that the train got me here early. I walked up. It was a good walk. I think I even miss the City a little bit."

"Oh?" she said.

They found a table and sat down.

Small talk: How do you like your new place? Fine. How's Sue? Good. Keeping busy? Yeah, I don't know where the time goes. The newspaper doing well? The owners seem pleased. Lots of ads? Yeah. Sue, huh? Frankly I would be dead without her. A pause and then, "Beth?"

Beth looked at him.

"Do you have any idea why I'm here?" he said.

Beth hesitated, looked down, played with her fork, and then looked up again.

"I don't, Andy," she said. "Why are you here?"

He didn't know. He was hoping for an answer. He knew he wanted to talk with Beth, but he didn't know why. He didn't know what to talk about. It all sounded familiar. He thought of all the missed opportunities, the times when he simply turned away. Finally, Beth said his name, and he came back from his thoughts. He looked at her, waiting for her to say more.

"Look, Andy," she said, "there's something you should know. I'm not going to be here forever. In fact —"

Andy interrupted. "Not yet," he said. "Let's just talk for a while. You promised."

She nodded and took a drink of water.

Silence. Finally, Beth said, "Andy, even you can do better than this. What is it? The Jacob and Sarah thing? Is that what's bothering you? Is that why you came all this way to talk with me?"

"I don't know," Andy said. "I feel pretty good, actually. I think I'm beginning to understand Jacob now." He paused, folded and refolded his napkin, leaned back in his chair, and added, "The only problem is that I'm beginning to see I'm much more like him than I care to admit."

Beth looked at him, but Andy didn't see the small surprise on her face. She asked him if he was also beginning to understand Sarah, what she's been through, and why. Andy cleared his throat and sipped his beer. He said, no, he couldn't put himself in her place; he could not understand. He could only accept her decision.

"Her decision?" Beth asked, "About Jacob or about you?"

Andy protested that he was talking about her decision to remain separate from Jacob, that he understood why he had to stay away from her. And then, changing his approach, he asked Beth if she thought it was possible to love two people at the same time. Beth didn't hesitate. She said no, that it's unfair to one, maybe both. Andy agreed with her, but he knew that until that moment he had thought—hoped—it was possible.

Andy thought it might be time to be going, but he didn't know how to end it.

"How are you doing?" he asked.

Beth looked at him, again surprised. "Why do you ask?"

Andy was hurt. "It matters," he said.

"Ironic, huh?"

Andy agreed. There's more than enough irony to go around, he thought.

Beth changed the subject and asked him if he still thinks of his grandfather. Andy asked where that came from.

"You used to talk about him," she said. "I've been thinking of my grandfather lately."

"You never talked about him," Andy said.

"You never asked. He's buried in Queens. At least I think he is."

"You think? Don't you know?"

"I heard they were moving the cemetery. Making room for a shopping center. Maybe they did. That's why I was thinking of him. I was wondering where he might be."

"I visited my grandfather last spring." Andy said. "His grave, I mean. On a hill overlooking Sunbury and the Susquehanna. I think maybe that's why Sarah began to mean something to me then. I missed him. I had forgotten what that is."

"What?"

"To miss someone you care about. Love, I suppose."

"Now you know?"

"I think so," he said.

They sat for a while, not looking at each other. Finally, Andy said, "Beth, I can't believe we never talked like this. This is —"

"Careful, Andy. Remember you're on the rebound."

"Rebound?"

"From Sarah. And now you find your ex-wife interesting. This is too weird."

Andy laughed and agreed.

More small talk. They both seemed to enjoy talking, barely touching their food. And then Andy heard someone, a man, say Beth's name. It was a voice he had not heard before.

"Oh, hi," Beth said, a different tone to her voice. She smiled and moved over on the bench. The man sat beside her, close to her. Andy said nothing.

"Oh, I'm sorry," Beth said, "this is Andy Simpson. Andy, this is Mel Friedman."

Mel began to offer his hand. Andy hesitated, and Mel withdrew his hand midair.

Mel was older, mid-50s Andy guessed, with a short beard—mostly white. He was tall, a bit overweight, but not much for his age. He moved easily, taking Beth's hand.

Beth began: "Andy, Mel is —"

"I know," he said, "I know." He looked at Mel and then away. He wondered why Mel was here, invading his time, invading his good-bye.

"Good to meet you," Mel said.

"Yeah," Andy said.

Mel looked at the two of them. "Look," he said, turning to looking at Beth, "if this is awkward, I can leave."

"No, it's fine," Andy said, with calm forced into his voice. "Beth and I," he paused, thinking what that really meant, "were just talking. Nothing serious."

After another awkward pause, he said, "I was just in the City and we decided to have lunch." He added, "Look, I was just leaving."

"No need," Mel said.

Andy thought that Beth must have asked Mel to stop by at this time in case things were going badly. Andy looked at Beth; Beth half smiled back, embarrassed Andy thought.

Mel turned from Andy and asked Beth how her morning had gone. It was a harmless question, but Andy sensed Mel's sincerity. Beth said it went well, obviously pleased to be asked. It was clear they understood what it was that was good about the morning and didn't need to say more. As usual, Andy was a spectator to the events surrounding him, and also as usual, he was confused by them. "I really should go," he said.

"No," Mel said. "Don't rush off just because I'm here. Why don't I leave? I'm on my way back to my office."

"Neither one has to leave," Beth said, "unless you really want to." She looked back and forth from Andy to Mel.

They sat there, neither one knowing exactly what to say, how to begin.

Finally, Mel said, "Beth told me about the trial. I can't imagine what that must have been like. Those poor people. How are they?"

"I don't know," Andy said. "I haven't seen them since just after the trial. But I think they'll be okay. They're both strong people."

Mel complimented him on the story. Andy thanked him and realized Beth must have gotten a copy of his story somewhere and shared it. He looked at her but said nothing. She smiled and shrugged her shoulders. He smiled back and relaxed a bit.

"Beth said you cared about them," Mel said. "It must have been tough to be objective. I really admire how you pulled that off. I couldn't have done it, I know that."

Andy said nothing.

"Oh, Beth," Mel said and turned to her. "I almost forgot to tell you. I looked at that dress and I think you should get it. It's perfect."

Andy didn't know that Beth cared much about her clothes and was surprised that Mel did.

"Thanks," she said, and glanced nervously at Andy. "I think I will. I need something for the convention next weekend."

"I was thinking," he said. "I can come out to the airport with you."

"You don't have to do that," Beth said.

"No. No problem. I switched a couple of meetings. The staff seemed relieved to have me out of the office for a few hours." He laughed. Beth smiled.

Beth and Mel talked of other trivial matters, a movie they hoped to see, a new exhibit at the Guggenheim, Beth trying to involve Andy in the conversation, unsuccessfully. As Andy sat there watching this couple completely at ease with each other, saying things, asking questions when it was already clear they knew what the responses would be, but still needing those responses, that connection, he felt himself receding further and further from them. Or perhaps they were simply sealing off the rest of the world, including himself, from their own small, intimate world, a world of two, which they had created by the simple fact that they were together. They didn't seem to intend this, but it happened, and Andy was fascinated to watch it. He realized it was possible.

Finally, Beth looked at Andy and apologized for ignoring him.

"No, that's fine," Andy said. "I'm just pleased things are going well for you. For both of you."

Beth said she had to get back to the office, and Mel said he would walk along. They offered to walk Andy part way to the train terminal, but he said no, he would just sit there for a while and finish his coffee. He had a bit of time until he had to be at the station. He watched them leave, Mel opening the door for Beth, who gave one small wave to Andy and then was gone. So that's it, he thought, that's how it's done. Nothing could be simpler.

Andy asked the waitress for a refill, which he paid for. He thought about this couple he had just met and decided he liked them, perhaps because they liked each other. He realized there were many things he still didn't know, but he also realized the list was getting smaller. He sat there for a while, alone at the table, stirring his coffee, sipping at it, watching the people, satisfied to be there, at least at that moment, in that place.

The return to Lancaster was uneventful, one more look, brief, at the Amish country, one more thought, brief, of Beth walking back to the motel, almost on him before he even realized who this woman was. He thought he might drive along Route 340 to Intercourse and take the back road to the turnpike and then across to Carlisle, but it was already getting dark. No point to that, he thought. Too late.

The next morning Andy didn't go directly to his office. Instead he walked slowly down Main Street and stopped at Harry's for a cup of coffee, lingering too long, getting a refill, then another, chatting with a few of the regulars about the weather, about the Senators now that their season was over. What a difference, he thought. When the subject of the trial came up, as it always did, he excused himself and walked back to his house to get his car, telling himself that he should drive to the office since he might have to use the car later in the day. He didn't stop at the office, however; instead he drove past it and out onto Route 15. He wanted to see Sarah one last time, just as he had wanted to see Beth one last time, but he also knew she would not yet be at the market, so he drove down Route 15, past the market, and soon found himself pulling into the parking lot of Kreider's Church. He sat there, thinking he could wait until Sarah was likely to be at the market. It was quiet; he lowered his window and heard the birds in the trees, crows, nothing unpleasant. Occasionally a car went by. This is wrong, he thought. It would only make matters worse, at least for Sarah, probably for himself. He looked at the church, and thoughts came back to him. He got out of the car and walked over to the entrance. He tried the door. It was unlocked, as always, so he walked in, quietly, not knowing why but not wanting to disturb anyone who might be there. He stood in the back and looked down the aisle, the same aisle that Jacob had walked down, denouncing the bishop and the church members, embarrassing Sarah. He walked toward the front, toward the pew where Sarah had buried her head in his shoulder, where he had kissed her, where she had kissed him, powerfully. And then, as he neared the front of the church, near the pew where he and Sarah had sat, he noticed a figure, a female with a white bonnet, sitting at the end of the pew. He thought at first it might be Sarah and could not decide whether to say something. At that moment the woman turned to Andy. It was not Sarah. Andy began to apologize, stuttering, stumbling, embarrassed, but the woman smiled and said it was fine. He can be here if he wishes. The door is open to all God's children. Andy tried to explain that he was simply looking for a place to rest, that he had some time to kill, and then realized that that sounded even more ridiculous than whatever reason he might have for being there. He was relieved she didn't seem to recognize him from his time in the church with Jacob. She asked if he lived nearby or was just traveling through the area, and seemed pleased when he said he lived in Carlisle. Maybe she just didn't want another tourist gawking at her, Andy thought. Finally, he said he should be going, but the woman insisted that he stay.

"There is room for all of us here," she said and looked around the church. Andy looked too but felt terribly out of place. She asked him to sit and he did, at the opposite end of the pew.

"I love this church," the woman said. "I come here often in the morning, after my chores are done. Sometimes I see other people; sometimes I sit alone. I like the church either way."

She then turned to look at Andy. "Have you been here before?" she asked.

"Well, yes," Andy said. "One time, twice really. I mean it wasn't official or anything. I mean I was just —"

"It does not matter," she said. "The important thing is that you decided to come here now."

"But I didn't, really," Andy said. "I just happened to be here. I'm not sure why."

"Same thing," she said.

Andy realized this woman could be from another planet, she was so foreign to him. She was certainly speaking a foreign language, and yet, somehow, she put him at ease. They spoke of other things, of her children, of the coming cold weather, of autumn flowers, of friends. Andy relaxed and talked easily with this woman he didn't know. He felt he didn't need to defend himself, did not need to impress her, did not need to feel uncomfortable because she is a woman and he is a man; he could simply be himself, whatever that is. It was easy.

Finally, she said she had to be going. Other chores, she said. He thanked her, and she smiled. Will you be back, she asked. Andy said he thought not. When she had left, he sat for a few more moments in the church, knowing that he didn't belong there, but feeling strangely at ease.

As he drove back up Route 15, he thought about the woman in the church and about how easy it had been to talk with her. Although at some point in this drive he always glanced over the mountain to see the vapor, always ominous to his mind, coming from TMI, this time he forgot all about it. He was thinking of other things, of the future. He did think about stopping at Souders Market, but decided not to do that. It's better, he thought.

Rather than continuing up Route 15, Andy decided to take one of the back roads up to Carlisle. There were many ways of getting there, he thought, and while they were different, they all got him to where he wanted to go. For no reason he stopped along the side of one of the roads and lowered his window. He was on a small hill, which looked out over the countryside with its patchwork fields, its neat houses and white barns, its gently rolling landscape, reminding him of his grandfather's place, corn stubble still in place, wheat cut and baled, cows standing in groups, under trees, eating lazily, knowing that all this will be here again next year. He got out of his car and leaned on the wooden railing, feeling, for the first time, part of the countryside. He thought of how comfortable he felt there. He thought of Sarah and of her strength. He thought of Beth and was happy for her new life. He remembered sitting in the Mexican restaurant the day before, after Beth and Mel had left, sipping his second cup of coffee.

"Another one?" the waitress had asked.

Andy had looked at her and smiled. "Maybe so," he said. "Maybe now it's time to begin."

Arthur L. Ford is professor emeritus of English and playwright-in-residence at Lebanon Valley College in Annville, Pennsylvania, a small town on the edge of Amish country. Before retiring from the college in 2001, he taught a variety of literature and composition courses as a member and chairman of Lebanon Valley's English Department, and he later served as the college's dean of international programs.

Dr. Ford earned his bachelor's degree from Lebanon Valley, and his master's and PhD degrees from Bowling Green State University in Bowling Green, Ohio. He has traveled extensively throughout his career and lived abroad for three-and-a-half years, including two years as a Fulbright professor—one year in Syria and one in China.

In addition to the usual publications associated with academia, he has published his own poetry and short fiction, as well as plays and libretti for operas. In 2007, Lebanon Valley College published his non-fiction book, *Cinderella and the Seven Dwarfs: The Lebanon Valley College 1952–53 Basketball Team's Improbable Run to the NCAA Sweet Sixteen*.

Dr. Ford lives in Annville with his wife, Mary Ellen. They have three grown children and six grandchildren. *Shunned* is his first published novel.